"Full reverse." Sulu moved quickly, [...] the urgency in the captain's voice without understanding the reason for it.

"Course, Captain?" Chekov sounded puzzled.

"Away from . . . that!" Kirk gestured toward the main viewscreen, which now was showing streaks of exploding gas in the far distance. "Spock—any chance your figures could be wrong?"

"No, Captain, I've checked them twice. We are now retreating from the effects of a primal explosion identical to the one that gave rise to the universe we are living in."

Kirk didn't like it; he didn't like it at all. "So what we're seeing is a new universe in the process of being born," he said heavily.

"Inside our uniwerse?" Chekov protested. "But ve vere here first!"

Look for STAR TREK Fiction from Pocket Books

STAR TREK®

THE THREE-MINUTE UNIVERSE

BARBARA PAUL

POCKET BOOKS

New York London Toronto Sydney Tokyo Singapore

This book is a work of fiction. Names, characters, places and incidents are either the product of the author's imagination or are used fictitiously. Any resemblance to actual events or locales or persons, living or dead, is entirely coincidental.

An *Original* Publication of POCKET BOOKS

POCKET BOOKS, a division of Simon & Schuster Inc.
1230 Avenue of the Americas, New York, NY 10020

Copyright © 1988 Paramount Pictures. All Rights Reserved.

STAR TREK is a Registered Trademark of
Paramount Pictures.

This book is published by Pocket Books, a division of
Simon & Schuster Inc., under exclusive license from
Paramount Pictures.

All rights reserved, including the right to reproduce
this book or portions thereof in any form whatsoever.
For information address Pocket Books, 1230 Avenue
of the Americas, New York, NY 10020

ISBN: 0-671-74358-9

First Pocket Books printing August 1988

10 9 8 7 6 5 4 3

POCKET and colophon are registered trademarks of
Simon & Schuster Inc.

Printed in the U.S.A.

THE THREE-MINUTE UNIVERSE

Chapter One

"THE GALAXY IS ON FIRE," said Captain James T. Kirk.

The grim look on his face told his officers he was not joking. Of the six others in the briefing room of the U.S.S. *Enterprise*, four looked astonished, even shocked. But First Officer Spock, who already knew the facts of the case, showed no expression at all—as he rarely did in any event. And Lieutenant Uhura, the ship's communications officer, merely looked resigned; she'd been dreaming of flames and blistering heat for the past three nights.

"You are going to explain that, Captain, aren't you?" The skepticism in Chief Medical Officer Leonard McCoy's voice was even heavier than usual.

"You all know that for over a week we've been getting measurements of extreme heat from the direction of the Beta Castelli star system," Kirk said. "Until recently. A few hours ago our telemetry probes stopped transmitting."

"They must have been defective," suggested helmsman Lieutenant Sulu, who'd sent out the probes himself. "All systems were operative our end."

"How many probes did we use altogether, Mr. Sulu?"

"Six," the helmsman admitted. Probes were normally sent out in pairs. When the first pair had stopped sending back data, Sulu had launched another. And then another.

"And you're seriously suggesting the *Enterprise* was fitted with six defective probes at the same time?" the captain persisted. "I've never seen even *one* defective probe, not in all my years in the service. Six at once is out of the question. No, the reason those probes stopped transmitting is that . . . they melted."

Uhura shuddered but said nothing.

"Here, now, Captain!" Chief Engineer Montgomery Scott objected. "Those probes are cased in tempered alphidium! Why, for those hulls to melt, the heat'd have to be—"

"Unmeasurable." Spock spoke for the first time. "Unmeasurable by our probe instrumentation, that is. And therein lies the difficulty. The last few readings we did receive revealed temperatures at the extreme end of the telemetry capability. The readings held steady for twenty-one minutes, seventeen seconds precisely. Then the transmissions stopped. The most reasonable conclusion is, as the captain has stated, that the heat was extreme enough to melt our probes."

"Mr. Spock!" Scott's eyes were large, his face disbelieving. "D'ye have any idea how hot it'd have to be for *alphidium* to melt?"

"Yes, Mr. Scott. I do."

"Hot enough to melt us, too," Kirk pointed out. "The *Enterprise* could turn into a pressure cooker. Everything in sector 79F is in danger. And the heat is advancing, spreading out more and more the farther it gets from its source."

"Vhat about Zirgos?" It was the ship's navigator,

Ensign Pavel Chekov, who asked that. Zirgos was their destination, the third of four planets orbiting Beta Castelli.

"Zirgos is gone," Kirk said bluntly. "Even before our probes stopped working, we were getting no planetary readings from the Beta Castelli system at all. None whatsoever. The whole star system has vanished." He paused. "Including the star itself."

There was a stunned silence. Then Chekov asked, "You mean the star vent supernova?"

"Not possible, Ensign," Spock said. "The star was not yet in its death throes." The Vulcan used the library computer to call up a schematic of the star system in question. "Beta Castelli was an ordinary G2 main sequence star of a minus twenty-seven magnitude. Although the star was consuming hydrogen at the rate of five hundred million tons per second, its fuel supply was in no danger of immediate exhaustion. The general estimate was that Beta Castelli would not reach its helium flash point for another five billion years. In addition, the star massed only point nine solar, insufficient to attain supernova state. Any explosion could be only minor, certainly insufficient to obliterate all traces of every one of its orbiting bodies."

"It was too young and too small," Kirk translated. "No, something else caused it. Something came along and incinerated an entire star system."

Uhura made a sound of dismay. "But what is hot enough to burn up a *star*?"

Kirk nodded. "Exactly. That, I'm afraid, is what we have to find out. So we're going to go in as close as we can and measure whatever's left to measure. Maybe there's enough residue to give us a clue."

"Excuse me for being dense," Dr. McCoy drawled, "but shouldn't we be heading in the *opposite* direction? Anything hot enough to fricassee a star should be able to vaporize the *Enterprise* from lightyears away. Just where is this thing anyway?"

"Unknown, Doctor," Spock said. "We are not even sure it is a 'thing'—it could be a phenomenon of nature that we know nothing about. We need more data."

"And so we go jump in the furnace to see how hot it is," McCoy grumbled.

"Not quite, Bones," Kirk smiled. "We go up to the outside of the furnace and read the temperature gauge."

"Captain," Scott said worriedly, "what about the Zirgosian people? Did they get away?"

Kirk sighed heavily. "I don't know, Scotty. There've been no distress signals . . . Uhura?"

"Nothing," Uhura confirmed. "Nothing but static from that entire sector."

"So they dinna make it?"

Chekov shook his head. "Incredible. An entire race of people . . . viped out."

"Maybe not," Kirk said. "Zirgos did have colonies. Spock?"

"The Zirgosians colonized two of the other three planets orbiting Beta Castelli," the Vulcan said. "The third was a gas giant. But all four planets are gone now. However, Zirgos did colonize one world outside its home star system. Presumably there are survivors there."

"So the race isn't extinct?" Sulu asked.

"We'll find out," Kirk said. "But right now let's go see what's causing this unbelievable outpouring of heat. Engineer, we'll be putting a strain on the ship's coolant system. You're going to have to monitor the dilithium couplings for overload."

"Aye, sir."

"Lieutenant Uhura, notify Starfleet Command what we're up to. And send a subspace message to that other world the Zirgosians colonized—what's it called, Spock?"

"Holox, Captain."

"Holox. Ask them what they know about this."

"Yes, sir." Uhura rose and followed the captain out of the briefing room. Chief Engineer Scott headed toward the dilithium reactor room on O Deck, but Dr. McCoy tagged along after the others to the bridge. The ride up in the turbolift was a silent one. They were not only disturbed over the fate of the Zirgosian people but also concerned for their own safety, a mixture that made casual conversation impossible.

They'd been on a routine inspection mission, checking to see if the Klingons were honoring their truce and not violating Zirgosian space. Zirgos was one of a number of Federation worlds the *Enterprise* was scheduled to visit, to make sure the planet's star lanes remained inviolate. Watchdog duty was generally unexciting, but it was important; now, however, it would have to be postponed for as long as this unexplained and continuing flow of heat threatened them all. This time, the Klingons could wait.

On the bridge, Spock, Uhura, Chekov, and Sulu silently moved to their posts. But instead of taking the command chair, Captain Kirk stood with his hands on his hips staring at the main viewscreen, which told him nothing. A normal-looking starfield was displayed—not glowing red or smoking or giving any other indication that it was on the verge of being incinerated. But the life-destroying heat was out there.

"Mr. Chekov, lay in a course that takes us toward the center of that heat."

The young navigator studied his instruments. "But Kepten . . . vhere *is* the center? I cannot find it—the heat is too diffuse!"

"Ensign Chekov is correct, Captain," Spock interposed. "That high a temperature is beyond our instrumentation's ability to pinpoint."

"All right, then, pick a spot."

Nervously Chekov picked a spot. "Two one one mark four."

"Ahead full, Mr. Sulu."

"Ahead full," the helmsman repeated.

Dr. McCoy cleared his throat. "Is it my imagination, or is it beginning to get warm in here?"

"It's your imagination," Kirk told him. "We're a couple of days away from the point where we should start feeling the heat."

"I'm already feeling the heat," McCoy muttered. "Jim, even if we do get in close enough to get a measurement—what's that going to tell us that we don't already know?"

"Cause? Source? Duration? We won't know until we get there. How would you go about investigating a fire-related catastrophe?"

"I'd call the fire department."

"Bones, *we*'re the fire department."

McCoy threw up his hands. "I'll be in sickbay." Clearly this was one of those times it didn't pay to argue with James T. Kirk.

The captain watched him step into the turbolift, vaguely wondering whether McCoy's well-known worrywart tendencies might in fact prove to be justified this time. He sat down in the command chair and said, "Mr. Spock, any discernible increase in temperature readings yet?"

"Decidedly, Captain." The first officer was also the ship's science officer; at the moment they were both bending over the sensors viewer. "The readings indicate an unmeasurable wave of heat is headed our way at high speed. At our present rate of progress, we will meet the leading edge of the heat front in thirty-one point six hours. We will start feeling the effects of the heat long before that, of course."

"Of course," Kirk murmured. He stared out at the starfield. Now there was nothing to do but wait, wait and wonder what could be out there that was hotter than a star.

Uhura looked at her bed with revulsion. She needed sleep if she was to continue performing at peak efficiency. But the last three nights had been filled with terrors—alternating periods of nightmares and sleeplessness. She knew it would be the same this time.

And the periods of sleeplessness were filled with remembering. She was recalling details that had remained buried deep in her unconscious despite her best efforts at exorcising her own particular demon. Smells as well as images came creeping back. The stench of a computer console as it burned and threw out sparks. The sinus-burning smoke from a window curtain that disappeared bit by bit as the flames crawled upward. The sweet, pungent odor given off by a small, delicate, wooden gazelle her grandfather had carved for her, its legs burning away from under it one by one.

And the one image she could never forget: T'iana,

caught under a fallen beam, calling out to Uhura for help, crying as only a terrified child can cry. Uhura, only ten years old herself, blinded by the smoke, trying to fight her way through the flames to reach T'iana, while adult voices screamed at her to get out, screamed at her that her hair was on fire . . .

Her first dream, three nights ago, had been of the adults slapping at her head with their hands, trying to smother the flames that were eating up her hair. But in the dream it had gone on a lot longer than it had in fact, and the flames had proved more stubborn; they'd run down her arms, her back . . . while the adults kept slapping at her head, slapping hard. That was the first time she'd wakened in a sweat, so shaken it had taken her two hours to get back to sleep again.

One of the doctors who'd treated her at the time warned her she would have related dreams of the fire—as indeed she did, for almost a year after T'iana died. But gradually the dreams had grown less intense and had begun to occur less frequently; by the time Uhura reached adolescence, she had recovered from the trauma.

Or so everyone told her. She'd even witnessed another fire at the age of sixteen without any undue panic. Uhura knew it was guilt over not having been able to save her friend that was behind the nightmares; she was still haunted by a memory of responsibility not fulfilled. She'd long since come to terms with the fact that there had been no way that she, a burning child herself, could have saved the other burning child. She forgave herself for not being able to perform the impossible. She'd done all the psychmed had told her she must do.

And it hadn't made one bit of difference.

It still hurt to think of T'iana, of her laughing face,

of her mind full of creative mischief. They'd met at the Institute for Advanced Mathematics, which vigorously operated a special program for gifted children. None of the children there had a private room; since each of them worked basically alone for six hours every day, the Institute insisted upon shared rooms as a way of counteracting the propensity toward isolationistic traits that could so easily develop in their scholarly young minds. And so Uhura and T'iana had been more or less arbitrarily thrown together, and to their mutual joy and delight they quickly discovered they pretty much operated on the same wavelength. They'd formed a bond that was not broken even yet, all these years after the ugly and terrifying death one of them had suffered.

A memory of responsibility not fulfilled.

Then three days ago on the bridge Mr. Spock had calmly announced the probes had encountered a field of heat so intense their instruments were incapable of measuring it. Uhura had watched impassively as the first pair of probes failed, then the second, then the third, knowing instinctively they had all been incinerated out in what was supposed to be the cold of space. Even before Captain Kirk told them about the planet Zirgos and its star, Beta Castelli, she knew she was about to face the biggest fire of her life. And the dreams had started.

She stared at her bed hopelessly; it was no use. She couldn't stay awake forever, but the dreams were even worse than not sleeping. Something had to be done. Uhura dressed quickly and left her quarters. *Dr. McCoy,* she thought. He'd help.

When she got to sickbay, the doctor was busy in the examination room. She waited in his office, sitting in a chair that faced McCoy's empty desk. It was quiet there; the hum of the ship was muted and even the intercom remained silent. Uhura's eyes slowly began to close and her head tipped forward. She jerked herself awake with an effort.

"Well, Lieutenant, something I can do for you?" McCoy came in and perched on the corner of his desk facing her. "You're looking a little peaked."

Uhura hesitated, then blurted out: "I want you to give me a dream-suppressant."

McCoy's eyebrows rose. "I can't do that. The dream-suppressant drugs are used only for treating manic depressives in immediate danger of harming themselves. Those drugs are illegal on a lot of worlds. They're habit-forming and they're dangerous."

"I'm not asking for any kind of full-scale treatment. I want just one dose, Doctor—for tonight. Sometime tomorrow we'll be meeting that wave of heat and I must be alert for that. I need one night of uninterrupted sleep. Just one dose."

He shook his head. "Absolutely not. Even one dose is addictive, and believe me, the withdrawal treatment is a lot worse than any nightmares you might be having. But that's only a secondary danger. The real danger is that it works—you end up not dreaming at all. And do you know what the medical prognosis is for the dream-deprived?"

"No," she said with a sigh. "Tell me."

"They go looney tunes," Dr. McCoy said bluntly. "We have to dream. It's what keeps us functioning." He paused, and then said more gently, "Why don't you tell me about it, Uhura? What are the dreams about?"

"Fire," she responded dully. "I keep dreaming of fire."

McCoy nodded sympathetically. Only three people

aboard the *Enterprise* knew of Uhura's traumatic childhood experience with fire—the captain, the first officer, and the chief medical officer; it was part of Uhura's medical record and would follow her as long as she remained in the service. McCoy asked, "Old memories coming back? Or new kinds of fire?"

"A mixture of both. They all start out as memories, but then they balloon out into something even worse. Something that's . . . unstoppable. I keep waking up covered with sweat, four and five times a night. I'm afraid to go to sleep."

"How long has this been going on?"

"Three nights, ever since we first learned of that all-consuming heat we're racing to meet. Tonight would be the fourth. Dr. McCoy . . . I just can't face another night of it."

"You won't have to," he smiled. "I can't give you the dream-suppressant you want, but I have a nice compromise that should let you get a good night's sleep." He pressed a button on his intercom. "Nurse Chapel, prepare a hypo of Tridocane. Lieutenant Uhura will be out in a moment."

"Yes, Doctor," said the voice on the intercom.

"What I'm giving you," McCoy said to Uhura, "is a new tricyclic compound that shifts some of the time you spend in REM sleep over to delta sleep. The REM state is where most dreams occur, so you'll be dreaming less. But Tridocane has a little something extra that should do you a world of good. It lets you stop a dream that turns threatening."

Uhura looked startled. "How?"

"You just think 'Stop!' It works as a chemo-hypnotic. The drug and your brain chemistry co-operate to give you a limited control over your unconscious thought processes, and that includes dreams. That way you aren't totally at the mercy of whatever your unconscious chooses to throw at you. Something scares you, you think 'Stop'—and it will stop. You may have to run through the beginnings of half a dozen dreams before you find one that looks safe, but you will be able to decide which one you'll finally dream. And best of all, you won't end up a dream-deficient basket case in need of extensive therapy before you can function again."

Uhura smiled, the first time in days. "It really will work?"

McCoy smiled back. "It really will work. This is only a temporary measure, you understand. It won't cure what's causing the dreams, but it will let you get some sleep. Come see me tomorrow."

Uhura thanked him and went into the examination room, where Christine Chapel was waiting with the Tridocane. After she'd administered the hypo, Nurse Chapel said, "Some patients find this works faster if they keep repeating the word 'Stop' to themselves just as they're falling asleep. Why don't you try that, since this is your first time."

"All right, Christine. Are there any side effects I should know about?"

"No, none—no groggy feeling the next day or anything. The only problem with Tridocane is that it tends to lose its effectiveness after the third or fourth use."

Uhura was dismayed. "So this will help me only four nights at the most? That's all?"

Nurse Chapel put a hand on her friend's arm. "It's only a temporary measure, Uhura. Didn't Dr. McCoy tell you?"

"Oh. Yes, he did say that," Uhura admitted. "Well, I suppose it's better than nothing. Thanks, Christine."

Uhura went back to her quarters and quickly prepared for bed. She lay down and closed her eyes and did what Christine Chapel had told her to do. *Stop,* she thought, a bit desperately.

Stop. Stop.

Captain James T. Kirk forced himself to stand still and not pace. The bridge temperature was the highest he'd ever felt it, and unnecessary movement could only increase his personal discomfort. Thirty hours had lapsed since he'd first announced that the galaxy was on fire, and now the *Enterprise* itself felt ready to burst into flames. The ship's coolant system was overtaxed, small electrical fires had broken out in four or five places, and Scotty was calling every two minutes to say the ship couldn't take much more. Everyone on the bridge was sweating—except the Vulcan first officer. Kirk could feel the heat through the soles of his boots.

"How much farther, Mr. Spock?" he demanded.

"We're almost within sensor range now, Captain. Just a little closer."

Kirk strode over to the communications station. "No answer from Holox yet?"

"No, sir," Uhura said. "I've repeated the message on every comnet frequency open to this sector. They must have received it by now." The colonized planet had remained stubbornly silent. Another mystery.

Chekov called out, "Tventy-two minutes to heat front!"

Twenty-two minutes, Kirk thought. He sat in the command chair. "Mr. Spock?"

"Readings coming in now, Captain." The Vulcan studied the symbols scrolling through his viewer. "Temperature beyond our capability to measure, but

13

gas analysis is in. Twenty-five percent ionized helium and seventy-five percent ionized hydrogen, plus trace elements." Spock straightened up from his viewer. "Fascinating." His voice had a seldom-heard edge to it.

"Captain Kirk!" Scott's voice erupted from the speaker system. "We canna take any more! The——"

Kirk slapped a button on his armrest control panel. "Not now, Mr. Scott! Why 'fascinating', Spock?"

"The three-to-one hydrogen-helium ratio—that's exactly what our universe consisted of when it was approximately three minutes old. Even the trace elements had begun to appear by three minutes after the colorfully named Big Bang had taken place. And now we find those conditions precisely duplicated right here."

Kirk thought that over . . . and his eyes widened as he realized what it meant. "Helmsman, full reverse! Get us out of here, Mr. Sulu, and fast! Now!"

"Full reverse." Sulu moved quickly, responding to the urgency in the captain's voice without understanding the reason for it.

"Course, Captain?" Chekhov sounded puzzled.

"Away from . . . that!" Kirk gestured toward the main viewscreen, which now was showing streaks of exploding gas in the far distance. "Spock, any chance your figures could be wrong?"

"No, Captain, I've checked them twice. We are now retreating from the effects of a primal explosion identical to the one that gave rise to the universe we ourselves are living in."

Kirk didn't like it; he didn't like it at all. "So what we're seeing is a new universe in the process of getting itself born," he said heavily. "It's more than the galaxy that's on fire!"

"What's that?" Uhura exclaimed, startled. "A new universe?"

"Inside *our* uniwerse?" Chekov protested. "But ve vere here first!"

Without looking away from his viewer, Spock remarked, "You'll find the laws of nature have little respect for squatters' rights, Ensign, if I understand that term correctly. But it's unlikely the new universe had its origins within our own. Ours is only one of countless numbers of universes, all residing in a larger superspace that has been swelling outward for an unimaginably long period of time, a superspace that is ferociously hot and immeasurably dense. To use an analogy, we're but one bubble in a sea of foam—a sea with no surface, and no bottom. And bubbles in that sea of foam occasionally touch."

The bridge personnel all fell silent, depending on their instruments to tell them whether they were about to be burned alive or not. There was nothing in their universe to shield them from the heat generated by a neighboring universe's Big Bang; their only hope was to outrun it.

Spock's image of touching foam bubbles persisted in Kirk's mind. Could one of the bubbles burst the other? Could the bubbles just bounce off each other? Or would the abrasive action of two universes grating against each other wear a hole in both of them, to create an interspatial portal allowing matter and energy to flow from one universe to the other? And if they had to bump into another universe, why couldn't it be a mature one? Why did the collision have to come only three minutes after the other universe's primal explosion, an explosion that spewed out heat intense enough to vaporize every star system, every galaxy, every supercluster . . .

"Temperature is dropping!" Chekov cried out jubilantly. "Half a degree, one—"

He was interrupted by an outbreak of cheering. "Let's hold off on the celebrating," Kirk said. "All we've done is buy some time." He rose and stepped between the navigator's station and the helmsman's. "Sulu, I want you to match the rate of our retreat as closely as you can to that of the heat front's advance. Chekov, keep feeding him temperature readings. Don't let the front get too close."

"Understood, sir," Sulu said.

The speaker crackled to life. "Ah, Captain," sighed Chief Engineer Scott, sounding much relieved. "Thank ye."

Kirk smiled wryly. "Just for you, Scotty," he murmured and moved over to his first officer's station. He hesitated, looking for the best way to frame his question. "Spock, is there any possibility this is an *un*natural phenomenon we're witnessing? That is, could it have been manipulated from this side of the front?"

The Vulcan's right eyebrow rose. "Triggering a primal explosion? Not by any technology known to us, Captain. Do you have some reason to suspect such an unlikelihood?"

Kirk shook his head. "Just a hunch. Never mind the technology—somebody's always developing new technology we don't know about yet. But is it possible *in theory*?"

In the years they'd served together, Spock had developed a healthy respect for his captain's hunches. And he'd done so in spite of the fact that even the idea of hunches went against the grain of Vulcan thought processes. Inspired guesswork grated against all of Spock's training as well as against his own natural proclivity to reason things out and ignore the insights that sprang from the exercise of instinct and imagination.

But he'd learned the captain didn't depend upon either instinct or logic exclusively, and Spock himself had frequently benefited from Kirk's more oblique approach. So now he put his mind to the problem his commanding officer had posed. "If it's true that every universe is a vacuum fluctuation—then yes, theoretically at least, such a triggering event might be possible. But one would have to develop some sort of gravity manipulator of far greater potency than the antigrav units we use on the *Enterprise*."

"Why gravity?"

"Gravity is unique, Captain. It is the very warping of space-time that we have encountered in the past. There are moments in time that cease flowing smoothly into the next moment, and there are points in space that fail to connect logically with adjacent points. During these off-moments and at these non-points, space-time itself literally does not exist. But if one of those non-moment-points could be captured gravitationally . . ."

"Big Bang?"

"Big Bang. But Captain, who would wish to trigger an uncontrollable destructive force of such magnitude?"

"Klingons," Sulu muttered from the helm.

Kirk was thinking. "This heat explosion—it'll go on until it consumes our universe?"

"Unknown, Captain. Since we have no instruments capable of measuring the intensity of the heat or the size of the gaseous mass, it's impossible to say how far out in a concentric circle the original explosion will travel before it begins to cool down. There is this, though—the explosion would travel outward in all directions from a central point. It would not travel in just one direction, toward us."

"So we're getting only a piece of it?"

"I assume so, Captain. We would not be able to outrun it if we were receiving the full blast . . . we would have been consumed immediately otherwise. That does not mean it is any less dangerous. However, there is always a possibility that this new universe will prove to be smaller than our own, in which case the survival of at least part of our universe would be assured."

"Looking on the bright side, Spock?" Kirk asked sourly. "What if it's larger than ours?"

"Then we are indeed in trouble."

Abruptly Kirk swung around and started pacing. After a moment he stopped as suddenly as he'd started and said, "It all began near the Beta Castelli system. What if someone were determined to wipe out the Zirgosian race? Wouldn't this be a sure-fire way of doing it? No pun intended. This big an explosion got not only Zirgos itself but two of its colony planets as well."

Spock raised an eyebrow. "Earth humans have an expression that covers such an eventuality," the first officer said archly. "I think it is something about shooting off a cannon to kill a gnat."

"Yes, yes, it would be overkill—it would be suicidal, in fact. But maybe something went wrong. Maybe the energy released is greater than what was anticipated. Maybe a lot of things. We need some answers. One thing in our favor—if someone did set out to kill off the Zirgosians, they could have missed a few. Let's see if the Zirgosian colonists can tell us what happened here." Kirk returned to the command chair.

"Mr. Chekov! Lay in a course to Holox. Mr. Spock, how much longer before we've learned everything we can learn here?"

The Vulcan peered into his viewer. "The data are repeating now, Captain. We can leave any time."

A few moments later Chekov announced, "Course to Holox laid in. Two point five parsecs."

"Ahead warp five, Mr. Sulu," Kirk said. "Lieutenant Uhura, notify Starfleet where we're going and why. And feed through the data from Mr. Spock's computer—we want them to know all about our three-minute universe. Starfleet has some decisions to make."

"Yes, sir," she said. "Do you think they'll try evacuating this sector?"

"Where would they evacuate *to*, Lieutenant?" Kirk muttered.

The question hung ominously in the air. The *Enterprise* hurtled onward toward a small planet called Holox, where questions bigger than that might find their answers.

Chapter Two

CAPTAIN JAMES T. KIRK woke to find he'd been sleeping on his stomach, something he hadn't done since he was a boy. Was he that afraid of what was coming—to revert to childhood in his sleep?

What woke him was an audible signal that he was wanted. He rolled off the bed and hit the intercom control. "Kirk here."

It was Sulu. "We're approaching orbit, Captain. But someone got here ahead of us. There's another ship circling Holox and I can't identify it."

"Is Mr. Spock on the bridge?"

"No, sir."

"Get him. I'm on my way."

In the turbolift Kirk rubbed his eyes; he wasn't fully awake yet. From the lift's speaker came the sound of Sulu's voice summoning Spock to the bridge. An unidentified ship? Must be some mistake. He stepped off the lift—and woke up completely. On the bridge's main viewscreen was displayed a piece of flying hardware the likes of which he'd never seen before.

Long and lean, what was almost a perfect rectangle lay stretched out to form a thick gray bar across the deep black of space. No deflector dish, no nacelles. No identification markings.

"Increase magnification," Kirk ordered. The closer picture showed him weapons hatches, closed ports, exterior ship structures hidden behind unrevealing casings. Whatever that ship had, its occupants weren't displaying it for casual passersby to examine at their leisure.

Uhura was standing by her station, hypnotized by the sight of the ship on the screen. "What is it, Captain? They don't acknowledge our signal."

"Don't know, Lieutenant. Keep sending. Mr. Chekov?"

The young navigator was at the science officer's station, peering into the viewer. "Mass, three hundred forty-one point one million kilograms. Length . . . nine hundred meters exactly!"

"Nine hundred meters!" Sulu echoed disbelievingly. "How can they maneuver?"

"So they're three times as long as the *Enterprise* and twice as heavy," Kirk mused. "And they don't want to talk to us?" He glanced at Uhura.

"Still no response."

The turbolift door hissed open and Spock stepped out on to the bridge. The Vulcan's only visible reaction to the strange ship on the screen was an arched eyebrow. Wordlessly he moved over to his viewer; Chekov resumed his navigator's seat.

"Interior visuals, Mr. Spock?" Kirk asked.

"Unable to scan, Captain. The ship has some sort of shielding we can't penetrate. It's too large for a battle cruiser, yet it's obviously armed. Maneuverability must be limited."

"And slow," Sulu added. "Even a simple ninety-degree turn would take forever."

"Not quite forever, Mr. Sulu, but an inconveniently

long period of time if the ship were under attack," Spock remarked. "They must depend heavily upon their shielding for defense."

Kirk strode over to Communications. "Ship-to-ship."

Uhura flipped two switches and pressed a button. "Ready."

"This is Captain James T. Kirk of the U.S.S. *Enterprise*. We represent the United Federation of Planets and our mission here is a peaceful one. Please identify yourself."

No one made a sound as they all waited for the strange ship's response. There was none.

"Are you sure they got the message, Lieutenant?" Kirk asked.

"Yes, sir," Uhura said. "The receptor echo was quite clear."

"Repeat," Kirk ordered. "We—"

"Kepten!" Chekov cried. "Look!"

They all looked. The ship appeared to be in the process of growing mechanical arms and legs, but what it was in fact doing was unfolding itself. The top aft portion lifted, extended itself, and divided into four sections, each connected by dorsals with every other section as well as with the main body of the ship. Elsewhere on the ship the same process was taking place. In a few minutes the ship had changed from a long, monolinear slab into an ovoid composed of intricate, connecting parts. Then it moved. Following the curvature of the world below, it swiftly and gracefully slipped out of sight.

"Well, that answers the question of maneuverability," Kirk remarked dryly. "Where is it, Spock?"

"On the other side of Holox . . . and it is now

matching its orbit to ours. They're keeping the planet between us, Captain."

"Must be shy," Sulu grimaced.

Spock looked at the helmsman curiously. "Shy, Mr. Sulu?"

When Sulu realized the Vulcan was taking him literally, he hastily withdrew his suggestion and asked a question instead. "Why do they bother with that long, thin form anyway? The ovoid can do whatever they need to do."

"Probably to conserve power," Kirk guessed. "That ovoid shape has got to put a bigger drain on their resources than the more compact form. Maybe the colonists on Holox can tell us who they are. Lieutenant—"

"Sir, they're still not answering," Uhura said. "I've been transmitting continuously."

"Here's something, Captain," Spock said quickly, examining the sensor array monitor. "A point of great heat on the planet's surface, and in an area the colonists have not yet settled. No volcanic activity or other known natural phenomenon responsible."

"A hot spot with no cause?"

"With no *known* cause, Captain."

"Let's see." Kirk stepped over to the monitor. He studied the surface imaging on the screen and then read the numbers displayed across the bottom. "Could it be a forest fire? Does wood burn that hot?"

"It is an unforested area, mostly desert. There's nothing there to burn."

"Then there shouldn't be any hot spot."

"Correct, Captain. But it is indisputably there."

Kirk growled. "I don't want any more mysteries!

Come along, Mr. Spock—let's go see what's going on down there. Will we need suits?"

"No, sir. Holox has a nitrogen-oxygen mix we can breathe. And we can move faster—gravity is only point nine Earth normal."

"Mr. Sulu, you have the conn," Kirk said. "Lieutenant Uhura, notify the transporter room. And tell Mr. Scott to meet us there with a security detail. Make that a double security detail." He charged into the turbolift, followed closely by his first officer.

In the lift on the way to G Deck, Spock was aware that Kirk was growing increasingly annoyed—and deliberately did nothing to relieve his captain's frustration; the Vulcan knew how effective Kirk could be when he was angry. "Jim, you must be aware the odds are that the Zirgosian colonists on Holox will know nothing about what happened to their home planet. They are probably as uninformed as we are."

"Don't tell me the odds. Holox is the only lead we've got—unless you have a better suggestion?"

"At this juncture I have no suggestion. I merely point out the Zirgosians on both planets must have been caught by surprise."

"Yes, they must have been," Kirk agreed. "They're a technologically sophisticated people, but what technology can protect against the birth of a new universe?"

Spock had no answer.

Transporter Chief Kyle had their phasers and communicators ready for them. "I've set the coordinates for an exterior location, Captain. You'll be materializing in the primary street of the only major settlement. Is that satisfactory?" He looked worried.

"Quite satisfactory, Mr. Kyle," Kirk said. "Is something the matter?"

"I'm sure the figures are correct, Captain, but I was unable to get confirmation from anyone on the planet."

"Yes, they're not taking any calls today." Kirk turned to see Scott coming in, followed by six security guards. "Scotty, did you get a look at that ship out there?"

"Aye, I saw it."

"So? What do you think?"

The corners of Scott's mouth turned down. "An energy-guzzler, if y'ask me." He took a phaser and communicator from Kyle.

Kirk raised an eyebrow at Spock. "It seems our engineer doesn't think much of the mystery ship."

"Oh, it's fancy enough, I gie ye that," Scott said, stepping on the transporter platform to join the others. "But it's bound to have problems. For instance—"

"Later, Scotty. And in detail, when we have the time." Kirk nodded to the transporter chief. "Now, Mr. Kyle."

The first thing they saw on the surface of Holox was a dead body.

The security team immediately drew their weapons and formed a rough circle around the three officers. Spock knelt by the dead man. "Rigor mortis not far advanced," he said. "He's been dead only a few hours."

"A few hours!" Scott echoed in outrage. "They left him lyin' in the street for *hours*?"

"'They' who, Scotty?" Kirk asked. "Look around. Do you see anybody?"

The street they were standing in was a wide avenue lined with tall ornamental trees of a species unfamiliar to the landing party; the trees' feathery lavender branches were in constant motion even though there was no breeze. The buildings for the most part were prefabricated zyroplex structures, tall and shimmering in the bright light of Holox's sun. Down the side streets could be caught an occasional glimpse of a building constructed from substances native to Holox, all blues and purples and greens; but for the most part the Zirgosians had brought their building materials with them from their homeworld. But of the Zirgosians themselves, the only one in evidence was the dead man at their feet.

"Look at all the hovercraft," Kirk pointed out. "A dozen vehicles at least, and all of them at rest. The walkways are moving, but no one's riding them." He led the landing party to the nearest building and peered inside; it was some sort of administrative center, and it looked empty. "It's the middle of the day here—this should be a busy time for them. Where are all the people?"

"Where indeed," Spock said. "Since the structures are intact, it would appear Holox has not been the target of an assault, nor is it the victim of some natural catastrophe such as earthquake. But there is another possibility. Captain, we may need to undergo decontamination when we return to the ship."

"Disease? A plague?"

"That man we found back there—I could see no visible wound. He could have died from the natural failure of some essential bodily function, but precautions would seem to be in order just the same."

Kirk whipped out his communicator. "*Enterprise*, come in."

"*Enterprise* here," Transporter Chief Kyle's voice answered.

26

"Beam down Dr. McCoy immediately," Kirk ordered. "And have him suit up—we may have been exposed to something contagious down here."

"Right away, sir."

While they were waiting for McCoy, Kirk ordered a search of the administrative center. "They can't all have disappeared. Teams of two, and spread out."

They didn't have to look far. "Captain!" Scott called. "In here!"

Scott and one of the security team were in a conference room. Six wall-mounted display screens were running columns of unfamiliar symbols, probably Zirgosian numbers. Around the conference table three figures lay slumped over their consoles; a fourth was stretched out on the table as if reaching for something, and a fifth lay huddled on the floor.

Scott was lifting one of the figures at the table upright. "Captain, this lady's alive!" She began to slide out of her seat; Scott caught her and lowered her gently to the floor.

Kirk hunkered down beside her and felt for a pulse—very faint, but still there. The woman's eyelids fluttered and opened. She said something in a language Kirk didn't know. "Don't worry," he told her, "help is on the way. Hang on."

Her eyes focused on him, and with great effort she whispered a word. "Sackers."

A chill ran down Kirk's back. "The Sackers?"

"Here," she gasped. "On Holox."

Kirk and Spock exchanged a look. "They did this to you?" the captain asked. "Where are they?"

"Building . . . structure." She breathed shallowly for a moment and then said, "Heat . . . structure."

A heat structure, Kirk thought. "There's your hot spot, Mr. Spock." To the woman he said, "Don't talk any more. Just lie quietly until medical assistance arrives."

But the woman forced herself to say one more word. "Ship."

"Ship . . . that's a Sacker ship in orbit?"

The woman mumbled something in her own language and reached up to grasp the front of Kirk's uniform feebly with one hand. "Stop . . . them." She lost consciousness.

Scott bent over and picked her up. "Ah, poor lady! I'll take her outside. Dr. McCoy must be here by now." He carried the unconscious woman out.

The leader of the security team, a woman named Berengaria, looked up from the side of the figure huddled on the floor. "Captain, the other four are all dead. But if one woman is still alive . . ."

"Then there might be others," Kirk finished for her. "Let's find out. Take your team and search these other buildings, Lieutenant. And don't waste any time about it."

"No, sir!" Berengaria turned to the rest of the security team. "Hrolfson, you take Franklin and Ching and cover the north end of the street. You other two come with me." She started out, followed by the others.

But the one addressed as Hrolfson, a blond giant with pale blue eyes, hesitated. "Captain, if there is disease down here—"

"Then we're already exposed to it," Kirk snapped. "Get going, mister!"

"Yessir!" Hrolfson stepped out smartly.

When the captain and his first officer were left alone, Spock said, "Sackers, Jim."

Kirk grimaced. He knew of the Sackers, although as far as he was aware no one on the *Enterprise* had ever seen one. The Sackers were an enigmatic race that had never shown any overt hostility in the entire time their existence had been known to the Federation, a period of about fifty Earth years. Their contact with Federation worlds had been limited mostly to the exchange of information, and they had earned the reputation of being equitable and fair traders. They were peaceful, courteous, and always respectful of other people's laws . . . and their visits were dreaded by every world in the Federation.

"This can't be the work of the Sackers," Kirk said, "not from what I've heard of them." He shivered in spite of himself.

"Then why did the Zirgosian woman warn us against them?"

"I don't know. But they're supposed to be nonviolent, aren't they?"

"And so they have been," Spock replied, "but no one really knows much about them. I do not know whether that is because the Sackers do not wish to reveal information about themselves, or whether they have simply never been asked. It could well be that no one has had the courage to face them long enough to ask questions."

"Or the stomach for it."

The Sackers were cursed with a physical appearance repugnant enough to turn even the strongest stomach. In addition to their nausea-evoking exteriors, they gave off an overpowering stench; most people of other races became violently ill in their presence, vomiting uncontrollably until removed from the sight and smell of the Sackers. And to top things off, Sacker speech was shrill and piercing, causing excruciating pain in their listeners' ears. This standard response to the Sackers was purely a physiological one, and it couldn't be helped. But even after half a century of exemplary behavior, the Sackers still found that their presence inspired reactions ranging from uneasiness to near-violent disgust wherever they went.

"They've never hurt anyone before," Kirk mused. "So far as we know, they've never fired a shot in anger. And now this? It doesn't make sense. Spock, we'd better look through the rest of this building."

Their search was a disheartening one. They found thirty-one more people, all of them dead. One man had been trying to reach a communications console when he was struck down. Whatever had hit them had acted fast enough to keep them from sending out a call for help; no wonder Uhura hadn't been able to raise an answer. "Someone really has it in for the Zirgosian people," Kirk murmured. "First their home planet, and now Holox." Even Spock looked more grim-faced than usual.

Outside the building, they caught sight of Dr. McCoy in his spacesuit kneeling in the street beside a row of eight or nine recumbent people. At the head of the row was the Zirgosian woman who'd spoken to them. Even then the security guard named Hrolfson was carrying a man over to be placed at the end of the line. Kirk noticed that McCoy had removed his helmet.

But before he could ask, McCoy looked up and said, "Jim, there's no disease here. These people have been poisoned! Every one of them."

"Poisoned!"

"It tests out a common alkaloid poison—we ought to be able to save most of those who are still alive, if we can find them in time. I've called down a full medteam and supplies."

"That won't be enough. Spock, order all off-duty

personnel to beam down and help search for survivors." He knelt down next to the Zirgosian woman while Spock spoke into his communicator. "What about this woman, Bones? Will she make it?"

"Borderline, Jim. Can't say yet."

"When you've got things under control here, beam her up to the ship with you. I want to talk to her."

"If she makes it," McCoy cautioned.

"If she makes it."

Just then they heard the humming sound and spotted the shimmering air that announced a beamdown was in progress. The medteam materialized, led by Nurse Chapel; they took one look at the row of patients waiting for help and hurried over to them.

Lieutenant Berengaria jog-trotted up to them, a child tucked under each arm. "I found a school, Captain," she said heavily.

Kirk winced. "Many of them survive?"

"Very few."

"Smaller body mass," Spock offered. "Children would have less resistance to the poison."

"Poison?" Berengaria said. "Is that what caused this?"

"Afraid so," Kirk answered grimly. He thought a minute. "Where's Mr. Scott?"

"He's helping us look."

"Find him, and round up the rest of your team. I've got a job for you. There'll be others beaming down to do the looking."

Berengaria took out her communicator and started calling.

Soon the settlement was swarming with *Enterprise* crew members searching every building for survivors. Scott returned, his face filled with pain. "Ah, Captain!

Have y'ever seen such a sad sight?" He wiped a forearm across his eyes. "The lass said y'wanted me."

"There's something I want you to do, Scotty. We'll wait until the security team gets here."

Kirk looked along the row of poisoned Zirgosians. Some were moaning softly, others were trying to move their heads. The woman who'd warned them was still breathing shallowly. "Bones?"

"I still don't know, Jim. I'll have her beamed up as soon as someone is free."

The rest of the security team returned. "Mr. Scott," Kirk said, "you heard what this woman said about the Sackers building some sort of heat structure here. It's probably a hot spot Mr. Spock detected on the sensor array—he has the coordinates. I want you to take three of the security team and go find it."

Spock removed the tricorder from around his neck and handed it to Scott. "The location is locked in. Just follow the beam indicator."

"Thank ye, Mr. Spock." Scott took the tricorder and studied it. "That way," he pointed, off toward the southwest. "And when we find it, Captain?"

"Make no contact with the Sackers. Don't even let them know you're there. Just find out what that thing is they've built. Study the layout and report back. But no contact!"

"Y'don't have to tell me twice, sir," Scott replied with a shudder. "I've heard about those beasties— contact with *them* is the last thing I want." He looked at the security team. "Ye three," he said, pointing, "y'come with me." He turned and headed off toward the nearest grounded hovercraft, followed by Hrolfson and two of the others.

"And my job is?" Spock asked. He knew his captain.

"Your job is to investigate this mass poisoning. Find out how the poison was disseminated—through the food, the water, perhaps the air-circulation systems inside the buildings. Was it accidental or deliberate. Find out as much as you can."

"Where will you be?"

"On the *Enterprise*. Remember the maxim 'Know thine enemy'? I'm going to see how much our record banks can tell me about these strange beings we call Sackers."

Captain Kirk sat alone in the briefing room, staring with disgust at the image of a Sacker on the viewscreen.

All his training and all his natural tolerance seemed to have deserted him. Meeting alien races had been an integral part of his adult life; he would feel as if he'd lost a part of himself if it were to come to an end. Contact with new races was often demanding, always exciting, and sometimes dangerous. But it was his job, and he'd always been able to do it without the feeling of repugnance that the sheer differentness of other peoples sometimes evoked in the human race. It was one of the things that made him a good starship captain.

But *this* race . . . just a two-dimensional image of one of its only technically humanoid members was enough to make him feel queasy. What must it be like to see one in the flesh, if that stuff hanging on their outsides could be called flesh? Their real race-name was unknown; they'd been dubbed Sackers because each of their bodies was encased in a semi-transparent membrane similar to an amnion—a "sac". It wasn't a smooth-surfaced sac, though. The computer's record banks quoted a human observer's comment that the

Sackers all looked as if they were constantly molting; another had remarked they appeared to be in a state of "self-regenerating decay". Kirk acknowledged the aptness of the seeming contradiction: *self-regenerating decay* was just what it looked like.

And the sac was hot to the touch, the record banks said, fiery hot by human standards. Even a casual brushing together of Sacker and human arms was sufficient to result in second-degree burns to human flesh. No wonder no human being had ever shaken hands with a Sacker. The computer noted that the prolonged touch of a Sacker finger was sufficient to ignite an ordinary sheet of paper.

Inside the sac was a colored fluid, purpose unknown—possibly a nutrient or a lubricant. The colors varied from one individual Sacker to another, and frequently within the individual as well. The Sacker on the briefing room screen had a fluid that was primarily yellow with streaks of a particularly nauseating shade of green running through it.

The records were full of speculations about the Sacker body structure—speculations based on observations that had all been made at a distance. No one really knew anything about Sacker physiology. No medical practitioner on any world had ever treated one. The best method of learning about them would have been through post-mortem examination, but that had proved impossible. The reason for that was simple: no one had ever seen a dead Sacker.

If one looked closely—and Kirk forced himself to do just that—it was possible to catch glimpses of a Sacker's internal organs and even observe them functioning. The Sacker internal arrangement included a multitude of small, white, sluglike organs that seemed to be mobile; even as Kirk watched, one broke loose from a larger organ and slithered a few centimeters away to attach itself to a body part not completely visible. Messengers? Chemical carriers? They looked for all the world like blind worms feeding on a corpse.

Kirk tasted bile in his mouth. *Fascinating,* as Mr. Spock would say. The computer mentioned the smell the Sackers gave off, a stench so overpowering it brought a bilious taste to human mouths. Personal communication between Sacker and human was possible only when the latter wore a breathing mask of some kind. Kirk had no idea what the smell was like, but his body had been visually stimulated to produce the same physiological reaction the olfactory stimulus was supposed to produce. He turned his back to the screen until the vile taste began to fade.

When he could look again, he said to the image on the screen, "You are without a doubt the ugliest son of a bitch I've ever laid eyes on."

The Sacker language was unknown, mostly because there were very few races that could bear to hear it spoken—and those races could endure it for no longer than a minute or two. Sacker speech was high and shrill . . . and painful; continued exposure to it was enough to pierce the tympanic membrane in the human ear. This barrier to communication had been solved by the Sackers themselves; they all wore translator devices that muted their earsplitting tones, modulating them to a level tolerable to the ears of their listeners. They accepted the name "Sackers" for themselves, just as individual Sackers accepted names given to them by others not of their race.

Kirk found that interesting. Perhaps they were a group mind, in which case the concept of individual identity would be meaningless to them. Or if they were individuals, did they have so little self-respect that they didn't consider themselves worthy of bearing names? *No,* Kirk told himself sternly, *you're projecting your own negative reactions on to them, anthropomorphizing with a vengeance.* The computer suggested a more mundane explanation: probably Sacker names were simply not translatable into other languages.

Kirk switched off the screen and summed up what he'd learned. The appearance of a Sacker was disgusting to human eyes and his smell offensive to the human nose; both sight and smell could bring the taste of bile to a human mouth and cause the poor observer to lose his dinner. Touch one, and you get burned. Listen to one, and your eardrums are punctured. Sight, sound, smell, touch, and taste—without meaning to, the Sackers managed to offend *every one* of the human five senses. Without those senses, humanity was a race of machines. With them, humans could never approach the enigmatic race derisively known as Sackers.

There didn't seem to be any answer.

Instead, there were new questions, bothersome questions that Kirk could see no answers to. Why would a hitherto peaceful race suddenly turn violent? Could the Zirgosian woman be mistaken and was unknowingly blaming the wrong people for the havoc wreaked on Holox? *Were the Sackers somehow responsible for bringing the three-minute universe into our own?* Did that last question belong with the first two?

"McCoy to Captain Kirk," the speaker said.

Kirk pressed a button. "Kirk here."

"Just wanted you to know I'm back, Jim. And I brought the woman with me, the one you wanted to talk to."

"I'll be right there," Kirk said, and broke the connection before McCoy could tell him not to bother.

Lieutenant Uhura didn't want to be in sickbay. "My problems are nothing compared to what's happened to those poor people down on Holox," she insisted. "I can wait."

"Uhura, I called *you* in, remember?" McCoy said tiredly. "The situation on Holox is under control, and it looks as if those we reached in time are going to pull through. Now tell me about the dreams. Are you getting your sleep? You look more rested."

"I am, thanks to you. I'm still dreaming of fire now and then, but the dreams are, well, different."

"Different how?"

"I'm no longer dreaming of . . . *that* fire, the one I was caught in when I was ten years old. I dream of other places burning. Do you remember the palace on the planet Platonius?"

"Very well."

"I dreamed it caught fire. It never has, so far as I know. The games arena on Triskelion—I dreamed of it burning. And the space station where I got that first little tribble? Burned. Does that mean that on some level I'm convinced fire is uncontrollable? If I'm letting it burn up every place I've ever been?"

"No, I don't think so, Uhura," McCoy smiled. "What you're doing is depersonalizing the fire that hurt you. You're substituting other places, other details for the ones that cause you pain. It's a way of controlling the memory—you've taken a big step. I'll bet you that the dreams start coming farther and farther apart now. You'll see."

"You think so?"

"I do indeed. And you won't need drugs to help you sleep."

Uhura sighed happily. "That's the best news I've heard in a long time." She got up to leave. "I thank you, Dr. McCoy."

"That's what we're here for."

They walked together out of McCoy's office into the examination room. Uhura looked around. "Where's Christine?"

"Down on the planet. The doctoring is done—it's all nursing from now on."

Suddenly the doors whooshed open and Captain Kirk came charging in. "Where is she? Oh—sorry, Uhura. Where is she, Bones?"

"In intensive care. She's sleeping, Jim."

"Can I talk to her?"

"Not yet. She's sleeping a natural sleep, one of the best healers in the world. Right now treatment consists of sustaining life while the antidote has time to clean all the toxic residue out of the system. We can't rush it, Jim. I'll call you when she wakes."

Uhura looked puzzled. "Who is it you're talking about?"

"A Zirgosian woman, I don't know her name," Kirk said. "She's the one who warned us about the Sackers."

"Ah. No one else said anything?" Uhura asked.

"No one else was in any condition to talk—none that I saw, at any rate. Bones, that heat front is still advancing, and if the Sackers had anything to do with it I've got to know about it!"

"If we wake her now, we may interfere with the healing process. Just a couple more hours, Jim."

Kirk shrugged and accepted it.

"There's still no answer from the Sacker ship, Captain," Uhura said. "If only we knew their language!"

"Doesn't matter—they know ours. Or at least they have translators they can use. They're not answering because they don't want to answer. And they don't want to answer because they're planning something. Something that's not going to do any of us any good. You can bet on it."

Uhura and McCoy exchanged an uneasy look, said nothing. Captain Kirk was disturbed, and that was reason enough for both of them to feel disturbed as well. The captain wasn't in the habit of seeing problems where none existed.

They had trouble.

Chapter Three

"ALL RIGHT, two lads and a lass," Mr. Scott said, "what're ye called?"

"Hrolfson."

"Franklin."

"Ching," said the lass.

They were in a Holox hovercraft heading southwest from the settlement. The security team member named Franklin was at the controls and the ride was getting a bit bumpy, but Scott didn't say anything about it. He studied Mr. Spock's tricorder resting on his knee. "A wee bit to port, lad."

Franklin edged the craft over to the left. "What are we looking for, Mr. Scott?"

"We're lookin' for an unaccounted-for source o' heat out in the middle o' nowhere. The captain is thinkin' it may be a Sacker structure."

The hovercraft lurched, then straightened out again. "Sackers?" Franklin gulped. "On Holox?"

"That's what we're to find out, lad."

"My sister saw a Sacker once," Ching remarked from the seat directly behind Scott's. "She was sick for a week."

Scott swiveled around to face her. "Aye? Where was this?"

"On Elas. The Elasians wouldn't let them inside the cities."

Scott grunted. "Smart o' them. We'll not be havin' contact with the Sackers, so rest easy. We're just to see what they're up to."

They rode in silence for a while. Then Hrolfson said, "Am I getting nervous, or is it getting warmer?"

"It's getting warmer," Franklin said, tugging at the neck of his uniform.

Scott read the tricorder. "We're almost there."

"Could it be a military structure, do you suppose?" Ching asked.

"Maybe it's a supply base," Franklin said. "They might need a place to store things."

"Perhaps they just want to settle here," Hrolfson suggested. "Holox has a lot of unused land area."

Mr. Scott said nothing.

"Wait here, Mr. Spock," Lieutenant Berengaria ordered.

Spock halted obediently. So far they'd run into no sign of danger in any of the Zirgosian structures they'd entered on Holox, but the lieutenant was just being thorough. Spock approved.

Berengaria barely met Starfleet's minimum height requirement for security work, but she always managed to look bigger than she was. The hard, muscled arms helped, as did the pouf of hair standing straight up from her head and adding inches to her height. But what made most people forget her size was the air she exuded of knowing exactly what she was doing. Spock was quite content to wait while she checked out the building.

Berengaria and the other two members of her team

cautiously made their way into the structure, which bore no indicator on its façade as to its function. So far, the investigation had proved fruitless. Spock had looked over the rows of patients the medical teams from the *Enterprise* were treating, but he'd found only two of the poisoned Zirgosians who were able to speak. They'd barely had time enough to gasp out that they had no idea what had happened before Nurse Chapel showed up to shoo Spock away. One of the medteam's members was even then at work analyzing the food and water; Holox's air had already tested out safe.

Spock took a few steps back to get a wider view of the building he was to search next. On the whole the Zirgosians built well; they balanced function and aesthetics in a proportion that was especially pleasing to Vulcan eyes. A very civilized people, the Zirgosians; they'd never once initiated hostilities against another world in all the time they'd been a spacefaring race. They were probably as close to being enemy-free as any modern culture could be, and Spock had thought Jim Kirk mistaken in his suspicion that an attempt was being made to eradicate the entire race. But after the evidence of the mass poisoning on Holox, he could no longer deny the likelihood.

Spock walked to the corner of the building and looked along the side. This building was different from the others. Most of the Zirgosian buildings they'd visited had been supersolid structures designed to look light and airy, soaring and pristine. Zirgosian tastes in color ran to cool blues and whites, complementing perfectly the clean lines of their architecture.

But the building in front of him would have looked more at home on Argelius II. Dark and asymmetrical, it was evidently quite labyrinthine on the inside—if the exterior shape of the building was any guide. What colors Spock could glimpse through the windows were dark and rich, maroons and deep greens with an occasional dash of gold trim. He spotted a tapestry hanging on one wall but it was too far away for him to make out any of the detail. His communicator beeped.

"Spock here."

"Mr. Spock, the lab analysis is finished," Christine Chapel's voice said. "It was the water! The food hasn't been tampered with, but the water is loaded with a toxic alkaloid bonded to a delaying agent."

"A delaying agent? That rules out accidental poisoning, then."

"Yes, sir. Evidently whoever is responsible didn't want a few of the Zirgosians falling ill immediately after drinking the water and thus warning the others."

"That would seem a logical conclusion. Thank you, Nurse."

So now there was evidence of malicious intent. Spock was not surprised. Spock was rarely surprised. He was concerned, however. Under normal circumstances the *Enterprise* would stay in orbit around Holox until the colony was back on its feet. Jim would undoubtedly want to help find the poisoner; but unless they could discover a way to stop the advancing heat, there wouldn't be any Holox left to help. Yet he knew Jim would refuse to leave until enough Zirgosians had recovered to the point where the colony could function again, at least on a minimal level.

Berengaria came out of the building. "It's a hostelry, Mr. Spock, for off-planet visitors. I'd say it was for folks who didn't feel comfortable in the Zirgosians' usual antiseptic kind of building."

"Did you say 'antiseptic', Lieutenant? Are you speaking medically or aesthetically?"

"Aesthetically," she smiled. "I think I'd be happier in this building myself. We don't all like *that* kind of architecture." She gestured dismissively toward the nearest Zirgosian structure. "We haven't checked everything, but there aren't any booby traps lying around. I think it's safe."

"Did you find anyone inside?"

"Nobody yet."

Spock followed her into the building. The old-fashioned beamed ceilings were lower than in other Zirgosian structures, and the rooms were over-crowded with furniture, all of it richly colored and soft-looking. Tapestries and paintings and niches containing small sculptures took up most of the wall space; it was all too fussy for Spock's taste. "Where have you looked?"

"Just downstairs."

Spock started to climb a circular staircase—an affectation, he concluded, since the building had only two stories. The staircase ended at a narrow hallway with a ceiling so low he had to bend over when he entered. Even Lieutenant Berengaria, who was much shorter than Spock, had to stoop a little. Spock had been right about the labyrinthine structure; the hallway made three turns and dropped five steps before leading to a wider area with a number of doors opening off of it. He reached out to open the first door.

"Better let me do that, Mr. Spock." Berengaria pushed past him and cautiously opened the door. The bedchamber was empty.

So were the next three rooms they tried, but the fifth door opened on to just about the last sight they expected to see in a settlement that had recently lost well over half its population. A man stood poised on a wooden chest, a rope looped around his neck with the other end thrown over a ceiling beam and anchored to a bed. When he saw Spock and Berengaria, he gasped . . . and stepped off the chest.

Berengaria got there first. The man hanging by the neck kicked out at her, but she managed to grab him and support his weight, grunting from the effort, until Spock got there to help. Even with the two of them holding on to him, the hanging man continued to fight until Spock reached up and applied the Vulcan nerve pinch. All the fight went out of the would-be suicide; he slid quietly and bonelessly to the floor.

"Whew!" said Berengaria. "That was close. He weighs a ton."

"Let's try to make him more comfortable." Spock stooped down and hooked his arms under the man's arms, but even with his great Vulcan strength he had to strain to lift the unconscious man. Berengaria took the man's legs, and between the two of them they got him on the bed.

"He's awfully heavy for such a short and squat fellow," Berengaria panted. "Who is he, Mr. Spock? He doesn't look like a Zirgosian."

"That, Lieutenant, is an inhabitant of the planet Gelchen, if I'm not mistaken," Spock said. "A high-gravity planet—one point eight five Earth normal, if I remember correctly. All those who dwell there have that same low, compact body. Heavy mass."

"Wonder what he's doing here? Look, he's coming around."

The man opened his eyes and stared at them blankly for a moment. Then he remembered and turned his head to the side and began to cry. His body heaved with big, racking sobs.

Berengaria was appalled; instinctively she reached out to place a comforting hand on his shoulder. "Oh, don't—there's got to be a better answer than killing yourself." She turned to Spock. "You don't happen to speak the Gelchenite language, do you, Mr. Spock?"

"Unfortunately, I do not."

But it didn't matter; the Gelchenite understood English. "You should not have interfered," he choked out, and covered his face with both arms.

Spock and Berengaria waited; finally the Gelchenite got himself under control. He sat up in bed and looked at their uniforms. "You're from a Federation starship."

"The *Enterprise*," Spock acknowledged. "I am First Officer Spock—this is Lieutenant Berengaria. And you are . . . ?"

"I am Borkel Mershaya ev Symwid, of the Gelchen Transgalactic Trade Commission." He took a deep breath. "You might as well take me into custody. I am the one who poisoned the water supply. It was I who killed all those good people." His head drooped forward on his chest.

Berengaria made a strangled sound and stepped in closer to the bed.

Spock's left eyebrow rose. "Mr. ev Symwid, do you understand what you are saying? You deliberately poisoned the Zirgosian colonists?"

"Yes," the Gelchenite answered dully. "I can't live with what I've done. You should have let me die."

Spock turned to Berengaria. "Lieutenant, summon your team." He took out his communicator. "*Enterprise*, come in."

"*Enterprise* here."

"Five to beam up. On my signal."

* * *

The Gelchenite, Borkel Mershaya ev Symwid, slumped in his seat in the *Enterprise* briefing room. Dr. McCoy had given him a stimulant to keep him from succumbing to depression, but the man remained passive and resigned. Lieutenant Berengaria stood behind him, arms folded. Mr. Spock sat quietly at the briefing table calibrating the new tricorder he'd checked out of Stores, to replace the one now in Mr. Scott's possession.

The briefing room door opened and Captain Kirk walked in, his face a mixture of revulsion and curiosity. He stood before the disconsolate Gelchenite and gave him a good looking-over. "Borkel Mershaya ev Symwid," he said. "I'm told that is your name. Is it a name you're proud of?"

The Gelchenite lifted his head. "I was once," he said. "But not now."

Kirk stared at him a moment and then took his seat at the table. "I'm Captain Kirk. I want you to tell me why in the name of all you hold holy you poisoned those people. And make it good, mister. Don't hold back anything. Why did you do it?"

The Gelchenite sighed deeply. "The Sackers. They forced us to. They—"

"Hold it," Kirk commanded. "You're saying it was the Sackers who wanted the colonists dead? Why?"

"The Zirgosians had denied the Sackers permission to build that thing out in the desert, whatever it is. So the Sackers took three of us—"

"Us? Start at the beginning, ev Symwid. Why were you on Holox to start with?"

The poisoner ran his tongue over dry lips. "I was part of the Gelchen Transgalactic Trade Commission. We were here to set up offices to administer a trade agreement recently drawn up between Holox and

Gelchen. Then the Sackers came. They beamed down in the desert and started building without so much as a by-your-leave. When the Holox authorities went to their site to tell them Holox was a Zirgosian colony planet and they were not welcome to build here, the Sackers killed them."

"Killed them! What did the rest of the Zirgosians do?"

"They're not a combat-oriented people, Captain, so the first thing they did was try to contact their home planet. But they got no answer. So they started arming themselves. They weren't decided as to whether they should attack or defend, or whether they should just try to contain the Sackers until they could contact either Zirgos or a Federation starship."

Kirk held off on telling him why they couldn't reach Zirgos. "Then what?"

"Two other members of the trade commission and I were about to beam up to our ship—we were thinking of leaving, frankly. All the others were already on board. But the Sackers . . . kidnapped us, I suppose it was. We didn't have a chance."

Berengaria snorted.

"Did you say something, Lieutenant?" Kirk asked.

"No, sir."

Spock spoke for the first time. "How did they go about kidnapping you, Mr. ev Symwid?"

"I don't really know. All I remember is this horrible smell—and I started vomiting . . . the other two were doing the same. Then I lost consciousness. When I came to, I was wearing a helmet of some sort—it kept out the smell. We were on the Sacker ship. They told us they wanted us to poison the Zirgosian water supply. They even supplied the poison."

"Just this one settlement?" Spock asked. "There are at least a dozen others on Holox."

"Just this one. Because it's close to where they were building, you see, and they didn't want the Zirgosians bothering them. So their solution to that was to kill them. We refused, of course. But then the Sackers told us that if we did not, they would attack *our* homeworld. And to prove they meant what they said, they destroyed our ship."

Kirk pressed his lips together. "Survivors?"

"None." The Gelchenite covered his eyes with one hand. "They *teased* us, Captain. They fired over our ship first; then they fired to starboard a couple of times. This went on for several minutes before they got bored playing with us and blasted our ship out of the sky."

"Didn't your ship fight back?" Berengaria asked, appalled.

"Yes, of course—but their weapons didn't even begin to penetrate the Sackers' shielding . . . that ship's impregnable. I've never seen one like it. Anyway, all the other Gelchenites were dead except the three of us on the Sacker ship, and the Sackers told us that's what would happen to Gelchen if we didn't poison the Zirgosian colonists for them." He swallowed. "So we did it."

There was a long silence. Then Spock said, "Mr. ev Symwid, why didn't the Sackers destroy the settlement themselves? They obviously have the firepower."

"I don't know, Mr. Spock. They didn't explain their reasons."

Kirk asked, "Where are the other two of you?"

The Gelchenite lifted his shoulders, then let them

drop. "Gone. Maybe they fled to one of the other settlements."

Berengaria was seething. "And you did it? You just went ahead and *did* it?"

The Gelchenite's head jerked up at her accusing tone. He heaved his stocky body out of his seat and faced her. "Yes, I did it. I'm ashamed of what I did, and I'm ready to die for it. But what choice did I have? Should I have sacrificed my own people to save the Zirgosians? What would you have done? It's easy to pronounce judgment."

Berengaria stood toe to toe with him. "What would I have done? First I would have looked for a way to contact Gelchen and warn them a Sacker attack was imminent, and then I would have refused to poison the Zirgosians. If I failed in my attempt to warn Gelchen, I would still have refused. Gelchen isn't defenseless. Your people aren't stupid, are they? They know when they're being attacked? At least your people would have had a fighting chance—which is more than you gave the Zirgosian colonists. Or, I would have accepted the poison and looked for a way to use it against the Sackers. If I failed at that too, then I would have taken it myself. You ask me what I would have done? *That's* what I would have done."

"That will do, Lieutenant," Kirk murmured, not entirely disapproving of her outburst.

Berengaria turned her back to ev Symwid and said no more. The Gelchenite appealed to Kirk. "Do you think I'm making excuses? I'm telling you the truth, Captain, I swear I am! I'll submit to any electric or chemical memory probe you like!"

"Oh, we have a quicker way than that. Mr. Spock?"

Spock put down the tricorder he'd finished calibrating and went over to ev Symwid. "I have to touch you, Mr. ev Symwid. There is no pain involved." He spread the fingers of his right hand and placed them on one side of the Gelchenite's face. The latter evidently knew of the Vulcan mind meld because he remained still and did nothing to disturb Spock's concentration. A minute passed. Then another. Spock dropped his hand. "He's telling the truth, Captain."

The intercom unit on the table came to life. "Captain Kirk. Acknowledge, please."

"Kirk here. What is it, Uhura?"

"Captain, the Sacker ship is receiving a message," she said. "And Captain—it's coming from the *Enterprise.*"

"Can you isolate it?"

"G Deck—that's as close as I can pinpoint it."

"We're on G Deck," Kirk said.

Spock was reading his tricorder. "Captain, I'm getting a signal . . . within this room." The Vulcan moved the tricorder to home in on the signal—which led him directly to the Gelchenite. "The point of origin seems to be Mr. ev Symwid's arm."

Puzzled, the Gelchenite raised his arm. "Me?"

"An implant," Kirk snapped. "What did they put in there, ev Symwid? A homing device? A voice transmitter?"

"I . . . I don't know. This is news to me, Captain. It must have been done while I was unconscious."

Kirk spoke to the intercom. "It's all right, Uhura, we've got it. Kirk out." He cleared his throat. "Lieutenant Berengaria, escort Mr. ev Symwid to sickbay. Tell Dr. McCoy to remove the implant as quickly as possible."

"Yes, sir," Berengaria said. "Come on, you." She

gave the Gelchenite a tap on the shoulder and they both left the briefing room.

Kirk and Spock exchanged a long look. The latter said, "An entire race doesn't change its nature overnight, Jim."

"I was thinking the same thing myself," Kirk nodded. "Whatever turned the Sackers into such callous killers must have been building for a long time. Either that, or they've been planning this all along."

"But exactly what are they planning? We have no evidence that the Sackers are responsible for releasing the new universe's energy into our space. The two could be entirely unrelated."

"They could, but I'll bet you my retirement pay they're not."

One corner of Spock's mouth lifted. "Your retirement pay, Jim? Really?"

"*Half* my retirement pay, half. A fourth."

"You are fortunate that I am not a betting man. Not to mention the very real possibility that neither of us will be around to collect."

"I've been trying not to think of that. That heat front's still moving . . . Spock, is there any way of stopping that thing?"

"I would say no. But if you are correct that the release of energy was precipitated by person or persons unknown, then that person or persons might also have the means of stopping it. It would have to be a way of sealing up the rupture between the two universes, and I for one know of no way such a monumental undertaking could be accomplished. Not even theoretically. But if the Sackers do possess this knowledge, they would have to use it eventually to prevent their own extinction."

"Yes . . . you're right, Spock. What are they after? They must have some goal in mind. Maybe that woman we found in the Holox administrative center can tell us something when she wakes up. And isn't it about time Scotty reported in?"

"Indeed, Mr. Scott is overdue."

The intercom spoke with the chief surgeon's voice. "McCoy to Captain Kirk."

"Here, Doctor."

"I've got this gizmo out of the Gelchenite's arm. What do you want me to do with it?"

"Take it to the bridge—we'll meet you there." Kirk broke the connection and stood up. "Let's go, Spock. You're about to get your first close-up look at Sacker technology."

"What is this thing, Jim?" Dr. McCoy asked. "A transmitter of some sort?"

"Looks like it," said Kirk. "Mr. Spock, is there some way to hook this thing up to the ship's computer?"

"I shall try, Captain." Spock took the Sacker device that had been implanted in the Gelchenite's arm and examined it curiously. "Minuscule circuitry. Lieutenant Uhura, I will require your assistance."

"Yes, sir. Microwaldoes?"

The two got to work, with McCoy peering over their shoulders. Kirk sat in the command chair and said, "Status report, Mr. Sulu."

"The Sacker ship is still keeping the planet between us, Captain. And they're still refusing communication."

Kirk nodded, not expecting anything else.

Chekov swiveled around in his seat. "Kepten, are

the Sackers responsible for poisoning the colonists on Holox?"

"Yes, through unwilling agents. They kidnapped three Gelchenites and forced them to poison the water supply."

The young navigator looked puzzled. "But . . . but vhy? Vhat do they gain?"

"That," sighed Kirk, "is the question, Mr. Chekov. What do they want here at all?"

"What's their homeworld, Captain?" Sulu asked.

"Nobody knows."

"Maybe something happened to it, and they're looking for a new one," the helmsman suggested. "Maybe they just want a place to live."

"Ve hef a wery nice place at home vhere they are velcome to live," Chekov said. "Ve call it Siberia."

"Ready, Captain," Spock announced.

"All right, what've we got?" Kirk looked at the viewscreen's display of light impulses generated by the Sacker transmitter. "They look like scratch marks. Is this what the Sacker ship is receiving?"

"Yes, sir," Uhura said. "It will record in their computer banks in this form. The signal must be bouncing off one of Holox's communication satellites."

"Tricky device. Those markings keep changing . . . Spock?"

"Our computer does not recognize the code, Captain. I am initiating cryptographic analysis."

Uhura's eyes narrowed. "There is a pattern here . . . wait, let me isolate this part." She froze ten lines of the Sacker symbols and transferred them to a smaller screen while the larger viewscreen kept running a changing array of what Captain Kirk had called scratch marks. "Look, see this symbol?" Uhura said. "It always stands alone, never part of a larger grouping. See here . . . and here . . . and here? Like a connective, or possibly whatever the Sackers use for punctuation."

"That's a start," Kirk acknowledged. "Cryptoanalysis?"

"None, Captain," Spock answered in a distinctly unhappy tone. "The computer cannot break the code because it is unable to find a starting point. The most it can do is transmogrify these symbols into approximations of English-language word groupings." He touched a few keys and a series of what looked like nonsense words appeared on the screen.

"Stop talking!" Uhura suddenly cried. "Captain? Everybody . . . please stop talking!"

They all looked at her in surprise, but at a gesture from Kirk the bridge was suddenly silent. The big viewscreen went blank.

"There, you see!" Uhura cried triumphantly, and the viewscreen showed a new set of words.

"Those are *our* words up there on the screen?" Kirk asked.

"Yes, sir! This device we hooked up to the computer is a translator as well as a transmitter. That's the Sacker language we're seeing on the screen!"

"Good going, Uhura!" Kirk exclaimed, pleased. "Now we've got something to work with!"

"Excellently done, Lieutenant," Spock said more quietly.

"No wonder the computer couldn't break the 'code'," said Kirk. "It has no Sacker words in its memory bank. And another thing—the Sackers can no longer pretend they're not receiving our messages."

He raised his voice. "Sacker ship—this is Captain James T. Kirk of the U.S.S. *Enterprise*. We request immediate communication and an accounting of your part in the poisoning of the Holox colonists. Respond immediately."

They waited. There was no answer.

"Keep replaying that message, Lieutenant," Kirk instructed. "Mr. Spock—can the translator part of that device be separated from the transmitter without damage?"

"I shall attempt to do just that, Captain. Doctor, if you could take just two steps backward . . . ?"

McCoy moved out of the way. They all waited in silence, now that they knew every word they spoke was being translated into the Sacker language and broadcast to the strange ship on the other side of Holox.

Finally Spock lifted his head from his task. "Much of the circuitry is integral, Captain, used mutually by translator and transmitter. To keep one without the other would mean destroying one of them. I assume it is the translator part you wish to keep?"

"You assume correctly," Kirk said. "Do it."

A few minutes more and it was done. They all breathed a sigh of relief, all except Spock who was too caught up in examining the disassembled parts of the tiny transmitter to think of anything as mundane as a feeling of relief. "Truly a remarkable piece of microengineering," the first officer said.

"Now why did the Sackers plant that thing in the Gelchenite's arm?" McCoy mused. "Were they expecting him to get caught? Did they expect *us* to catch him?"

"Probably all three of the Gelchenites had implants," Kirk said. "In case something went wrong or the Gelchenites tried to run away. The Sackers would want some way of keeping track of them."

"So eavesdropping on us was just a little extra bonus?"

"Evidently." Quickly Kirk ran over in his mind everything that had been said in the briefing room before the implant had been discovered. He concluded nothing had been revealed that the Sackers didn't already know. "Lieutenant Uhura, since you're the one who discovered the secret of the translator, why don't you . . . ?"

But she was already at work on it. "Starship," she said into an isolated microphone she'd connected for the purpose. A word appeared on the screen, and Uhura keyed its meaning into the computer.

"Ah . . . yes, something like that," Kirk smiled. "Well, Doctor, do you suppose your patient has had enough of that 'natural' sleep you think so highly of?"

McCoy grinned. "Let's go see, shall we?"

Uhura looked back over her shoulder. "I could use some help, Captain."

"I vill help," Chekov volunteered. He was bored with having nothing to do so long as the ship stayed in a stable orbit.

"There's your assistant, Lieutenant," Kirk said. "Let me know when you think you have a handle on it. Mr. Spock, I'll be in sickbay if you—"

He was interrupted by the intercom. "Dr. McCoy to the transporter room! Dr. McCoy to the transporter room! Emergency!" Transporter Chief Kyle's voice was high and frightened-sounding.

McCoy hit a button on the command chair arm rest. "What is the nature of the emergency?"

"Burn case! The worst I've ever seen!" Kyle's frightened voice said. "It's Franklin, one of the security men. I . . . I never saw anyone burned so badly! Hurry, Doctor—hurry!"

The examination room of sickbay reeked with the odor of charred flesh. Captain Kirk stood by helplessly as Dr. McCoy worked quickly to save the young security man. He'd sprayed a coolant foam over the horrendously burned body to give Franklin some immediate relief and now was treating him for shock. Liquids and whole blood were being pumped into his body after some initial difficulty; McCoy had had trouble finding an undamaged vein. Franklin was breathing shallowly through an oxygen mask.

"That coolant foam has an antiseptic in it, so that should guard against infection for the time being," McCoy muttered to himself. "But is the body tissue getting enough blood? Dammit! All the nurses are down on the planet." He moved over to the intercom. "Bridge."

"Bridge," Spock's voice acknowledged.

"Spock, I need Nurse Chapel. Right now."

"I will summon her immediately, Doctor."

Franklin began to groan. McCoy hurried back to his patient and sprayed more foam over his body. "This stuff's only for temporary relief," he growled. "I need to get him into a burn bath—a proqualine solution. But I don't want to leave him alone long enough to prepare it."

"Can I help?" Kirk asked. "Tell me what to do."

"Watch his readings. If his respiration indicator begins to drop, call me." He hurried away to the intensive care unit.

Kirk watched the respiration indicator. It wavered for a moment but then recovered. He looked down at what used to be a nice-looking young man and felt himself fill with a fury so intense that it made his vision blur. He shook his head and focused again on the indicator.

"Ka-un."

Captain. Kirk looked down at Franklin's face; the young man was trying to talk . . . but his lips had been burned away. "Franklin?"

"S-Sackers . . . did this to 'ee." He couldn't say the *m*-sound. "Ching . . . dead. Ih-ciherated her." *Incinerated her.*

Kirk gritted his teeth. "Mr. Scott? And the other security man?"

"Don't . . . know. They ha'—" Franklin broke off to concentrate on the difficult problem of breathing.

"Don't talk any more," Kirk said. "Lie as still as you can."

The door opened and Christine Chapel came in. She gasped at the sight of Franklin. "Burn bath," she said.

"Dr. McCoy's preparing it." She hurried off to the intensive care unit.

McCoy came back pulling an antigrav gurney. "You'll have to help me move him, Jim. Put on a pair of gloves—behind you, on that table."

They got Franklin on the gurney. Nurse Chapel came back and said the bath was ready; she carried the transfusion equipment while Kirk and McCoy steered the gurney into intensive care. They lowered Franklin into the bath, and waited.

After a few minutes Franklin opened his eyes and said, "That 'eels 'etter." And saw three faces grin down at him.

"Feels better, does it?" McCoy said. "Ah, the resiliency of youth! You'll get sick of that bath soon enough." Nurse Chapel started sponging some of the solution on Franklin's face and head. "Just let yourself float. Relax every muscle as completely as you can."

"Bones, will it hurt him to talk?" Kirk asked.

"One minute. No more."

"Franklin, what happened down there? What did you find?"

"Sackers . . . 'uilt a 'lister do'."

"Blister dome?"

"Sea'less." Franklin thought that wasn't clear and tried again. "No sea's."

"Seamless, I understand."

"Looking 'or entrance. Couldn't 'ind one. Caught us."

"A seamless blister dome with no visible entrance, and the Sackers caught you looking. Then what?"

"S'ell . . . aw'ul s'ell." Franklin began to gag just from the memory of the smell. When he'd recovered, he said, "They use . . . 'ire 'eh'ons. Killed Ching, thought they killed 'ee."

"Fire weapons? Did they use them on Mr. Scott?"

"Don't know . . . I 'lacked out."

"Minute's up," said McCoy.

Kirk stepped back from the bath. McCoy gave Nurse Chapel some instructions, and then he and the captain went back out into the examination room. "I don't know how in the world he managed to call the ship, Jim. His hands are practically useless."

"Will he make it?"

"Fifty-fifty chance, I'd say. But he's young and he's healthy . . . maybe the odds are a little better than fifty-fifty."

Kirk nodded at this one little piece of good news. "They're not going to get away with this."

"What are you going to do?"

"McCoy, one of my people is dead, another is critically burned, and two are missing. What do you think I'm going to do?"

McCoy was aghast. "You're not going to attack that monster ship, are you?"

Kirk shook his head. "That's not the way. They could probably destroy us as easily as they destroyed the Gelchenites' ship. I'll have to think of something else. But I'm going to get those bastards—count on it."

McCoy looked at him closely. "You're worried about Scotty, aren't you?"

"Of course I'm worried about Scotty! I don't know whether he's alive or dead! He could be lying abandoned somewhere, too badly burned to work his communicator. He could be a prisoner . . . I don't even know whether the Sackers take prisoners or not! But if Scotty were in any position to contact us, he would have by now."

"I know. I'm worried about him, too."

Kirk's hands were fists. "I haven't figured out how yet, but those ghouls are going to pay for what they've done." His face hardened. "Believe me. They'll pay."

Chapter Four

UHURA SLAPPED AT her console in frustration. "*Mi*ster Chekov! I really do not think the Sackers would have a word in their language for *borscht*."

"Oh? Vhy not?" Chekov asked in all innocence.

"You know perfectly well why not. Besides, there's no point in arguing about it—look at the screen."

The screen was blank.

Chekov screwed up his face in mock concentration. "Maybe thet is the Sackers' problem. Poor nutrition."

Uhura growled low in her throat. "Let's go on. And please don't say *chicken Kiev*."

"You are the vun who suggested ve try food."

"I meant food the Sackers might eat."

"I do not know vhat food the Sackers might eat."

"Excuse me, Chekov, but aren't you supposed to be *helping* me?"

"I *am* helping you. I chust do not know vhat the Sackers are heffing for dinner tonight."

Uhura sighed. "Maybe we'd do better to look for variations of the word 'fire'. When I tried 'fire', the screen showed eighty-six words. Imagine—they have eighty-six different ways of saying 'fire'."

"If you vish," said Chekov, all agreeable cooperation. He thumbed on the microphone. "Blaze."

Sixteen symbols showed on the screen.

"Well, that narrows it down some," Uhura murmured, keying them in. "I wish I had some way of knowing which of these words are nouns and which are verbs. Keep going."

"Conflagration."

Three words.

"Ha!" Uhura cried. "Now we're getting somewhere. Let's try—wait a minute, Chekov. I have an incoming message." She listened carefully, recording the message at the same time. "*Enterprise* here. We acknowledge." She switched over to an intraship channel. "Bridge to Captain Kirk."

"Kirk here," came the immediate response.

"A message from Starfleet Command, Captain. It's bad news. Two more stars have been destroyed by the advancing heat front, and—"

"Did they have planets?"

"One of the stars had two planets, but neither was life-sustaining, fortunately. But some of the outpost stations are beginning to register sharp rises in temperature." She paused. "And Captain, Starfleet says the Sackers on other worlds have all departed. No one knows where they've gone."

"Damn. That's ominous. Do I have new orders?"

"Yes, sir. You are ordered to . . . *hurry up*." There was a silence. "Captain?"

"I heard you. Kirk out."

Uhura broke the connection. She turned to Chekov, and the two exchanged a long, grim look.

The navigator picked up the microphone, all business. "Combustion." Uhura barely had time to key it in before he said, "Ignition." Then: "Incineration."

No more kidding around.

* * *

Captain Kirk turned away from the intercom in the chief surgeon's office to see McCoy standing in the doorway. "Did you hear that?"

The doctor nodded. "The heat's getting closer and the Sackers are in hiding. Which problem do you tackle first?"

"They may be the same problem, if the Sackers are responsible for letting the three-minute universe in."

"It's no longer only three minutes old, of course," McCoy said. "But it still has a few billion years to go."

"Don't remind me."

"Jim, how long has it been since you've had some sleep? You don't exactly look fresh and ready to go."

"Ah . . . I don't know. I lost track."

"Better find time for a nap, then. You can't put out a fire when you're dead on your feet."

"I'll find some time."

"You know, I've been thinking about that," McCoy said. "We must not be getting the full blast of the new universe. If it explodes outward in all directions . . ."

"Then we're getting only a part of the explosion. Spock suggested the same thing. Not that it matters— the amount of heat we're getting is enough to cook us good. Did you hear my new orders? Starfleet wants me to *hurry up*." He snorted. "Bones, I have got to talk to that Zirgosian woman!"

McCoy grinned broadly. "That's what I came in to tell you. She's awake. And she's in good condition. Her vital signs check out positive, and she's clear-headed and articulate." Then, as if he'd just thought of it: "Why don't you go in and see her, Jim? Might do you both good."

Kirk glared at him and charged in to where the Zirgosian woman was sitting up in bed. He halted abruptly, struck by the thought that he was going to have to find the words to tell this woman that her homeworld had been destroyed. He temporized. "How are you feeling?"

She managed to muster up a smile. "Much better, thanks to your Dr. McCoy. He tells me I'll be 'up and around' in another day or so." She tilted her head and looked at him closely. "I remember you. You were one of the people who found me."

"I'm Jim Kirk—I'm the captain of this vessel. You warned me about the Sackers, remember?"

Her smile disappeared. "Sackers."

"They're the ones who poisoned you." He pulled a chair up next to her bed and sat down. "They strong-armed three men into doing the job for them, but the Sackers are behind it. We caught one of the poisoners—do you know a man named Borkel Mershaya ev Symwid?"

"No. That's not a Zirgosian name."

"He's a Gelchenite. He was on Holox as part of a trade commission." Kirk explained how the Sackers had forced ev Symwid and two of his fellow commissioners to poison the Holox water supply.

"Are the Sackers still on Holox?"

"Unfortunately."

Her face was anguished. "You must stop them! You can't let them do it!"

"Do what? Can you tell me what's happened? What do you know about the Sackers?"

It took a while, but eventually the whole story came out. The woman said her name was Dorelian, and her home was Zirgos, not Holox. She'd come to the colony planet to oversee the installation of and instruction in the use of some new mining equipment Zirgos had developed. At the time she'd left home, Sackers had been on Zirgos and were involved in a controversy about something they'd commissioned to be built.

"Their ship," Kirk said.

Dorelian looked surprised. "How did you know?"

"Someone had to build it for them. Their homeworld is not within the range of Federation worlds, so wherever it is it's too far away to be of much use to them in practical matters such as shipbuilding."

She nodded. "The ship had not been fully tested, and the builders were not ready to turn it over to the Sackers. But the Sackers didn't want to wait, so they just took it. The ship was built in orbit, so all they had to do was beam over from their old ship. It's a very special kind of ship, Captain Kirk. For one thing, it can transform itself into different shapes."

"We've seen two of them."

"Ah, then you know. The compact form conserves power that's needed for their life-support system—the Sackers require a great deal of heat, you know. That's why they never stay overnight on most planets if they can help it—it's physically taxing for them."

"I didn't know that."

"The expanded forms of the ship are its combat and maneuvering modes, and they take a great deal of power to operate—power that must be diverted from life support."

"So they can't stay in combat mode for extended periods?" Kirk said. "They'll need to go back to the compact form to, er, warm up?"

"That's right. As I understand it, that was one of the areas the builders thought could be improved. But the Sackers were in a hurry. And right before I left Zirgos, we all found out why."

She paused, trying to get her thoughts in order. "Ships aren't the only thing built on Zirgos, Captain. To put it briefly, our scientists have made a tremendous breakthrough. They learned how to tap into the energy of adjoining universes."

Kirk caught his breath. "Go on."

"You understand what this means? It would be a limitless source of free energy, not only for Zirgos but for the entire Federation—*if it could be controlled*. For that purpose the scientists developed a device called a baryon reverter that's supposed to seal the breach between universes or limit its size, I'm not sure which. Perhaps both. Neither instrument has ever been tested, of course—how do you test something like that? Then the Sackers . . ." She stopped to swallow a couple of times.

"The Sackers stole both instruments," Kirk finished for her.

Dorelian pressed her fingertips against her eyes. "They're going to use them, Captain—I'm sure of it. Evidently they've been trying to find out the details of their operation ever since construction first began." She dropped her hands into her lap. "It may be the Sackers only want to keep all that nice free energy for themselves. But those instruments in the wrong hands would make an unstoppable weapon. And fire is the Sackers' natural weapon. So you see, you've got to stop them before they use it."

Every once in a while, a moment came along in which Captain James Kirk hated the things his job required him to do. This was one of those times when he would rather have been anywhere in the galaxy other than where he was at that moment. But someone had to tell her, and it looked as if he were elected. "You don't know how it distresses me to have to tell you this," he said to Dorelian as gently as he could, "but they've already used the first device."

Her face filled with horror. She opened and closed her mouth wordlessly a couple of times and then cried *"No!"* so loudly that Dr. McCoy came running. "Are you sure?"

"What's wrong?" McCoy asked.

"I'm sure," Kirk said sadly.

"Did they use the baryon reverter too? Did they stop it?"

Kirk slowly shook his head.

McCoy watched Dorelian closely, wondering if he was going to have another case of shock to treat.

"Where?" she whispered. "Where did they . . . ?"

They were the hardest words Kirk had ever had to utter. "In the Beta Castelli system," he said, hating what he was doing to her. "I'm sorry . . . Zirgos is gone."

She stared at him a long time—and then she began to scream. Silently. Over and over she screamed, without making a sound. Kirk took her hand, wanting to comfort her. McCoy took the other and tried to soothe her. Her grip was like a metal vise.

"Sedative?" Kirk asked.

McCoy said no. "Her system's just been purged, Jim—it's too soon. Besides, she's doing the right thing. Let her get it out."

Kirk wondered what he would do if he'd just been told that Earth and all the people who lived there no longer existed. What must that feel like? He couldn't imagine it, and he doubted that he'd behave as well as Dorelian. Eventually the silent screaming stopped and the Zirgosian woman lay there sobbing, exhausted from her exertions.

"Dorelian," Kirk said, bending over her bed, "can

you hear me? I want you to listen. I promise you right now that I'll find a way to stop them. They won't get away with what they did to Zirgos. I give you my promise. Do you hear?"

She looked at him with an unreadable expression, and then slowly nodded her head.

"I'll stay with her until she falls asleep," McCoy said. "Why don't you, uh." *Get lost,* his expression said.

Kirk took the hint and left them alone. In the corridor outside sickbay, he went to the nearest intercom. "Spock—where are you?"

"In my quarters, Captain."

E Deck. Kirk rode the turbolift up two levels and headed straight for the Vulcan's quarters.

Spock was seated at his library computer terminal studying the same material about the Sackers that Kirk had read earlier. "Jim—has something happened? You look distraught."

"I just told the Zirgosian woman she no longer had a homeworld to return to." Kirk plopped down in the nearest chair.

Spock frowned. "The Holox colonist we found in the administrative center?"

"She's not a colonist. She lived on Zirgos." Kirk went on to repeat everything Dorelian had told him, from the Sackers' premature occupation of their new ship to their stealing of the instruments that could open and close portals between universes. "I didn't tell her the universe the Sackers tapped into was a brand-new one—I figured she had enough grief. Anyway, now we know how it happened . . . but not why."

"More to the point, Jim, we also know there is a way to turn off the heat, so to speak. A baryon reverter.

What a fascinating approach . . . if its name is a true indicator of the way it functions. I don't suppose the woman told you any of the details?"

"I don't think she knows them—she's a mining engineer of some sort. But figuring out how the reverter does what it does is a pleasure we'll have to postpone. Right now all we have to worry about is whether the damned thing works or not. It's never been tested."

Spock raised an eyebrow. "That's not quite all we have to worry about. There is only one baryon reverter in existence, and it is aboard a Sacker warship. We cannot attack, because we might damage or even destroy the reverter in the process."

"No, no—attack is out." Kirk didn't bother to explain he'd already decided against a direct assault. "They won't talk to us, they won't acknowledge our messages. If we try beaming a security force aboard, they'll simply roast us on sight. Dorelian said fire was their natural weapon, and they aren't going to hesitate to turn it on us." That reminded him. "Have you seen Franklin?"

"I visited him briefly. Nurse Chapel says his chances for recovery are good."

Kirk nodded. "What happened to Franklin—that's the kind of greeting we have to expect from the Sackers. Warm, to say the least. But we have to risk it, Spock. We simply must make contact with them."

"A rather formidable undertaking, I would say, since they steadfastly refuse to acknowledge our existence."

"Ah, but all the Sackers aren't in the ship. There's one other place where we might get at them."

"On Holox?"

"Right. In that blister dome that Scotty's team

discovered." Once he'd mentioned Scotty's name, Kirk's whole body began to sag. He'd kept his worry over the chief engineer pent up too long, and now it all came spilling out. The two men had been together for so long . . . Kirk couldn't imagine the *Enterprise* without his old friend ruling over the engineering section like some benevolent laird of the manor. It was unthinkable.

Spock left his seat and crossed over to lay a gentle hand on the captain's shoulder. "We had better prepare ourselves, Jim. There's a very real possibility that he may be dead."

Kirk lifted his head. "From what we now know of the Sackers," he said heavily, "maybe we'd better pray that he is."

Chief Engineer Montgomery Scott felt his right cheek pressing against something hard, flat, and cool. He labored mightily and managed to get one eye open. He saw he was lying on the floor. *Now why d'ye s'pose I'm sleepin' on the floor?* he wondered vaguely. After a time he worked the other eye open and saw the floor didn't have the familiar carpeting that covered the deck of his quarters. He gravely considered the possibility that someone had stolen his carpet, but then rejected that surmise in favor of the more likely explanation that it was someone else's floor he was sleeping on. It must have been a hell of a party.

He'd struggled up to a sitting position before it all came flooding back. The Sackers. Holox. Ching and Franklin. He stood up too quickly; a pain shot through his head and he almost succumbed to a wave of dizziness and nausea. When his eyes could focus properly, he saw he was not alone. He knelt by the recumbent body of the blond security man called

Hrolfson and shook him by the shoulder. "Laddie! Wake up! Are y'all right?"

Hrolfson opened his eyes and blinked, and then went through the same slow remembering process Scotty had just gone through. He sat up and held his head. "Where are we, Mr. Scott?"

Scotty looked around. "We're inside the Sacker blister. An' it looks as if they built a special little cell just for us."

The cell was a perfect cube made of some sort of transparent plastiform; one wall held a door. Inside the cell an old-fashioned generator-powered refrigeration unit chugged away in the corner under a gridded vent. Other than that, the cell was empty.

"What happened to Ching?" Hrolfson asked. "And Franklin?"

"I think they're dead, lad," Scotty said leadenly. "Heaven only knows why we're still alive."

When Scotty thought his stomach could stand it, he forced himself to look outside their cell. The cell's transparent walls were smoke-colored, of a shade that blurred outlines and cut down on details. For this small mercy Scott rendered thanks; without some sort of muting effect he would never have been able to look at the Sackers directly. Even so, he felt his stomach turn over when he picked out one Sacker and examined him (her?) closely.

He saw a semitransparent membranous sac that looked tougher than leather; it made him think of the mole rat, one of the most repugnant-looking life forms Earth had given rise to. The sac was wrinkled, lumpy, and loose, like a poorly fitted space suit. The Sackers all looked as if they were molting but still carrying their dead skins around with them; Scotty watched several of them walking but none of them left pieces of themselves behind on the floor. That molty, moldy look was their natural state, then. Scotty heard Hrolfson gag once or twice and hoped he could hold it in; their cell contained no cleanup facilities. "Y'are not goin' to be sick, are ye, lad?" he asked.

"I'm all right, Mr. Scott," Hrolfson replied greenly.

The chief engineer turned back to his examination of their captors. The sac fluids were all different colors. One color seemed to dominate in each individual Sacker, though, making it relatively easy to differentiate among them. *Color-coded monsters,* Scotty thought. It was hard to think of these creatures as men and women. They resembled human beings only superficially, primarily in their bifurcated structure; in all other respects they were as alien as any creepy-crawly Scott had ever encountered in all his travels in the galaxy.

"What are they doing, Mr. Scott?" Hrolfson asked. "What are those vats for?"

The two men from the *Enterprise* could see waves of heat rising outside their refrigerated cell; whatever the Sackers were doing, it took a lot of steamy heat to do it. Six huge plastiform-sided vats filled with a cloudy liquid were bubbling away. The Sackers kept checking the gauges on the outside of the vats; the Sackers were slow-moving, Scotty noted, although not clumsy. Once in a while one of them would add something to one of the vats—*a nutrient?* Scotty wondered. He squinted and tried to make out what those small forms were he could see floating in the cloudy liquid. They looked for all the world like . . . fetuses?

"I think," he said slowly, "I think they're growin' new Sackers."

Hrolfson drew in his breath sharply. "Baby Sackers? This is how they reproduce?"

Scott shrugged. "Why not? The males donate sperm, the females donate eggs, they come down here and . . . aye, now, why is that? Why not do all this on their ship?"

"Those vats are pretty big."

"But not so big that their monster of a ship couldna accommodate them. It might be the heat—but that shouldna be a problem either. Why do they need Holox?"

They watched a while longer until Hrolfson said, "Oh-oh. We've got company."

A seven-foot green Sacker was heading straight for their cell. He was followed by a gray Sacker and a brown one who were towing an antigrav carrier loaded with equipment of some sort. The green Sacker opened the door, letting in a blast of heat that drove Scotty and Hrolfson to the farthest corner of the cell. The Sacker took a few things off the antigrav carrier, tossed them inside, and closed the door.

On the floor lay two breathing masks attached to small air tanks and two pairs of smoky-lensed goggles. "I guess we're supposed to put those on," said Hrolfson.

Scotty sighed. "Brace yourself, laddie. I'm afraid we're in for a close encounter of the worst kind." They put on the masks and goggles and waited.

Outside the cell, the green Sacker was putting on a floor-length hooded robe. He pulled the hood forward to hide most of his face. "So we won't throw up all over him," Hrolfson commented dryly. The Sacker strapped a translator around his waist and slipped some kind of attached headpiece inside his hood. The other two Sackers unloaded a piece of equipment and a solid plastic cube and pushed them through the door. The hooded green Sacker stepped inside.

Even with the breathing mask on, Scotty still caught a whiff of the creature. He sternly ordered his stomach to stop churning.

The Sacker looked the two humans over and then indicated Hrolfson. "You," a mellow male voice said from the translator at the Sacker's waist. "Sit there." He pointed at the plastic cube.

Hrolfson hesitated. "What do I do, Mr. Scott?" he asked through his breathing mask.

Scotty took a step forward. "What d'ye plan to do with him?"

"I probe the memory. There is no pain, and no danger."

If that was the worst the Sackers had planned for them, they could survive that. "Do as he says, lad. But don't let him touch ye."

Hrolfson sat uncertainly on the cube. The Sacker used tongs to place a metal band bristling with electrodes on Hrolfson's head. Then he went around behind the instrument to read the results of the probe. He went on studying the results long after the probe was finished. Hrolfson took the metal band from his head.

Then without warning the Sacker moved over to the security man and grabbed his upper arm. Hrolfson screamed from the burning pain. The Sacker opened the door and thrust his human captive out. Scott let out a yell and started after him, but the green Sacker slammed the door shut and stood in front of it. "Get out o' the way!" Scott demanded, but the Sacker didn't move.

One of the two Sackers who'd stayed outside the refrigerated cell—the gray one—had a weapon in his hand. Without further ado he pointed it at Hrolfson . . . and set him on fire.

Scotty screamed and tried to push his way past the green Sacker, who wrapped his robe around one arm and used it to knock him away. Outside, a tongue of flame caught a passing Sacker in the arm; he jerked back and said something to the Sacker wielding the weapon. What would have destroyed a human arm merely made the Sacker wince.

But the human security man was now barely visible inside his coat of fire. Hrolfson was jerking spasmodically as the flames reached his nerve endings; finally all movement ceased as he collapsed into a heap that went on burning and burning. Scotty fell to his knees and beat against the plastiform wall with his fists, moaning as he watched the younger man die.

"You are connected?" The Sacker's pseudovoice sounded puzzled.

"Ye heathens! Why did y'do that?" Scotty cried in anguish. "Y'dinna have to kill him!"

"I do not comprehend your pain. Was he your kin? You do not share characteristics."

"No, he was not me kin! He was me *shipmate*—if that means anythin' to ye!"

"But if he was not your kin, his going should not cause distress."

"Oh, that's the way your so-called minds work, is it? If he's not a relative, kill him?" Scotty wiped his eyes. "Well, y'can kill yourselves off that way if y'like . . . an' the sooner the better! But y'have no right to be takin' our lives away from us. Y'have no right!"

"If I had let him go, he would have called your ship. We are vulnerable here."

Scotty got to his feet. "We're not all as bloodthirsty as ye, y'great green blitherin' blob! Y'dinna have to kill him!"

The Sacker was silent for a moment. Then he asked, "What is 'blitherinblob'?"

"Look in a mirror," Scotty snarled.

The Sacker thought that over, but instead of answering simply pointed to the plastic cube.

Scotty sat and snatched up the electrode headband. "I'll put it on meself." He did.

When the probe was finished, Scotty took off the headband and stood up. The Sacker said, "You are the chief engineer of the U.S.S. *Enterprise*?"

"I am. What about it?"

"You know much of the *Enterprise* engines?"

"Much? I know *everythin'* about 'em."

"Interesting similarities exist between your engines and ours. This information will be of much use."

"So glad to be of service," Scotty said sarcastically.

"Your willingness to cooperate will be noted."

Scotty threw up both arms. "Cooperate! Y'dinna give me a choice! Y'probed me mind, remember?"

"You are skilled in adapting engine functions to various alternate purposes as well as in maintaining and operating them?"

"Aye."

"I?"

"*Yesssss,*" Scotty hissed. "Yes, I am skilled."

"In—"

"In anythin' you can name havin' to do with the *Enterprise* engines! Have I made meself clear?"

The Sacker considered a moment and then said, "Aye."

Scotty shot him a sharp look, wondering if he was being made fun of. The Sacker started pushing the memory probe machine toward the door. "Here, now, where'll ye be goin'?"

"This temperature distresses me. I must momentarily return to my own environment."

"Momentarily. That means ye'll be comin' back."

"Aye."

The green Sacker went out, taking the probe machine with him. The minute the door was closed, Scott ripped off his goggles and mask. He sat down on the plastic cube the Sacker had left behind and tried to think.

Clearly it was his technical expertise that was keeping him alive. If he could convince that green monster that one Montgomery Scott would be a valuable asset to have around, he just might hang on until Captain Kirk could think of a way to get him out. He didn't see there was much he could do to get himself out, locked in this now quite chilly cell as he was. A thought struck him. He got up and tried the door. Locked was right. The only other possible way out was through the gridded vent over the refrigeration unit, and he'd never get his shoulders through that small hole.

Poor Hrolfson. What a dreadful way to die—the lad didn't deserve such an ugly fate. No more did Ching or Franklin. Those two had gone down fighting, though; Ching had kept firing her phaser even after the Sackers had set her ablaze. Brave people; Scotty was proud to have known them, even though for so short a time. Now he was the only survivor of that ill-fated team, and his own future wasn't exactly what he would call secure. There he was, the only human being in this furnace of Sackers, creatures who killed easily and with no concern for the rights of others. What could one lone human do?

"I can do a lot," Scotty said out loud, in a tone of wonder. Why, what an opportunity this was! If he could just get that green beastie to talk to him, he might learn all sorts of things that could be useful later. And there *would* be a later, Scotty told himself firmly. He started planning his strategy.

Ten minutes later the Sacker came back to find the chief engineer of the *Enterprise* seated on the cube, begoggled and bemasked, hands resting on his thighs. "Well, now, Mr. Green—come in, come in," Scotty said expansively. "It's time the two o' us were havin' a nice friendly little chat, don't ye think?"

Chapter Five

THE DOOR TO the captain's quarters opened to reveal a puffy-eyed James Kirk.

"Oh, my," said Dr. McCoy. "I tell you to get some sleep and then I come wake you up."

"I was awake, Bones. Come on in."

McCoy stepped inside. "Did you get any sleep?"

"Yes, several hours, in fact. Something up?"

"I wanted to tell you that most of the Holox poison victims are on their feet again and functioning, to a degree. Our people are starting to beam back up."

"Good. How's Dorelian doing?"

"She'll be all right—I want to keep her here one more day. She's starting to come to terms with the fact that she'll never see Zirgos again. It's going to be rough, but she'll make it."

Kirk massaged the back of his neck. "I feel bad about having had to tell her. I wish there was something I could do to help."

"Time is what she needs, Jim. Just give her time."

Kirk nodded and turned to the intercom. "Captain to bridge."

"Spock here," came the answer.

"Mr. Spock, Dr. McCoy tells me the poison victims on Holox are pretty much recovered and getting back to normal."

"I am heartily glad to hear that, Captain."

"Contact Holox and find out who's in authority now. Tell them we have one of the poisoners for them. Then instruct Lieutenant Berengaria to beam down with, ah, what's his name, ev Symwid—and turn him over to the appropriate Holox officials."

"Understood, Captain."

"Kirk out."

"You're going to let the Zirgosian colonists try him?" McCoy asked.

"It seems only fair, since it was the Zirgosians he poisoned. It could be considered a Federation matter—ev Symwid was acting as an agent for the Sackers. But Starfleet Command likes to turn these matters back to local authorities whenever it can."

McCoy grinned. "Besides, you don't want to be bothered with him."

"Right," Kirk laughed. "The Zirgosians are a humane people. They'll deal with him fairly."

McCoy was silent for a moment. Then he brought up the question that was really on his mind: "What are you going to do about Scotty?"

Kirk exhaled sharply. "I'm going to make one more attempt at contacting the Sackers. I wanted to give Uhura as much time as possible with the Sacker language, but something tells me I'd better not wait any longer. Coming?"

"Wouldn't miss it for the world," McCoy replied. In the turbolift on the way up, he asked, "What if they still don't answer?"

"Then we'll have to apply a little pressure."

On the bridge Uhura and Chekov were still compiling a Sacker vocabulary. Sulu was off duty, but Mr. Spock was studying the results of Uhura and Chekov's efforts. Kirk watched and listened for a minute until he got the hang of what they were doing. Then he said, "Lieutenant, if we should get a reply in the Sacker language, could you translate it?"

"It would be difficult, Captain," Uhura answered. "The words are easy enough, but the syntax and grammar are still a bit of a mystery."

"Let's give it a try. Cover your ears." She did. Kirk picked up the isolated mike and said, "I feel angry."

Sacker word-approximations appeared on the screen. Uhura studied them with a puzzled expression and translated, " 'I feel full of fire'?"

"Close enough," Kirk said wryly. "It's time we sent the Sackers a message in their own language."

"It will have to be visual only, Captain. I don't know how these words are pronounced."

"Visual will do. Blank the screen, please." Uhura cleared the Sacker words. Kirk spoke into the mike. "This is the *Enterprise*, calling the Sacker ship. You have killed one of our crew and grievously injured another. Two more are missing. You are also responsible for the mass poisoning of the Zirgosian colonists. We demand you account for your actions, and we further demand a meeting for the purpose of negotiation. If these demands are not met, we will open fire on the structure you have erected on the surface of Holox. Respond immediately." He switched off the mike. "Send that, Lieutenant."

Spock said, "You are not telling them we know of the baryon reverter, Captain?"

"Best not to show all our hand at once, Mr. Spock."

Spock thought a moment. "Ah. Poker."

"Are you really going to fire on that Sacker blister?" McCoy asked. "Scotty may be alive in there!"

"We'll lay down a ring of fire around the blister first. That may be enough to catch their attention."

"Light-impulse message coming in," Uhura said excitedly.

All talk ceased as every eye on the bridge was trained on the screen. Uhura's sketchy knowledge of the Sacker language was not needed; the message was in English.

AGREE TO MEETING WITH SHIP'S CAPTAIN NAVIGATOR AND COMMUNICATIONS OFFICER ONE KILOMETER DUE EAST OF DOME IN ONE HOLOX HOUR NO WEAPONS NO OTHER CREW

"No other crew!" McCoy said. "Do they think we're fools?"

"Mr. Spock," Kirk said, "how long is a Holox hour?"

"About forty-five of our minutes, Captain."

"And no weapons?" McCoy went on. "Jim, they're making the conditions impossible!"

"Only if we obey them, Bones. Lieutenant Uhura, tell Security to have twenty men in the transporter room as soon as possible. Notify Mr. Kyle where we'll be beaming down and then join us there. Mr. Chekov, the Sackers desire your presence."

"Hold it!" McCoy roared. Kirk glared at him. "Hold it . . . *sir.* You're not really going down there? They'll roast you alive! Remember what they did to Franklin? Don't do it—don't go."

"I don't have any choice. But we don't have to go *when* the Sackers tell us to." He told Chekov to go on down to the transporter room. "Bones, listen. We'll beam down now instead of waiting forty-five minutes. That'll give us enough time to stake out the place. Twenty armed men in concealment should give us an edge."

"Unless they've already got *thirty* armed Sackers hiding down there," McCoy muttered. "There's something else too. Let's get on the lift."

Spock stepped into the turbolift with them. "Captain, request permission to—"

"Denied, Spock. You're definitely staying here. We can't let the Sackers get a crack at both of us."

"Then allow me to meet them in your place, and you stay on the *Enterprise*. I could present myself as the ship's commander."

"Won't work. Our first messages to them were visual as well as audible—they know what I look like."

Spock had been hoping he wouldn't remember that. "Jim, I urge you to proceed with caution."

"Count on it," Kirk said grimly.

"There's something you may be overlooking, Jim," McCoy pointed out. "Uhura. Have you forgotten her childhood traumatic experience with fire? And if fire is the Sackers' natural weapon, she's about the last person you should be sending down there."

Before Kirk could answer, Spock said, "Unfortunately, Lieutenant Uhura is the only one of us with even a rudimentary knowledge of the Sacker language. Her services could prove invaluable."

The turbolift came to a stop and the three men stepped out into a corridor of G Deck. "What about Chekov?" Kirk asked.

"He knows a great many of the words," Spock admitted, "but it is Lieutenant Uhura who has been studying the language's syntax. If you find yourself in a position in which you need linguistic assistance, it will have to come from her."

McCoy shook his head. "It's a hell of a thing to ask of her. Jim, Uhura's afraid of fire almost to the point of incapacitation—and she has been for over twenty years. She's getting a handle on it, but she's not there yet. You put her in a situation where the Sackers are likely to start shooting flames at you and there's no telling what she'll do."

"It all comes down to how far you trust her," Spock said, "whether you take her with you or not."

The situation had an all-too-familiar ring to it, Kirk thought. How many times had the three of them stood like this, in a corridor of the *Enterprise*—Kirk with a decision to make, McCoy advising one thing, Spock another. *It all comes down to how far you trust her,* Spock had said.

"She's coming with me," Kirk announced.

They headed down the corridor toward the transporter room, where they found Lieutenant Berengaria waiting for them outside the door. "Sir," she greeted the captain.

"Berengaria," Kirk said. "Did you find someone on Holox to surrender ev Symwid to?"

"Yes, sir. The surviving Zirgosians have formed a pro-tem governing committee, and they were more than happy to take the Gelchenite off my hands."

"I'll bet they were," McCoy muttered.

"Sir, can you tell us what to expect down on the surface?"

"Angry Sackers. Spock, fill her in, please." Kirk hurried into the transporter room, trailed by McCoy. Chekov was standing on the transporter platform, ready to beam down; Berengaria's security people were milling about, filling the area to near-capacity. Transporter Chief Kyle was taking phasers out of the arms locker. "Chekov, get down off that platform," Kirk called out, picking up his phaser and communicator from Kyle. "Security is beaming down first."

The navigator stepped down just as Spock and Berengaria came in; the latter headed straight toward Kirk. "May I have your communicator, sir." Kirk gave it to her. "I'm activating your distress beacon, silent mode. That way Mr. Kyle will be able to track you if we don't prove to be enough protection."

"You're saying we need more security?"

"Let me check out the beamdown point first. I'll be able to tell better when I've seen the place. But don't lose your communicator, sir." She was very emphatic about that. "Don't let it out of your possession for a minute. Do you understand?"

"I think so," Kirk smiled. "Don't take too long, Lieutenant. We're under a time limit."

"Right." She hurried to the transporter platform, snapping out orders as she went. Kyle started beaming the security people down, six at a time.

Kirk felt a hand on his arm and turned to see Spock looking concerned. "Jim, a suggestion. Keep your thumb on the emergency signal button of your communicator. I intend to remain here with Mr. Kyle, in case you need to make a precipitous departure. Do not wait to verify any suspicion you might have. Press the button immediately."

Kirk smiled at his old friend. "I'm not going to take any chances, Spock—don't worry. I shall be the epitome of caution and discretion."

"*That*'s something I'd like to see," McCoy said dryly.

"Now, Bones. We'll have to talk to the Sackers from some distance anyway—the smell, remember. If they get too close, I have a feeling we'll all be beaming up mighty fast."

"This is a mistake, Jim," McCoy insisted. "You shouldn't be going at all."

"It is essential that we meet with the Sackers, Doctor," Spock pointed out. "They and only they hold the solution to the problem of how to stop the advancing heat front. If these are the only conditions under which they are willing to meet, then we have no choice but to accept them. With our own modifications, of course."

McCoy was working himself into a state. "It's wrong, I tell you," he snarled. "Something will *go* wrong. I . . . I feel it in my bones!"

Spock raised an eyebrow. McCoy glared at him belligerently, daring him to say something, ready to take on the entire crew of the *Enterprise* if necessary. Spock remained silent.

So did Captain James T. Kirk.

The transporter room door opened and Lieutenant Uhura walked in. She started to say something but noticed the dour looks on her shipmates' faces and thought better of it. She collected phaser and communicator and moved over to stand with Chekov, who greeted her by laying one finger against his lips. Transporter Chief Kyle found something urgent to busy himself with in the field equipment locker.

Almost ten minutes passed before Lieutenant Berengaria called in. Kirk stepped over to the control pod. "What's it like down there?"

"No Sackers in sight, sir. We can see their blister dome, and it's radiating heat we can feel from here. We're in an open area—not much cover, a few rocks and bushes."

"More security?"

"No, sir, there's no place for them to conceal themselves. We'll have to make do with what we have."

"Wonderful!" McCoy said through clenched teeth.

"Captain, we're in position now," Berengaria said. "You can beam down when ready."

Kirk waved an arm at Uhura and Chekov. "We're as ready as we'll ever be. Let's go."

The three positioned themselves on the transport pads. At the last moment Kirk thought of Lieutenant Berengaria's warning and slipped his communicator inside his tunic. "Energize, Mr. Kyle," he said.

Berengaria had posted a lookout about halfway to the Sacker dome, behind a small rise in the land, the only cover in the immediate area. So far the Sackers hadn't left their dome yet, if it was those Sackers they'd be meeting instead of the ones on the ship. She should have time to brief Captain Kirk as to where the members of her team were concealed.

The bushes hadn't proved much help—too thin and scraggly. They'd uprooted a number of them to combine with others, providing enough cover for four of her people. All the others were hunched down behind rocks that were too small, or stretched out on their stomachs behind hillocks that were too low. There wasn't a tree anywhere in sight; this part of Holox really was a wasteland. They could have dug in if they'd had more time, but the meeting hour set by the Sackers was almost upon them.

Berengaria was both edgy and curious. Like everyone else, she'd heard tales aplenty about the Sackers—most of them apocryphal, she had no doubt. Nevertheless, a certain amount of anxiety was to be expected when one was meeting for the first time a race of beings assiduously avoided by every other race in the galaxy. Fearsome they might be, but Berengaria sincerely doubted that they were phaser-proof. But if the phasers didn't do the trick, they'd brought along two photon grenade mortars that surely would.

She was the only one of the security team out in the open. She concentrated on not fidgeting, knowing the other team members were watching her. Then she spotted the shimmer in the air that meant a beamdown. The form of Captain Kirk and two others began to take shape. She stepped forward to meet them; but before she got there they faded out of sight again.

Berengaria whipped out her communicator. "*Enterprise*, come in."

"*Enterprise*."

"What happened? They were here and then they weren't. Did you have a malfunction?"

"No malfunction, Lieutenant," said Kyle's voice. "Please wait."

She waited.

"Lieutenant!" someone whispered.

"Hold your positions," she ordered sharply.

When next she heard from the *Enterprise*, it was Mr. Spock speaking. "Lieutenant Berengaria, summon your team and beam back aboard immediately."

"But what about the captain? If his party beamed down somewhere else, we'll have to form search teams to look for them."

"The captain is not on Holox, Lieutenant," Spock's unnaturally calm voice told her. "Captain Kirk is aboard the Sacker ship, as are the other two with him. Beam up immediately."

Chekov was throwing up all over the transporter platform. Uhura was down on her hands and knees, gagging. Captain Kirk was curled into a ball, trying to create a little pocket of air where he could breathe away from that overpowering, not-to-be-resisted, gut-wrenching, stomach-churning, heart-stopping, god-awful *smell*.

Kirk felt the taste of bile in his mouth, his sinuses, his nose; a war was being waged in his stomach, and he had to fight against passing out from wave after wave of nausea and dizziness. Sackers were around them everywhere, but Kirk kept his eyes averted; he knew if he looked at one of them directly, he'd be vomiting even harder than Chekov. He tried to check on Uhura but his vision was blurred; he struggled to his feet until a feeling very like vertigo brought him back to his knees.

And then a pain like nothing he'd ever felt before shot through both his ears—and it went on and on. Uhura and Chekov both screamed, but Kirk didn't hear them. A voice issuing from an apparatus strapped to the waist of one of the Sackers said, "Your translator!"—in a tone of reprimand. Kirk didn't hear that either; he was temporarily deafened.

Out of the corner of his eye he saw, but did not hear, the approach of two Sackers wearing waldoes. He tried to back away from them, but his legs had turned to rubber. One of the Sackers grabbed his arms with the waldoes and held him still while the other Sacker forced a liquid down his throat. It was thick and milky—an analgesic? Then a helmet was slapped over his head and Kirk found himself gulping in sweet, sweet oxygen. Gradually the furor in his stomach began to die down. His ears were still ringing and now his head pounded, an aftereffect of the pain in his ears. But he could live with that.

Chekov was sitting on the floor beside the transporter platform, his helmeted head down between his knees. Uhura was perched on the edge of the platform, gingerly touching the helmet resting on her shoulders. The helmets were shaded, Kirk noted, but he doubted if that would make the Sackers any more beautiful. He still couldn't bring himself to look at them directly. Unsteadily he made his way over to Uhura and put his hand on her shoulder. "Are you all right?" he asked.

Uhura said something. He could see her lips moving, but he could hear no words.

"Can't hear you—maybe it's the helmets," Kirk answered . . . and realized he couldn't hear himself either.

The expression on Uhura's face told him the same realization had just come to her as well. Kirk whirled around and faced the Sackers for the first time.

They were all cloaked, with hoods pulled forward over their faces. Only the scabrous hands that showed confirmed the identity of their captors as Sackers. "What have you done to us?" Kirk yelled, without hearing.

A grayish-blue hand that looked decayed enough to be falling off held out a stylus pad to him. Only three words were written there: *Deafness will pass.*

Kirk took the stylus pad and showed it to Uhura. When she nodded, he took it to Chekov. The young navigator's lips formed the word "Deafness?" He hadn't realized.

The Sackers were stirring around, moving slowly. Two of them held weapons, which they used to gesture toward a turbolift. *A lift right in the transporter room,* Kirk thought, automatically beginning to memorize the layout of the ship.

He and Uhura and Chekov were herded into the turbolift, and the doors closed after them. They were alone, a fact for which each of them rendered silent thanks. They looked at one another helplessly, unable to communicate and not knowing what awaited them when the lift completed its ascent.

What awaited them was four armed Sackers. One of them gestured imperiously, revealing a black arm with streaks of green running through it. Kirk and the other two stepped off the turbolift and followed the black Sacker down a corridor much wider and higher than any on the *Enterprise*. They were led to a stateroom and again left alone.

The room was stiflingly hot. A coffin-shaped vat stood in one corner. Other than that, it was an ordinary enough stateroom—slightly oversized tables and chairs, a console, something that might possibly be artwork on the walls. An open door revealed a washroom-toilet with a sonic shower. Three air mattresses with blankets folded on them were on the floor. Kirk went over and looked in the vat; it was filled with a pale green viscous material. Was that what Sackers slept in? Was the vat a Sacker bed?

Uhura sat down at the console and tried it. She raised her hands, palms up. Disconnected.

Chekov activated the door to the corridor and found himself facing an armed Sacker. He smiled wanly and closed the door.

Kirk cautiously lifted the helmet from his head— and hurriedly put it back on again. They might be alone, but the reek of Sacker was still in the air. The place was obviously an officer's quarters, vacated for their benefit. The air mattresses and blankets indicated they'd be staying a while. *So they're not planning to kill us right away,* Kirk thought. *Why?* He felt a rivulet of sweat running down his back.

Chekov pulled out a chair from a table and sat

down, carelessly banging the chair against the bulkhead. Kirk heard it. "Did you hear that?" he asked. Chekov made no response, but Kirk heard a kind of buzz from behind him. He turned to see Uhura mouthing *I heard it!* So their hearing was coming back.

Kirk plopped down on one of the air mattresses and leaned back against the bulkhead as well as he could; the helmet made it awkward. So now they'd met the Sackers. Physically they were even more disgusting than the *Enterprise*'s record banks had led him to believe; no wonder every world in the Federation dreaded their visits. And no wonder there'd been no advance in human-Sacker relations in over fifty years. How could you carry on negotiations with a race that, just by being in the same room with you, made you want to puke?

It was almost an hour before they were able to talk to one another. All three of their uniforms were stained with sweat, but they'd been unable to find a temperature control. "They want something of us," Kirk said. "But what? Why did they kidnap us?"

"Ransom?" Chekov suggested with an expression that indicated he didn't believe his own suggestion. "Vhile they are in the process of burning up the uniwerse? It cannot be."

"No, something else."

Uhura said, "Perhaps they're planning to use us as emissaries of some sort? Since they, ah, offend human beings themselves, perhaps they want to negotiate through agents that don't make other races throw up at the sight of them."

"Negotiate vith whom?" Chekov asked. "And for vhat?"

"With Starfleet Command, probably," Kirk answered. "That's not a bad suggestion, Uhura. What they want is anybody's guess. But with an exploding universe to use as a weapon, I'd say they had a pretty good chance of getting it."

"They took our phasers and communicators," Chekov said. "Ve can't fight them and ve can't call for help."

Kirk felt inside his tunic; his communicator was still there. He started to tell the others but stopped. For all he knew, the Sackers were listening to every word they said. And watching them. "Look for microphones," he told the other two. "And cameras. Any kind of bugging device."

They gave the room a thorough going-over but could find nothing. They were still looking when the door to their room opened. The tallest Sacker they'd seen yet walked in, rather grandly wrapped in a blazing scarlet cloak. Two other Sackers followed, both wearing black cloaks and both armed. One hand holding a weapon showed yellow fluid inside the sac, the other was gray. Kirk and the other two instinctively backed away from the door.

The red-cloaked Sacker spoke. "Your hearing has returned?" The voice was female.

"Yes," said Kirk. "What do you want with us?"

"The deafness was a mistake. One of us neglected to connect his translator correctly. It was the sound of his voice that deprived you of your hearing."

"You're speaking through a translator? That's not your own voice we're hearing?"

"The answer to both questions is yes. The voices we use when speaking to humans are computer-simulated."

"The voice coming out of the translator is female. Are you female?"

"I am female."

"Let me see the translator," Kirk demanded, and heard Uhura gasp.

The red Sacker didn't answer immediately. "To show you the translator, it would be necessary for me to remove my hood. We wear these garments to shield your eyes."

"Most considerate kidnappers I've ever met," Kirk said sharply. "Thank you—we appreciate the courtesy. Now show me the translator."

The Sacker did nothing for a moment; then she reached up and slowly pushed back her hood.

Chekov and Uhura immediately turned their heads away, but Kirk forced himself to keep his eyes on the Sacker. Gradually Chekov's head turned back; Uhura was the last, but eventually she looked too.

What they saw was the head of a seven-foot-plus creature whose molty-looking membranous sac was filled with bright red fluid streaked with gray here and there. Her brain looked red too, perhaps because it had to be viewed through the fluid as well as a semi-opaque skull. What caused the three from the *Enterprise* the most trouble was the sight of the little, white wormlike creatures moving around inside the brain. There were even some in the Sacker's face. Uhura and Chekov were both making noises of dismay. Kirk thought his original guess that the wormlike things were chemical messengers was probably right. His stomach was churning again, but he was determined not to let this big red monster see his distress.

Over the lower half of her face the Sacker was wearing an apparatus that was attached by two thin cables to another apparatus strapped to her waist. She pointed to the box. "The voice comes from here." She pressed a button and the voice emanating from the box spoke gibberish. She pressed the button again and said, "That time I was speaking our language. There will be occasions on which we will need to speak among ourselves in your presence. For that reason our translators have been equipped with a muting device, so that our voices will not cause you pain."

She paused. No one said anything. Then Chekov spoke up. "Ve thenk you," he said formally.

That was what she was waiting for. "You are welcome. We wear these translators for your benefit. And these outer garments also, for so long as is necessary."

"And how long is that going to be?" Kirk asked. "Why have you brought us here?"

"You are the captain of the *Enterprise*?"

"I am."

The Sacker pointed a red hand at Chekov. "You?"

"Navigator."

"And you?"

"Communications officer."

The Sacker wagged her head from side to side in a gesture they would come to recognize as the Sacker equivalent of a nod. "Your name is James T. Kirk, correct?"

"Correct. Who are you?"

"Their names, please?"

"Lieutenant Uhura and Ensign Chekov," Kirk said, indicating with a gesture which was which.

The Sacker slowly made her way over to stand directly in front of Uhura—who trembled a little but held her ground. The Sacker looked her over carefully, as if inspecting her for leaks. "You are a female?"

"You better believe it, Babe," Uhura said firmly.

The Sacker twitched and took a step closer. "Babe . . . baby? You call me a baby?"

"Uh, no," Uhura replied wide-eyed. "I'm not calling you anything. Babe . . . well, it's just a sort of nickname, that's all."

"Name? Do you say 'name'?"

"Yes," Uhura replied uneasily.

"Babe." Again the head-waggling gesture. "I am the commander of this vessel."

"So vhat is your name?" Chekov asked.

"You have heard. Babe."

Kirk made a quick gesture to silence the other two. "Commander Babe," he said, somehow managing to keep a straight face, "why are we here?"

"We have need of your assistance," the newly named Babe told him. "Our ship has recently suffered a disastrous accident. Every officer and crew member on the bridge was killed—not one of our command personnel survived. I am a commander-in-training only. We brought you here, Captain Kirk, because we need you to captain our ship."

Kirk felt his mouth drop open. He glanced at Chekov and Uhura; their mouths were hanging open too. When he found his voice again, Kirk exclaimed, "I don't know anything about this ship!"

"You are a starship captain, no?"

"I am a starship captain, yes. But this ship—"

"This ship has many similarities to Federation starships. There are differences in size and in some particular functions, but the basic structure was taken from Starfleet Command's Constitution-class vessels."

"And the *Enterprise* is a Constitution-class vessel," Kirk murmured. "I see. What if I refuse?"

"You will not. Are you aware of the fact that another universe is expanding within our own?"

"I am. I'm also aware that you are responsible for

its being here. And that you destroyed the very people who made it possible, and who built this ship for you, and who developed the baryon reverter."

At the words *baryon reverter* the two Sackers who'd come in with the commander raised their weapons and stepped toward Kirk. Babe said, "How do you know of the baryon reverter?"

He saw no reason not to tell her, but remained silent all the same.

"We have memory probes at our disposal."

Kirk shrugged. "Someone told me, obviously. A Zirgosian who was on Holox at the time you were busy poisoning the colonists. Why did you want to kill them?"

She ignored his question. "If you know about the baryon reverter, then you know it is the only way to seal out the other universe. The reverter, however, has a limited range. It will be necessary for us to return to the sector where the Beta Castelli star system used to exist. And that is why you will captain our ship. It is the only way you can stop the expansion of the other universe."

The three from the *Enterprise* exchanged uneasy looks; this was a development none of them had anticipated. *She's got me,* Kirk thought. *I'm going to have to do it.* "Why did you release the new universe in the first place?"

"That will be made clear in time."

"Who'd act as my first officer?"

"I will perform in that capacity. I know orbiting and docking, but my training had not advanced to the level of battle maneuvers when the accident on the bridge occurred. We are also weak in our handling of the ship's weapons systems. You will teach me, Captain Kirk, you will teach all of us. We have helmsmen, medicos, engineers, and soldiers, but we have no trainees sufficiently advanced to perform the functions of navigation and communications. The Chekov and the Uhura will complete the training in those areas."

"Oh, you've got it all figured out, have you?"

"I do not think I have overlooked anything. You three will be sufficient. Captain Kirk, do you still refuse?"

He hated being squeezed like that, but there really wasn't any question of what he should do. "No, I don't refuse. I'll captain your damned ship for you. When do we start?"

"Not for a time yet—we have preparations to make. Sustenance will be brought to you. These are your quarters—no one else will use them. A new air cycle has been initiated, so you will be able to breathe in here without your helmets before long."

"Thank goodness," Uhura murmured.

The Sacker commander pointed a red hand at some drawers built into the bulkhead. "In there is a selection of clothing we have acquired from various worlds. You should have no difficulty in finding some articles of dress that fit you. We understand that humans have an obsessive need for privacy. Therefore you will not be observed in any way so long as you remain here in your quarters. But you are not to go anywhere else in the ship without one of us in attendance. Guards will be outside your door at all times. When it is time for you to come to the bridge, you will be escorted to the turbolift. Is this clear?"

"Quite clear," Kirk said.

"If ve hef to stay in here," Chekov said, "do you suppose you could turn down the temperature?"

The voice from the box at her waist sounded surprised. "This is too warm for you?"

"Yes!" said three voices in unison.

"Strange . . . I am not comfortable in this chill. However, if you need a cooler environment, the temperature is controlled through the console in the corner. I will have that function restored." She paused. "There is one more thing. When you were first beamed aboard, we found three phasers but only two communicators. Which of you has the missing communicator?"

Kirk didn't even bother putting up a show of resistance. He took the communicator from his tunic and tossed it to her. "Here you are, Babe."

"Thank you, Captain Kirk. Is it necessary to use both names when addressing you?"

"No," Kirk said, "but the one you use is *Captain*."

"I understand. You are in command. But do you understand that any attempt at treachery on your part will result in the immediate incineration of one or both of your companions?"

"I do now," Kirk said, suddenly dry-mouthed.

"That is good. I am not tolerant of opposition, Captain, and we do not have time to spare. You will treat this ship as if it were the *Enterprise.* I expect no less of you."

Without another word the tall red Sacker and her two guards turned and left, leaving three stunned and uneasy humans in their wake.

Chapter Six

THE ZIRGOSIAN WOMAN'S STEP was firm and her eye was clear. Dorelian was ready to go back to Holox, to start building her life there.

"Remember," Dr. McCoy said as they walked through the corridor toward the transporter room, "nothing but bland food for another couple of weeks at least. Your system's had a pretty rough time, and you mustn't ask it to do too much for you just yet."

"I'll remember," Dorelian said. "Dr. McCoy, I don't know how to thank you for giving my life back to me. Anything I could say would be inadequate. But I want you to know I'll be grateful to you for the rest of my life. I owe you everything, you and the *Enterprise*."

"You don't owe us a thing, Dorelian. I'm just sorry we didn't get here sooner."

They'd reached the transporter room. Mr. Spock was waiting inside to do the honors himself. "I am pleased to see you in good health once again," he greeted Dorelian. "Your recovery was a matter of concern to all of us."

"Thank you, Mr. Spock," she said. "Thank you for everything. I especially thank you for keeping the Zirgosian race alive."

"You are most welcome. But we deeply regret the loss of so many of your numbers."

"Yes, it's a loss that will take a great deal of time to overcome." She lifted her head and smiled. "But we will overcome it, thanks to the *Enterprise*. I had hoped to say goodbye to Captain Kirk."

"Captain Kirk is . . . not on board at present," Spock said.

"A pity." She turned to McCoy. "Doctor, I hope we will meet again—under more pleasant circumstances."

McCoy smiled. "So do I, Dorelian, so do I."

She took her place on the transporter platform. "Please tell Captain Kirk," she said as the transporter machinery began to hum, "that I intend to hold him to his promise." And she was gone.

"I hope to be able to tell him," Spock said to the empty platform. "Even though I do not know what the promise is."

"He promised her he'd stop the Sackers," McCoy said.

"Indeed. What an extraordinary promise to make."

"Isn't it."

The transporter room intercom came to life. "Bridge to Mr. Spock! Bridge to Mr. Spock!"

"Spock here."

An anxious young voice said, "Mr. Spock, the captain's distress signal has stopped!"

"I shall be there immediately. Spock out."

"They're dead," Dr. McCoy gasped.

"Not necessarily, Doctor," Spock said calmly as they both hurried to the turbolift. "It is more likely that the Sackers have merely disengaged the distress beacon in the captain's communicator. *Bridge*." The lift started up. "If they had wanted to kill him, why would they have beamed him aboard their ship first?"

"How do I know? Nobody knows why Sackers do the things they do—not even you, Spock. But I knew something like this was going to happen! I said don't go! Didn't I say don't go?"

Spock sighed patiently. "Doctor, you *always* say don't go." The turbolift stopped. "The captain had to make the attempt to contact the Sackers—you know that as well as I." Spock headed straight toward the young man seated at the communications station. "Mr. Wittering, a message to Starfleet Command. Inform them that Sackers have kidnapped Captain Kirk, Lieutenant Uhura, and Ensign Chekov and that we are currently attempting to effect their release. Use channel A."

Wittering looked surprised. "The Sackers can intercept channel A."

"That is the point, Mr. Wittering. The Sackers need to be reminded that when they kidnap a starship captain, they can expect to have the entire fleet to contend with."

"Yes, sir. Channel A."

McCoy grunted. "And exactly how do you plan to 'effect their release'? As long as those three are aboard, you can't fire on the ship."

"First we try the obvious. Then if that does not produce results, we look for the less obvious." He picked up the microphone Uhura had connected to the Sacker translator. "Attention, Sacker ship," he said, watching the unreadable words appear on the screen. "You have taken aboard your ship Captain Kirk and two other officers, making a total of five *Enterprise* personnel you have made your prisoners. If you do not release all five unharmed within one Holox hour, we will destroy the structure you have erected on the planet surface. I repeat—you have one Holox hour to return all prisoners to the *Enterprise*." He put down the microphone. "Send that, Mr. Wittering."

McCoy was worried . . . and frightened. He'd seen Jim Kirk work his way out of hot spots before, countless times; but the captain had never been up against anything like the Sackers before. How do you reason with people who destroy whole star systems for no discernible reason whatsoever? And poison innocent colonists just to keep them from becoming a nuisance? And who seem to have no fear at all for their own safety? And now here was Spock threatening to level the Sacker structure on Holox . . .

"You know, Spock," McCoy said softly, "that threat didn't work before, when Jim tried it."

Spock pressed his lips together. "I am aware of that, Doctor," he answered quietly. "If you have an alternate course of action to suggest, I should be most happy to hear it."

McCoy was silent; he had no such suggestion. But now he was really frightened. The dependable Mr. Spock, the ever-resourceful Mr. Spock, the Mr. Spock who had all the answers—Mr. Spock didn't know what to do.

"I chust ate," Chekov complained. "Right before ve left the *Enterprise*."

"Eat again," Captain Kirk ordered. "The Sackers may go days between meals, for all we know."

They'd barely had time to shower and change out of their sweaty uniforms when a robed Sacker somewhat shorter than the others they'd seen had come in. The

Sacker had brought them something to eat and informed them they had twenty minutes to finish. When Kirk asked why the hurry, the Sacker had said their plans had changed and they were even then beginning to beam up all their personnel from Holox. Kirk guessed they must have heard from Spock.

The food was some sort of stew or thick soup and didn't taste half bad. When they'd taken their helmets off to eat it, they found that the air, while still faintly redolent of Sacker, was at least breathable now. The Sacker commander had kept her word and restored the temperature-control function to their console, so now they were all physically comfortable at least.

"The first thing we have to do," Kirk said between bites, "is find out what they're holding back from us."

Uhura looked up from her dish. "You didn't believe what the commander told us?"

Kirk shook his head. "There's something fishy there. According to her, all the command personnel were killed in the same bridge accident. That means every single Sacker on this ship with command status was on the bridge at the same time. Do you believe that?"

"No," said Uhura, realizing the unlikelihood. "The entire chain of command? That *is* fishy."

"So the accident wasn't confined to the bridge, or something else is going on. Maybe a mutiny? We're going to have to talk to these so-called people as much as we can, see what we can find out."

Chekov finished the last of his stew and said, "At least now ve know vhy they forced the Gelchenites to poison the colonists instead of blasting the settlement to bits."

Kirk had missed that. "Why?"

"Did that red commander not say they vere veak in the use of veapons? They did not fire upon the colonists because they vere not sure they could hit them."

"Chekov, you're a genius!" Kirk exclaimed. "Of course! They don't know how to launch an attack!"

"I am a chenius," Chekov told Uhura modestly.

"That poisoner we caught—ev Symwid," Kirk went on. "He told me the Sackers teased him and the other two Gelchenites by firing all around their ship before destroying it. But they weren't teasing—they were *missing*, and not on purpose. That was the best they could do. Hah. Now we've got something to go on! I'll have to find out from Babe just how much they do know."

"Did you hef to call her thet?" Chekov asked Uhura. "Babe is a cute sort of name, and that red monster is not vhat I vould call cute."

"Sorry. I had no idea she'd adopt the word as her name."

"Vhy did she? Is wery strange."

Kirk said, "The *Enterprise*'s record banks say they all do that—they accept names given to them by others outside their race. Even the name Sackers is just a label somebody pinned on them. They never tell anybody their real names, if they have any."

Chekov looked incredulous. "You can call them any name you like and they accept it? I cannot believe thet!"

"Here's your chance to find out," Kirk said as the door opened. "Try it."

The Sacker who'd brought them their food came in for the antigrav table they'd been eating from. The three from the *Enterprise* hastily donned their helmets. When the Sacker reached out a hand for the table, the robe fell away to show an arm encased in a sac filled with pale red fluid streaked with white.

Chekov stood up and bowed gallantly. "Thet vas wery good, Pinky. Ve thenk you."

The Sacker stopped. She turned slowly to face Chekov. "Pinky? Is that a name?"

"Yes, thet is a name."

The Sacker's head waggled back and forth. "Pinky."

"You do not like it? Then tell us your real name."

"Oh, no, I like it. Pinky is my name." Chekov threw up his arms and walked away from this incomprehensible state of affairs.

"Tell me," Uhura said, "are you a girl Pinky or a boy Pinky? Your computer voice is a bit androgynous."

"I am completely girl Pinky."

Chekov whirled around. "Vhat does your *mother* call you?"

Pinky hesitated, as if unsure of something. "Everyone will call me Pinky now."

"Give up, Chekov," Uhura smiled.

"Pinky," Kirk said, "we couldn't help noticing your coloring. Are you by any chance the commander's daughter?"

The Sacker suddenly started jiggling up and down in an alarming manner. The others didn't know whether to be afraid or to send for a Sacker doctor.

"Did I offend you?" Kirk asked worriedly. "Forgive me—I meant no insult. Is it forbidden to inquire about family relationships?"

The jiggling increased to near-violent proportions. "Kepten," Chekov said wonderingly, "I think she is laughing!"

Pinky eventually settled down a little. "Her daughter! Babe will not be permitted to donate life for years yet. She is my orthocousin." With that she took the antigrav table and left, still jiggling.

"Orthocousin?" said Chekov.

"She calls her Babe?" said Uhura.

Captain Kirk sighed. "We've got our work cut out for us," he said.

"Still no reply?" Dr. McCoy asked the communications officer.

"No, sir. Nothing yet."

Spock said, "I am sure Mr. Wittering will tell us the moment he receives a communication, Doctor. It is not necessary to query him every thirty seconds."

"Dammit, Spock, we have to do something!"

"I gave the Sackers one hour in which to respond, approximately forty-five of our minutes. They still have twenty-five minutes, thirty-seven seconds left."

"They're not going to answer, you know that!"

"I presume they will not, but I wish to give the Sackers every opportunity to avoid an exchange of hostilities. You must have noted, Doctor, that in a head-to-head confrontation between our two ships, the *Enterprise* would assuredly come out second best. We are outgunned, presumably outmanned, and definitely outshielded. All other alternatives must be tried before we embark upon what most assuredly would turn out to be a suicide mission."

McCoy knew Spock was right; he just didn't want to admit it. Spock for his part understood the doctor's anxiety—and even shared it to an extent, although he was careful not to show it. The bridge personnel were jittery enough as it was; they needed an acting commander who was steady and in control . . . or who appeared to be. Spock was struggling with the question of whether to fire on the Sacker blister dome on Holox or not. It was the next logical step to take, but Spock knew that in taking it he could well be signing Chief Engineer Montgomery Scott's death warrant.

No. He couldn't risk Scott's life when there was a way to better the odds. A ground attack on the dome might be just as efficacious as firing from orbit, and it would be safer for Scott and the security man with him, if they were still alive. *That,* Spock thought wryly, *is a rather large 'if'.* But until he had evidence to the contrary, he must proceed on the assumption that the two men were not dead.

Time was passing. McCoy was right; the Sackers were not going to answer.

Spock pressed a button in the arm panel of the command chair. "Security—full detail to the transporter room. Mortars and grenades. We shall attempt to penetrate the Sacker dome on Holox."

McCoy's face lit up. "Now you're cooking!"

"I am glad you think so, Dr. McCoy, as you are coming with us. Please pick up your medical kit and report to the transporter room."

"On my way."

"Mr. Sulu, you have the conn. Maintain monitoring of the Sacker ship and notify me immediately of any change in status."

"Yes, sir."

Spock quickly joined McCoy in the turbolift, wondering if he hadn't already left it too late.

Captain Kirk, Uhura, and Chekov crowded around the console screen in their quarters on the Sacker ship. Selected parts of the ship's schematics were being fed through to them, so Kirk would have a chance to familiarize himself with the layout before taking command. Notations were in two languages, English and one other that the three from the *Enterprise* assumed must be Zirgosian. Nobody knew the Sackers' language except the Sackers—and now Uhura, a little bit.

They read in silence for a while, and then Chekov gulped and said, "It is *big*!"

"Think of it as a bigger but not necessarily better *Enterprise*," Kirk said. "Remember, the Zirgosians weren't finished with it yet when the Sackers took over. That means there are still bugs in here somewhere that haven't been worked out. What we have to do is find them."

"And do what, Captain?" Uhura asked. "Correct them or exploit them?"

"Exploit them. Our primary objective is to get that baryon reverter aboard the *Enterprise*. If we do it the way Red wants us to—sorry, I mean Babe—then we'll have no control over what happens after the heat advance is stopped. Assuming the reverter works at all, that is. As long as the Sackers have possession of it, they're going to be a threat to the entire galaxy. But if we can beam the thing over to Spock . . . I wonder how big it is."

"Is there anything in here about it?" Chekov asked.

"Let me see." Uhura tapped a few keys. "No. They're not going to let us look at it."

"Let's go back to the engines," Kirk said. He studied the screen silently for a few minutes and then said "These are some engines. What can they do? How does the radiation-damping work? And what's this device here? Damn, I have a thousand questions and no one to ask! Uhura, how do I use this console to speak to Babe?"

"Press here, talk there."

Kirk pressed and talked. "Kirk to bridge." Immediately the image of the red commanding officer appeared on the screen—without either the concealing cloak or the translator mask. Kirk felt himself flinch, but he didn't look away.

She put on her translator mask. "Commander Babe speaking," she said. "You have a problem, Captain?"

"I need to talk to an engineer. There are parts of the engine plans that are not self-explanatory. Can you send someone to answer questions?"

"Very well, Captain, an engineer will be sent to you." Her image faded from the screen.

"Whew," Uhura breathed heavily. "I guess it's not so bad as long as you don't have to smell them."

"You think so?" asked a white-faced Chekov.

"Let's see what they use in place of a deflector dish," Kirk said. Uhura called up the data. "Hm, an enclosed unit. Very compact. I wonder if the *Enterprise* could use something like that."

But the *Enterprise*'s navigator wasn't impressed. "I am supposed to get navigational readings from *thet*?" Chekov protested. "Vhat is the feed route?"

Uhura tapped the keys—and all the data disappeared from the screen. Something unreadable appeared. Uhura said, "It probably means 'Access denied.'"

"Try the weapons system," Kirk said.

Here again they were given limited access, but Kirk was able to determine that the Sacker ship boasted no new superweapon. Of course, with the Zirgosian invention for opening doors between universes they didn't need one. Nevertheless, the Sacker armament still outweighed that of the *Enterprise* three to one; a battle between the two ships was to be avoided at all costs.

They were interrupted by the sound of the door opening, followed by an indignant voice loudly protesting, "Here now! I'm goin', I'm goin'! Nae need to be proddin' me with those things!" And a helmeted Chief Engineer Montgomery Scott was propelled unceremoniously into the room.

"Scotty!" Kirk yelled, happily abandoning decorum in his joy at seeing his old friend alive.

"Captain! Uhura! Chekov!" There was much pounding of backs and squeezing of shoulders. Scotty picked Uhura up and gave her a hug that took her breath away. "I'm glad to see ye, lass!" Then his expression changed to one of dismay and he held her off at arm's length. "Nae, I am *not* glad to see ye! What are y'doin' here? Captain, why did ye leave the *Enterprise*?"

"Ostensibly to meet with the Sackers, but the meeting was just a ploy to kidnap us. Scotty, how long have you been on this ship?"

"Just since yesterday. They kept me in that hothouse down on Holox until then." He took off his helmet. "Captain, do y'remember Hrolfson, the security man who was with me? They killed him. An' only because he dinna know anythin' about the operation of the *Enterprise*! That's all the excuse they needed."

Kirk looked sick. "That makes two. They killed Ching, too. Franklin survived."

"Franklin's alive? Ah! Thank heaven for that!"

"Scotty," Uhura said, "how did they kill him?"

"They incinerated him. Burned him alive. I watched 'em do it."

Uhura covered her eyes with her hand and turned away. She crossed the room and sat down at the table.

"Captain," Scotty said, "I'm sorry to have to tell ye,

but these beasties know everythin' about the *Enterprise* that I know. They used a memory probe on us, Hrolfson and me."

"Can't be helped, Scotty. Don't worry about it. What have you been doing since they beamed you aboard?"

"Checkin' the engines. Their chief engineer was killed in some sort of accident."

Kirk and Chekov exchanged a quick look. "Their enchineer too?" the latter said. "Also their navigator, their communications officer—and their kepten."

Scotty's eyes grew wide. "What's this?"

"It's true," Kirk said. "That's the reason we're all here. They want us to run their bloody ship for them."

For once in his life, Scotty was speechless.

"*Vhat* is going on here?" Chekov asked the room at large.

"Isn't this interesting," Kirk mused. "I ask them to send me someone to answer questions about the engines, and they send me a man who's never been inside this ship until a day ago. Scotty—*you* are their expert on their own engines?"

"I think I must be, Captain. Mr. Green is only a trainee an'—"

"Who?"

"Ah, that's me Sacker, the one who's been stickin' to me like glue. I call him Mr. Green. Anyhoo, he's only in trainin' but he knows more than any of the rest o' them. They don't have one real engineer on this ship. Not countin' me, o' course. But Captain, I have a lot to tell ye."

"Let's sit."

They joined Uhura at the table. "Mr. Green must be younger than he looks," Scotty said, "even though he looks as if he's been dead a coupla hundred years.

But he talks too much. D'ye know what they were doin' down on Holox? They were growin' baby Sackers!"

This was news. "Cloning?" Kirk asked. "In vitro?"

"In vitro. There were these huge vats of bubbly stuff kept at ultrahigh temperatures. Mr. Green says the entire Sacker race lives in clans o' one thousand individuals, but I couldna get him to tell me how many clans are scattered throughout the galaxy. An' Captain, they're totally nomadic. Somethin' happened to their home system some time back and they've been wanderin' ever since. Aboard ship is the only home the younger Sackers have ever known."

"And so they started making contact with Federation worlds," Kirk mused, "looking for a place to settle? And found they made every race they met sick at their stomachs. Go on."

"They're very strict about keepin' the clan number at exactly one thousand. When one o' them dies, they just put down on the nearest planet an' grow a new one. But Captain, I saw half a dozen vats down there! An' they were big ones—lots o' baby Sackers floatin' around inside."

"They're replacing all of their command personnel," Uhura told him. "Whatever that accident was, it took out everybody capable of running the ship."

"Ah. I see."

"Why do they have to go to a planet to incubate?" Kirk asked. "Why not do it on board?"

"The ship is certainly big enough to hold a nursery," Chekov remarked.

"Well, Mr. Green says infant Sackers canna survive in space," Scotty explained. "Sacker bodies have these wee white things crawlin' around inside—"

"We've seen them," Kirk said shortly.

"They're part o' the Sacker nervous system, an' they stay immobile for the first week or two o' life. Once these white things start movin' around, the Sackers beam the babies aboard an' they all go on to wherever they're goin' next."

Kirk nodded, thinking. "You know what this means? The accident that killed off their command personnel must have happened *after* they destroyed the Zirgosian system. Babe couldn't have directed an operation like that, not if she needs our help to run the ship."

"Babe? And who might Babe be?"

"The Sacker commander," Chekov grinned. "Uhura named her."

"Inadvertently," Uhura said.

"Uhura!" Scotty said in a tone of reprimand. "Callin' another woman 'Babe'!"

"She's not exactly another woman, Scotty," Uhura protested dryly. "Besides, I was being sarcastic."

"We probably have a bunch of people here trying to work outside their own fields," Kirk commented. "Geologists trying to be navigators, that sort of thing. This is good. They won't know when we're lying to them."

Just then the door opened and Pinky came in, carrying another air mattress and blanket. "The Scott is to stay here also," she said and was gone before they could get their helmets on.

When they'd finished gagging, Scotty said, "What was that?"

"Thet vas Pinky," Chekov explained. "She is *our* Sacker."

"All right, listen up," Kirk ordered, taking deep

breaths. "Here's the plan. Scotty, I want you to look for ways to sabotage the engines *a little bit.* Don't put them out of commission. Just make them sluggish in responding, or cause them to vibrate excessively—anything you can think of to buy a little time without incapacitating the ship. Can you do that?"

"Aye, Captain, can do. I'll work on the bleeder valves. That'll make the ship buck like a bad-tempered horse when we go into warp."

"Good! That's exactly what I want. Uhura, you are to try to find out as much as you can about this accident that killed off the command personnel. Get as many specifics as you can. They aren't telling us the whole story. Get the Sackers to talk, see what you can piece together."

"Yes, sir. Will I be instructing trainees?"

"It sounds like it from what Babe told us. Chekov—you've got the hardest job of all. I want you to find out where on the ship they're keeping the baryon reverter. As navigator you'll be within your rights to ask to inspect whatever unit they're using instead of a deflector dish—take advantage of it, look around. I know you won't have free run of the ship, but do the best you can."

"Yes, sir. If there is vun place on the ship none of us is allowed to go, thet is probably vhere the rewerter is being kept."

"Good point. Do you all understand what you have to do? Are there any questions?"

"One," Uhura asked. "What do you plan to be doing while we're doing all of this?"

"Who, me?" Kirk grinned. "Why, I plan to work on Babe, of course."

* * *

Mr. Spock checked his tricorder. No doubt about it; the heat the Sacker dome emitted was decreasing appreciably. "You are right, Doctor. The dome is cooling down."

"Thought so," McCoy said. "I was sweating when we first got here."

They were crouched behind a jumble of sandstone in the Holox desert. The security force Spock had ordered down had been able to advance to within a hundred meters of the dome without being challenged. There was no sound from the dome, no sign of activity.

"Don't they post guards?" McCoy asked, uneasy at being that close to Sackers.

"Possibly they depend upon sensors to warn them," Spock answered. "They may already be aware of our presence."

"Then why haven't they done anything?"

"I do not know, Doctor."

Spock's communicator sounded. "Berengaria here. We've circled the dome, Mr. Spock. We can't find an entrance."

"Then we shall make one, Lieutenant. Remain where you are and leave your communicator open. I shall join you." He turned to McCoy. "Wait here. Do not approach the dome unless I call for you."

"Count on it," McCoy shuddered.

Spock began to move cautiously, following Berengaria's communicator signal around the perimeter until he found her and several other members of the team kneeling in a natural depression in the ground. Berengaria had already ordered a photon grenade mortar into place, and the man handling it was taking point-blank aim at the dome.

"Any time you're ready," Berengaria greeted Spock.

"At your discretion, Lieutenant."

"Fire."

It took two shots, but a gaping hole appeared in the dome at ground level, the edges curling back as they burned. Spock pressed the stun select button on his phaser and started toward the dome, but a word from Berengaria made him fall back and let her team go in first. They slipped quickly around the still smoking edges of the hole to avoid being backlighted; Spock did the same and hunched down, waiting for his eyes to adjust to the dim interior. A decidedly unpleasant odor assaulted his olfactory senses, causing a twinge of nausea. The fetidness was uncommonly offensive.

"Stinks in here," Berengaria said.

The fresh air pouring in through the hole they'd forced in the side of the dome gradually made the smell bearable. The security team spread out, cautiously searching for the dome's inhabitants. Spock stuck to the wall, thinking that was where any lingering Sacker might be hiding. But he circled the entire interior without finding anyone.

"Nobody's home, Mr. Spock," Berengaria called out.

Even though the Sackers had gone, the dome was still uncomfortably warm for most of the *Enterprise* crew. They found evidence of equipment no longer there—probably generators and similar machinery. A transparent, cell-like cube stood opposite the entry they'd made, its purpose unclear. But what caught their attention was a series of enormous plastiform vats, six in all, with their pipes, tubes, and wires now unconnected to any machine or instrument that might have provided a clue to their use. The vats were empty.

"Now what do you suppose these are?" Berengaria asked, knocking on the side of one of them. "Storage bins?"

Spock was studying the control panel on the side, trying to decipher the purpose of the dials without knowing the language used for the notations. "I do not think so," he answered Berengaria. "They are more likely to be giant pressure cookers."

"Pressure cookers!"

Spock opened his communicator. "Spock to McCoy."

"McCoy here. What's happening, Spock?"

"The Sackers have departed, Doctor. Please come into the dome. You will find an entrance on the side opposite to where you are now."

Spock thought he knew what the vats had been used for. A hunch, Jim Kirk would call it. But while Spock trusted Kirk's hunches, he was leery of his own. He had them too seldom to have reached any conclusion as to their reliability.

He walked around the vat, inspecting the various gauges. Then he moved to the next one, and a quick look told him it was identical to the first. He abandoned the vats to look at the strange cell that seemed to have no connection with anything else. He located a door and opened it. The temperature inside was lower than that of the rest of the dome, which meant it had undoubtedly been even lower still before the Sackers removed all their equipment and the two temperatures began to equalize. Spock placed a hand against one of the walls. Decidedly cool.

What did the Sackers keep in here that required a lower temperature than the rest of the dome? Could it possibly have been a human being? Spock's heart beat a little faster at the thought that Mr. Scott might be alive after all.

"*Yucch.* What a smell!" Dr. McCoy had arrived.

Spock stepped out of the cell. "Doctor, I would like you to take a look at—"

"What about Scotty?" McCoy interrupted.

"I think he is alive and on board the Sacker ship." He explained about the cell and what he thought it had been used for.

"He's alive!" McCoy accepted it as fact. But then his face clouded. "Dammit, Spock, if we'd just come a little earlier—"

"We might all have been killed," Spock interrupted in his turn, "including Mr. Scott. Please inspect these vats, Doctor. Tell me if you know what they were used for."

McCoy glanced at the nearest one and said, "Why, they're incubation vats." He walked around the vat, peering at the control panel and the various gauges the same way Spock had done. "Yep, that's what they are, all right. So Sacker females don't gestate—they reproduce externally. These incubators were filled with some sort of chemical nutrient and the fetuses were grown right here."

Spock nodded, and filed the information away under *Hunches, Confirmed.* "Quite possibly the Sacker reproductive cycle adheres to a rigid time schedule, forcing them to stop everything else while they attend to their newborn. But it does seem odd that they would have started their assault on our universe so soon before such reproduction was due. No, there must undoubtedly be some other reason behind this. Why such an urgent need to reproduce more Sackers?"

"They're growing an army," McCoy growled.

Spock's communicator beeped. "Spock here."

It was Sulu. "Mr. Spock, the Sacker ship is leaving orbit!"

"Have us beamed aboard immediately, Mr. Sulu." He summoned Berengaria and her team.

They beamed up to the *Enterprise* and hurried to their posts. A shared sense of urgency kept them from speaking; the moment they'd both wished for and dreaded was at hand. The Sackers were at last making their move.

Chapter Seven

IT WAS CAPTAIN JAMES T. KIRK who had ordered the Sacker ship out of orbit.

Their first view of the Sacker bridge, glimpsed through the opening doors of the turbolift, had been an awe-inspiring and unsettling one. The bridge was about twice the size of the *Enterprise*'s, and it had four turbolifts as well as more manned stations. In the time they'd been on the ship, Kirk, Uhura, and Chekov had never seen so many Sackers gathered together in one place; the sight was enough to disconcert even the most stalwart of hearts. Their captors were cloaked and wearing translator devices, but a bulging green forehead here and a decayed-looking hand there were unnecessary reminders of what lay under those cloaks. All the Sackers had turned and were staring at the three helmeted humans standing uncertainly in the lift.

"This is it," Kirk muttered. "Let's go."

He strode out on to the bridge as if he owned it, but Uhura and Chekov followed a little less enthusiastically. "Commander Babe!" Kirk said in his best imperious manner. "I am ready to assume command."

"The command is yours, Captain," the red Sacker replied, and indicated a brown Sacker standing near her. "This one is to be my second-in-command and will learn with me." She moved slowly along the upper deck to where six Sackers were waiting. "These three are to learn communications. And these three, navigation."

Kirk acknowledged the entire student body and issued his first order. "Stations, please." He waited until Sackers and humans alike had positioned themselves and began a tour of his new bridge, trailed by the red commander and her brown companion. The temperature was uncomfortably high, but bearable.

Avoiding looking at his three trainees, Chekov slid uneasily into the navigator's seat. His station was all too close to that of the helmsman, an enormous blue Sacker who was staring at him with what Chekov hoped was ordinary curiosity. "Hello," he said faintly.

"Greetings," the Sacker's translator boomed. "You are the Chekov?"

"I am the Chekov," the navigator squeaked. He almost asked the blue Sacker's name but remembered in time. He gulped and said, "Nice ship."

"We like it."

Chekov's three trainees hovered behind him. Two were black and one was orange, a fitting Hallowe'en combination. Chekov turned to his navigator's board and started calling up various sets of data. He pointed to one display and asked the orange Sacker, "Do you know vhat this is?"

"No. Please instruct us." And the lesson began.

Captain Kirk had stopped by the science officer's station. An almost pure white officer stood at the Sacker equivalent of attention. "Status report," Kirk ordered.

"We're still in orbit around Holox, sir."

"That's no way to give a status report!" Kirk snapped. "I want specifics, and I want 'em fast, mister!"

"Mister?"

Kirk's eyebrows went up. "Ma'am?"

"Misterma'am?"

"Whatever."

The Sacker's head waggled back and forth. "Thank you, Captain!" He or she started reading off figures from the screen until Kirk called a halt. "Very good. Carry on."

He walked on out of range of the Sacker's hearing and turned to the commander. "Why did the science officer just thank me?"

"Because you paid him the honor of naming him, Captain."

"Naming him? I didn't name him."

"Is not Misterma'am a name?"

"I guess it is now," Kirk muttered. "Okay, so I named him. Babe, you're going to have to explain to me about this naming business. Why do you take any name we give you?"

She turned and consulted with her brown shadow before she answered. "It is permitted for you to know this custom. To give another a name is a sign of respect, or sometimes affection. When that name comes from one who is not of our race, the honor is doubled. It is our way of cementing loyalties."

"I see. So I just made a buddy for life back there?"

"Misterma'am will respect and honor you as long as you are with us."

That was a two-edged answer if ever he heard one, but Kirk decided not to pursue it. "As long as we're talking about names, what's the name of this ship?"

The commander seemed to hesitate. "This vessel has not yet been blessed with a name."

"Oh? Well, don't you think it's about time you gave it one?"

"It is not for us to provide the name."

"It isn't? Well, if not you, who?" Then it hit him. "You mean *me*?"

"That would be deemed appropriate, Captain." Both Sackers watched him, waiting.

So they want me to name their ship for them, do they? Kirk thought. He started considering appropriate names such as *Sacker Slaughterhouse* and *Zirgos's Folly*—but then stopped himself. If giving a name was a sign of respect, wouldn't withholding a name be an equal sign of *dis*respect? Was this a weapon he could use?

"I'll think about it," he said, and resumed his tour.

In the meantime, Uhura was trying to get used to the sight of three Sacker trainees hovering over her. She'd groaned inwardly when she saw the communications station. Touch pads. Uhura hated touch pads. She liked the feel of keys and switches clicking under her fingers, telling her that what she wanted done was in fact being done. With touch pads she always had to worry about whether she was pressing hard enough. Or, contrarily, pressing too hard; some of the pads were so sensitive that she had to be careful not even to breathe on them. At one time the entire bridge of the *Enterprise* had been refitted with touch pads, but everyone had complained so much they'd gone back to keys and switches.

Uhura's three trainees were yellow, lavender, and dusty pink. *Like garden flowers,* she thought sarcastically. They crowded around to watch as she began to familiarize herself with the board.

125

"The outgoing message channels are blocked," Uhura said in surprise.

The three Sackers exchanged looks. Finally the yellow one said, "We hope the Uhura will not be offended, but outgoing channels are controlled by the science officer."

"Oh. I see. Tell me, is there anything else I'm not to be trusted with?" She made no attempt to keep the irritation out of her voice.

"It was done by order of Commander Babe," the Sacker said unhappily. "All other functions remain."

"I'll *Babe* her," Uhura muttered under her breath. "All right, suppose you three show me how much you know about this board. What's the procedure for recording a ship-to-ship message?"

She was answered with a stream of gibberish that disoriented her until she realized the three trainees had switched off their translators and were consulting among themselves in their own language. She listened carefully, and heard a number of sounds that just might correspond to the words the translator had thrown up on the *Enterprise* screen. There was the word for *channel,* and for *playback,* and for *display.* They were trying to find an answer to her question.

Uhura turned her head away so they wouldn't see the look of elation she suspected had appeared on her face. She *could* learn this language! All she had to do was keep her mouth shut and listen. She got her face under control and turned back to do just that.

Finally the three Sackers switched their translators back to English, and the lavender one said, pointing, "You press there."

"Right. And next?"

Silence.

"And next?" Uhura repeated firmly.

126

The lavender one made a noise that might have been a Sackerian clearing of the throat. "You ask for help?"

She stared at them a moment. "I think you need a lot of help." Captain Kirk had said these would be people trying to work outside their own fields, but Uhura had expected them to know a simple thing like how to record an incoming message. How was she ever going to teach them the intricacies of rewiring a board?

First things first. "Pay attention, now. I'm going to show you one step at a time how to do this."

They got to work.

Captain Kirk had completed his inspection of the bridge. "Let's see how she handles," he said to Babe. He seated himself in the command chair, much larger than the one he was used to and made of the same material as the furniture in their quarters. *Probably heat-resistant,* he surmised. "You, there, Blue! Helmsman!"

The big blue Sacker seated next to Chekov swiveled to look at Kirk. "You call me Blue?"

Damn, thought Kirk, *I've done it again.* Bluff it out. "Yes, I call you Blue. Everyone who sits at the helm of a starship should be named, because the helm is a seat of honor. In battle, it is the helmsman who frequently means the difference between victory and defeat. Are you worthy of the post, Blue? Are you worthy of the name?"

"I hope so, sir."

"Let's find out. Take her out of orbit, helmsman."

The Sacker ship left orbit, rather slowly but without incident. Blue had obviously had some training, but Kirk responded by groaning and covering his eyes with his hands.

"Is something wrong, Captain?" Babe asked.

Kirk didn't answer her. He heaved himself out of the command chair and ponderously walked around to stand in front of the helmsman. "Blue," he said heavily, "that was *pitiful*."

"Sir?"

"That was the raggediest, bumpiest, *slowest* exit from orbit it's ever been my misfortune to witness!" He placed his hands on the helm and leaned his weight on his arms; his face was little more than a meter away from the Sacker's. "You want to be helmsman of this vessel? You want to guide this ship through battles and ion storms? You want to evade tractor beams and unfriendly sensor probes? *You?* I don't know, Blue, I just don't know. You're going to have to do much, much better than that!"

"I . . . I'm sorry, sir."

"*Much* better," Kirk repeated, a sinister gleam in his eye.

Ensign Chekov lay stretched out on one of the mattresses in their quarters, sleeping the sleep of the innocent. Captain Kirk was at the console, studying the ship's schematics again. He thought he had a pretty good idea of the layout of the ship by now, but pretty good wasn't good enough; he had to be sure.

The door opened and Scotty came in. He took off his helmet and said, "Where's Uhura?"

"On the bridge, finishing up something she'd started her trainees on," Kirk answered. "I wasn't sure about leaving her alone among all those Sackers." He laughed. "But she's taken this stern school-marmish attitude toward her Sackers—she's got all three of them jumping. So, Scotty, have you got any news for me?"

"Aye, sir, that I do. I canna stay long—Mr. Green's waitin' for me in the corridor. I told him I had to have a break. I think he thinks that's some kind of medicine." Scotty pulled up a chair and sat down. "Anyway, I diddled with the bleeder valves an' the piston boosters. The engines'll respond, but they'll be so sluggish ye'll have time for a round o' golf afore they'll be doin' what ye want 'em to do. An' when you give the order to go into warp drive, just be sure you're holdin' on to somethin', sir. Not that I'm sayin' the vibrations will be bad—but it would be best to be in a safe place just the same."

"That's perfect, Scotty," Kirk grinned. "I've already got the helmsman suspecting he's an incompetent boob. And that worries Babe. Anything that worries Babe can only help us. I left them to practice some simple maneuvers—quarter turn, full reverse, things like that."

"The engines'll handle that all right. They just won't be breakin' any speed records, that's all."

"What about trickier stuff, battle maneuvers?"

"Even slower still."

"Good! That's what we'll try next." He jerked a thumb toward Chekov. "Sleeping Beauty over there gave his Sackers some navigational problems to solve. When everybody's ready, we'll give it a go." Kirk paused a moment, and then said: "Scotty, this Mr. Green of yours—how does he treat you? Is he polite?"

"Polite! He could write the book, Captain. Me own men on the *Enterprise* don't treat me with that much courtesy, an' they're not a bad-mannered bunch at all. Mr. Green isna the only one, either. All the engineering Sackers are soooooo polite."

"It's not just the Sackers in engineering, Scotty. They're all like that, every one of them on this ship.

They treat us as if we were honored guests instead of four people they've kidnapped. You notice they never get on the turbolifts with us? Oh, they have somebody send us off and somebody else waiting to meet us. But we always ride alone. They know being in such close quarters with them would distress us—so they go out of their way to save us that little bit of discomfort."

"Aye, now that you mention it . . . we do ride alone, don't we? One horrendous purple beastie workin' in the intermix chamber told me he was honored to be instructed by the chief engineer of the U.S.S. *Enterprise*. At the time I thought it was so much fish oil, but maybe he meant it."

"He probably did." Kirk thought a moment. "There's something else. They don't seem to know very much about human beings. The Sackers have visited a lot of Federation worlds and they've come into contact with humans frequently, but *these* Sackers seem uncertain about the simplest things. Such as correct form of address. And the first time we met Babe, she had to ask Uhura if she was female. Scotty, they're acting as if they've never seen human beings before—and we know they have!"

"They know what kind o' food to serve us."

"Their computer could have told them that. But that means sometime in the past *somebody* knew enough about humans to put that information into the computer in the first place."

Scotty scowled. "The ones who were killed in the bridge accident?"

"Must be. But why is the commander of this ship so ignorant about humans that she's not sure of a female when she sees one?"

"Beats me, Captain. Maybe they restrict contact

with humans—only certain Sackers are allowed that privilege, if it is a privilege."

"But why?"

"Dunno. But Captain, did you know Babe was female before she told you she was?"

Kirk looked startled. "We knew from the computer voice she'd chosen for her translator—it was decidedly female. But you've got a point. I can't tell a male Sacker from a female just by looking."

"Well, then."

The door opened and Uhura walked in—backwards. "Scotty, there's a big green thing outside the door that wants you to come out."

"Aye, I best be goin'. Any further instructions?"

"Just make sure your sabotage can't be uncovered," Kirk said.

"Already taken care of, sir." He palmed the switch that opened the door. "Well, now, Mr. Green—time to be gettin' back to work." He left.

Uhura removed her helmet and dropped down in the chair vacated by Scotty. "Whew! I have had enough *Sacker* to last me the rest of my life."

"How's it going?" Kirk asked. "Are your trainees any good?"

She grinned mischievously. "They're hopeless."

"Wonderful! Don't explain things too clearly."

"I won't. Rose is the only one who seems determined to learn. The other two are just sort of *there*."

"Rose? You've named them?"

"They got mixed up when I just pointed and said 'You!'—so I pretty much had to give them names. They're such delicate little creatures that I called them Rose, Jonquil, and Iris."

He laughed. "Nice."

"But then I found out two of them are male. I didn't have any trouble shortening Jonquil to Jon, but when I told Iris I wanted to call him Irving instead—he objected. He likes Iris!"

Kirk thought of what he and Scotty had been talking about and asked, "How did you know they were male?"

"I eavesdropped. Captain, I can understand some of what they're saying! My three chatter in their own language a lot—and while I don't get all of it, I do pick up bits here and there. If I just had a little time . . ."

"Unfortunately, that's something that's in short supply just now." Kirk rubbed his eyes. "I found an escape chute during my tour of the bridge. It's located directly under the damage control monitors. Keep it in mind—we may need it."

"Yes, sir. Does Chekov know?"

"I told him right before he crashed. Uhura, I think we'd do well to follow Chekov's example. We may not have time to sleep later."

"That's not exactly a cheering thought."

"I know. But things are going to start heating up soon. We'd better be ready when they do."

Mr. Spock was studying Lieutenant Uhura's programming of the Sacker language in the *Enterprise* computer and thinking she'd built up a good, workable vocabulary. He sincerely hoped it would be of use to her in her present circumstances.

"Oh, Mr. Spock," Dr. McCoy began in his lightest, softest manner, "I hate to presume, and I do so hope you won't think I'm trying to tell you how to do your job, but considering the conditions that prevail at the moment, don't you think we ought to *DO SOMETHING*?" Every eye on the bridge turned toward him.

"Doctor, we are doing something," Spock answered reasonably. "We are following the Sacker ship. That is all we can do at present, so long as their shields are up. But even if the shields were down, we could not fire upon the ship without endangering Captain Kirk and the others. We cannot beam an armed force aboard for the same reason."

"Seems to me the odds of an armed party taking them by surprise would be pretty good. And there's got to be a weak spot in those shields somewhere."

Spock was aware that all the other personnel on the bridge were listening for his answer. "The odds *would* be good, if we knew exactly where on the ship the captain was. If we beamed aboard the bridge, for instance, and he turned out not to be there—the Sackers might very well kill him before we could get to him. Do you really think that is a chance worth taking?"

"Good Lord no," McCoy said in an abashed manner. "I'm sorry, Spock, I didn't think of that. It's just that the thought of Jim surrounded by those . . . those . . ."

"I understand, Doctor. It would be a different matter if we had interior visuals," Spock went on. "But the Sacker ship has a special shielding that blocks our sensors. The Zirgosians did too good a job with their new design, unfortunately."

McCoy shook his head. "Those poor people. At least they never knew what their supership was going to be used for."

There was silence on the bridge for a while, as everyone stared at the Sacker ship on the main viewscreen and wondered what was happening on board. Then Sulu said, "They're reversing, Mr. Spock."

"Follow suit, Mr. Sulu."

McCoy moved over to the helm. "Haven't they done that before, Sulu?"

"This is the fifth time. They make four slow turns and then reverse. Four turns, reverse. Regular as clockwork."

"Why? What are they doing?"

"I can't tell. Maybe they're just having trouble making up their minds where they're going."

"Where *are* they going?" McCoy asked. "Spock?"

"I do not believe they are going anywhere, Doctor. If it were not for the elementary nature of the maneuvers being performed, I would assume that what we are seeing is something in the nature of a shakedown cruise. It is a new ship, remember, and there might be some aspects of it that are not functioning satisfactorily."

"They managed to get all the way here from Zirgos."

"And perhaps encountered problems on the way. Yet these are such basic maneuvers they are performing, I have to suspect that something else is behind them. Until we find out what that is, we shall continue to track them."

"They're making a starboard turn, Mr. Spock," Sulu said.

"Follow suit, Mr. Sulu."

"We do not understand why another inspection of the navigational unit is necessary," one of the Sackers said.

"A good navigator must know his tools," Chekov replied pedantically. "And thet includes *all* the ship's equipment connected vith the navigation system. Here you are, in training to be navigators, and you still do not know the vorkings of the unit that sends you your readings! Disgraceful!"

The Sacker fell silent, chastened. They were in a corridor of the ship, Chekov flanked by the two black Sackers assigned to him while the orange one dragged along disconsolately in the rear. Sackers didn't move very fast, a fact that Chekov took advantage of by looking through every open door and hatchway they passed. He'd told his trainees that he needed to familiarize himself with the ship's layout; they saw nothing unusual in this, and consequently they took a different route every time they went to study the navigational unit.

They were approaching large double doors that were not only closed but guarded, by two armed Sackers who lifted their weapons slightly when they saw Chekov. "Vhat is this place?" he wanted to know.

"Ship maintenance section," he was told.

"Vhy is it guarded?"

Neither black Sacker said anything, but the orange one spoke up eagerly from behind them. "That is where the baryon reverter is kept!"

"Silence!" one of the black Sackers ordered. The orange one dropped back a few steps.

"Vhat kind of rewerter?" Chekov asked innocently.

"It has nothing to do with navigation."

Chekov went on asking questions and sometimes even listening to the answers. He already had *the* answer he wanted: ship maintenance. They reached the navigational unit, and Chekov forgot all about Sackers and burning universes in his fascination with this new substitute for the traditional deflector dish. An hour later they were ready to go back to the bridge.

But the orange Sacker blocked the hatchway. "Request permission to speak to the Chekov privately."

"Granted." He waved the two black Sackers back and followed the orange one into the corridor. The orange Sacker was the only female among Chekov's trainees, and right then she was trying hard to work up the courage to say something. "Vhat is it?" Chekov nudged.

She twitched once or twice and started to speak. "The Chekov has been instructing us in the arts of navigation for eight days. I wish to ask whether my work has been satisfactory or not."

Chekov chose his words carefully. "I think you are doing the best you can."

"Do I not heed every word you speak?"

"You pay attention, yes."

"Do I not follow your orders without question?"

"Quite so."

"Do I not solve all the navigational problems you give us?"

"Yes, yes you do."

"Then why," she wailed, "why have you given the other two names—but not me?"

"Ah, vell, ve must not rush these things," Chekov answered smoothly. "Do not despair. You may yet be named. It is something for you to vork toward." He turned his back and walked away down the corridor, grinning from ear to ear.

Divide and conquer.

Chief Engineer Montgomery Scott was roused out of a deep sleep by a smell that would have spoiled anyone's dreams. He opened one eye and saw a green nightmare standing in the doorway of the quarters the four from the *Enterprise* shared.

Scotty reached for his helmet and said, "What's the trouble, Mr. Green?"

"I apologize for disturbing the Scott's rest period," the Sacker said in what was almost a humble manner, "but the piston-booster power supply is slow in feeding through. It approaches critical."

Scotty was instantly awake; he'd been half expecting this. "Let's have us a look."

They made their way to the engine room, Mr. Green explaining along the way how he'd checked all the valves and the wiring but could find nothing wrong. *I certainly hope not,* Scotty thought.

The control panel for the piston boosters was on the upper level of the engine room overlooking the intermix chamber. The Sacker pointed to a dial; the needle was hovering just outside the red zone.

"Ah, now, wasn't it smart o' ye to notice that!" *Too smart,* Scott thought. "But y'need not worry, Mr. Green. I lowered the power feed meself. Keeps the mix purer, don't ye know."

"But . . . but if the helm should need power in a hurry . . . ?"

"Then the plasmicophic ferangulator kicks in. Nae need to worry."

"The plasmi . . . ?"

"Plasmicophic ferangulator. It wasna even hooked up when I first came aboard but it's workin' all right now. Come along—I'll show ye." He led the puzzled Sacker to a Rube Goldberg contraption he'd rigged a few days earlier. Scotty touched a finger to a button; the contraption started clicking and whirring, and rows of pretty lights began to blink on and off. "Y'see," Scotty explained, "the frammistan redirects the betagams through an ion-free calcimogrifying chamber, where they're mixed by the glockenspiel to regurgitate with zeta-minor demi-prostulances. Then the new mix spurts through the Fallopian tube into the Loch Lomond antimasticator—and ye know what that means, don't ye?"

Mr. Green was all agog. "What?"

Scotty threw up both arms and beamed. "Instant power! As much as y'want and as fast as y'want it! Ah, the ferangulator is a lovely instrument, it is! Saves energy and increases efficiency—what more could y'ask?" He lowered his arms and his face fell. "There's only one thing the matter with it."

"What's that?"

"It canna be serviced while operatin'. Y'take off any of the panels to get at the innards and—*zap!*"

"Zap?"

Scotty lowered his voice. "Y'get hit with all those nasty doubloons. By-products o' particle decay. Lethal nine times out o' ten. I wouldna be mentionin' it to the others, if I were ye—nae need to alarm them. But we're all safe as houses . . . as long as those panels stay in place." He was gratified to see the Sacker nodding soberly. "Well, if y'have nae more questions, Mr. Green, I'd like to finish me nap."

Mr. Green ordered another Sacker to escort the Scott back to his quarters, while he himself stayed to study the plasmicophic ferangulator.

"Too slow, Blue," Captain Kirk said wearily. "Much too slow."

"I initiated the turn the minute you gave the command!" Blue protested.

"You have to learn to anticipate these things, Blue. You have to develop a feel for the helm. Mr. Sulu would have had the *Enterprise* halfway to the next star system by the time you started your turn."

Blue twitched. For days the captain had been throwing the name of Sulu at him. The Sulu was evidently some sort of magician who could get the *Enterprise* to do anything he wanted just by wishing for it; Blue had to do it the hard way.

Kirk motioned the red commander closer. "Babe," he said in a voice just loud enough for Blue to hear, "you're going to have to do something about that helmsman. He's just not cutting it."

"I am sure he is doing the best he can, Captain." The voice coming out of her translator sounded worried.

"Maybe he'll take orders from you better than he does from me. Here, you try it." He slipped out of the command chair and stood to one side.

Babe lowered herself into the chair and the brown Sacker moved in closer. "Prepare for port turn with increase to mark two," she said.

"Preparing for turn," Blue said. "On your signal."

Kirk watched carefully until Babe was about to speak and then yelled, *"Now!"* Both Sackers twitched, as did the three standing around Chekov. "Too late!" Kirk cried, and threw up a hand in annoyance. "Babe, you're as slow as he is! You're quite a pair, you are."

"I was about to—"

"'About to' isn't fast enough, Babe. I've told you that before. You have to think at least five minutes ahead. You're not doing that. Are you?"

"I try to—"

"Try, try, try. Don't just *try*. Do it!" He glanced over to Communications and saw Uhura making a little signal with her hand. She had something! He gave her a barely perceptible nod.

Uhura stood up and said, "Captain, permission to leave the bridge."

"Granted."

"One moment please," Babe said. "Why do you wish to leave the bridge?"

"I have a slight headache. I'd like to go to our quarters and lie down for a few minutes."

"Do you require medical attention?"

"No, it's not that serious. If I can just get my feet up for ten or fifteen minutes, I'll be all right."

Babe consulted with the brown Sacker. "Permission granted."

Uhura left, and one of her trainees called down to have another Sacker meet the turbolift when it stopped. Kirk killed some time by finding ways to criticize Babe's performance. Actually, the red Sacker showed signs of developing into a fairly decent starship captain if given half a chance. Kirk was determined not to give it to her.

When he estimated ten minutes had passed, he too requested permission to leave the bridge.

"For what purpose?" Babe wanted to know.

"I have a personal matter to attend to in my quarters." That excuse had gotten him off the bridge once before.

Again Babe consulted with the brown Sacker. The consultation went on longer than usual.

Finally Kirk grew impatient. "Well? What does Brownie have to say?"

"Brownie?"

It was the first time he'd heard the brown Sacker speak. But now that he had . . . "I name you Brownie," Kirk pronounced solemnly.

Brownie wagged his head back and forth, which Kirk knew by now was a sign of acceptance and/or happiness. "I thank you, Captain."

"Don't mention it," he answered dryly.

More consulting.

Finally Babe turned to Kirk and said, "Do you wish to join the Uhura in your quarters for mating purposes?"

Of all the things she could have said, that was one which Kirk was in no way prepared for. "Well, uh, ah, umm," he mumbled. Which answer would get him off the bridge? Chekov seemed to be having a coughing fit.

Babe prodded for an answer. "We understand the human reproductive impulse is neither cyclical nor regimented to control population numbers. Is it true the urge to mate comes upon you without warning, at any time of the day or night?"

"Well, uh, yes, that's true," Kirk floundered.

"And is this urge upon you now?" Babe persisted.

Dammit. "Yes, it is!" he said loudly.

"Very well, you have permission to leave the bridge."

Kirk stepped into the turbolift and turned to see every one of the Sackers watching him. He hoped he didn't look as big a fool as he felt.

Chapter Eight

UHURA WAS WAITING in their quarters.

"What have you got?" Kirk said the minute the door closed behind him. He pulled off his helmet and sat down at the table opposite her.

"Captain, you know my Sackers talk freely in front of me," she said, "since they're not aware I can understand their language now."

"You overheard something."

"Yes. Today they were talking about the accident that killed off all the bridge personnel. Well, the 'accident' was a simple drop in temperature. Something went wrong in their environmental control section. When the temperature reached freezing point, their sac liquid turned solid."

"My God," Kirk said, horrified. "You mean their sac liquid froze? Ughhh, hell of a way to die. But wait a minute—why didn't they just leave the bridge?"

"The temperature failure was shipwide, Captain. You were right about that—all the command personnel were *not* on the bridge at the same time."

"But it didn't kill off all of them. Obviously."

"The way I understand it," Uhura said, "the older the Sackers grow, the more heat they need. Only the younger ones were able to survive that lethal drop in temperature."

"So all the elderly on this ship died off?"

"All the *adults*. The survivors who are running the ship now—most of them haven't even entered puberty yet. Captain, they're *kids*. We're dealing with a bunch of kids."

Kirk sat there open-mouthed. "Kids!"

She nodded. "The temperature failure came after the adults had destroyed Zirgos and everything else in the Beta Castelli system. The kids replenished the population as soon as they could, by putting up those incubation vats on Holox. Captain, over half this ship's crew is in a nursery somewhere on board here."

Kirk got up and began to wander aimlessly around the room. "Kids!" he cried, waving his arms in the air. "That explains so much! No wonder nobody knows how to do anything! They're a bunch of well-mannered, curious youngsters who are still at the beginnings of their educations. And no wonder they're so naive about human beings! All the contacts with other races must have been made by the adults. The only things they know about us is what their computer tells them." He started pacing. "They're unfamiliar with their own weapons system and too young to practice diplomacy, so they forced the Gelchenites to poison the colonists who threatened their incubation vats. They might be kids, but they're pretty bloodthirsty kids."

"They'd just seen their elders wipe out an entire star system," Uhura pointed out.

"Yes, there's that—they had to learn it somewhere. And Babe? Babe is a kid, too?"

"She's the oldest kid—I think she must be in early adolescence. But that's why she's the commander, because she's oldest. Iris—one of my trainees?—he's very bitter about that. He wants to command. He said that Babe and the brown Sacker both were taken out of their incubation vats less than an hour before he was, but those few minutes give them seniority."

Kirk was astonished. "That's the way Sackers determine chain of command? The oldest one is automatically in charge, regardless of ability?"

Uhura sighed. "That's the way these *kids* are doing it. I don't know if it's Sacker custom or not. I would guess not. Iris wouldn't be so rebellious if it were a long-standing custom. He's the only one of my three who's not even trying to learn communications. Rose has a natural aptitude, and Jon got off to a slow start but he's coming along nicely now. But Iris—I think Iris is just waiting for Babe to fall on her face, and the brown one along with her."

"Good. Encourage him in that kind of thinking. Tell him he was made to command, that kind of garbage. Ambitious also-rans always believe flattery. Anything we can do to shake the hierarchy these kids have set up has to work to our advantage."

"Yes, they can't be feeling as sure of themselves as they look."

Kirk thought a minute. "You know, Uhura, in a way these kids have done a pretty remarkable thing. They've stepped into their elders' shoes without being prepared to do so, and they're making it work. It's all very tenuous, but they sure as hell got the drop on us. Even that was pretty bright—they knew they needed help, so they went out and got themselves a starship captain and a communications officer and a navigator. They've got guts, and *they* weren't the ones who destroyed the Beta Castelli system. You could almost admire them, if it weren't for what they did to the colonists on Holox."

"And to us," Uhura added. "I don't mean the kidnapping, although that's bad enough. But when they've learned to run their ship without our help, they're not just going to send us back to the *Enterprise* with a polite thank-you."

"I know. Remember Scotty's story about how casually they incinerated the security man with him in the Holox dome? These kid Sackers don't have a whole lot of respect for human life. Whew. I'm going to have to get Scarlett O'Hara up there off for a private talk before long. But you've given me the handle I've been looking for, Uhura. Now that we know we're dealing with kids, we should be able to shake 'em up a bit."

"There's something else, Captain. I *think* I've figured out how to lower the interior visuals shield. If I'm right, we can let the *Enterprise* see what's going on here."

"Great! Audio too?"

"Audio too. But it's a four-step procedure, Captain. I could probably sneak in one of the steps or maybe two without one of my trainees spotting it—"

"Understood. I'll provide a distraction. Now I think we'd better be getting back. Oh—by the way, in case anyone says anything, the reason you and I are down here is for mating purposes."

"What?!"

Kirk shrugged helplessly. "It was the only way I could get off the bridge!" He put on his helmet and palmed open the door to reveal two Sackers waiting to escort them back to the turbolift. "Come on—and for crying out loud, Uhura, *stop laughing.*"

She did her best. But her suppressed mirth was so contagious that on the lift Kirk found himself first smiling, then beaming, and finally laughing out loud.

They were both laughing when the turbolift stopped at the bridge and opened its doors.

"Ah!" Babe greeted them. "I am happy to see your mating has restored the spirits of both of you."

Chekov fell out of his seat.

Kirk marched around the bridge, barking *"Status report!"* at every kid Sacker who happened to catch his eye. When he came to the science officer's station, Misterma'am was ready for him.

"Sir, the *Enterprise* is still tracking us. But I've calculated that it is now within firing range!" He stood there, waiting to be congratulated. Like a kid.

"Whose firing range, Misterma'am?" Kirk said in a deceptively soft voice. "Theirs or ours?"

"Why . . . ours, sir."

"Don't you think you should be worrying just a little bit about *their* firing range? Are you capable of comprehending how that might possibly have some bearing on the survival of this ship? An enemy vessel in pursuit, and you haven't figured out its range yet? *What the hell have you been doing over here—playing with dolls?*"

Misterma'am twitched at Kirk's blast. "I'll compute it now, Captain."

"You do that."

Babe yielded the command chair to Kirk. "Captain, you just now referred to your own ship as an enemy vessel."

And it hurt. "On this bridge, the *Enterprise* is the enemy."

"You do not expect me to believe you have changed allegiances, do you?"

"Of course not. What I want right now is to get that baryon reverter back to what used to be the Beta

146

Castelli system, and if the only way to accomplish that is to teach you to fly this ship—then I'll teach you to fly this ship. But I'm not on your side, Babe, and I never will be. You people are murderers."

The word fell like a bomb on the bridge. All talk ceased, and the Sackers stared at Kirk. Then Babe chanted in a singsong, "Killing will sometimes be necessary. It must be done neatly and quickly, remembering always that we are merely removing obstacles from our path."

Kirk turned his head and looked at her. "That sounded memorized, Babe."

"It is part of the Plan."

"What plan?"

But Babe would say no more. Kirk hesitated but then dropped it; this wasn't the time.

"Kepten."

"Yes, Chekov."

"Permission to go to the head."

"Granted." Kirk watched Chekov leave his seat and walk along the upper level toward the head. As he passed the damage control console, the young navigator took a look at the escape chute underneath—a large circular opening with a grab bar above it. Chekov was a little too obvious about it; Kirk would have to warn him to be more circumspect.

A black Sacker was now seated in the navigator's chair. "You, there!" Kirk said. "Navigator!"

The black Sacker turned. "Sir?"

"Have you been named?"

"Yes, sir!" the Sacker said proudly. "Ivan is my name."

As in Ivan the Terrible? Kirk thought. "That's a well-known name on Earth," he said, and coughed.

He looked at the other black Sacker standing beside Ivan. "And you?"

"I, sir, am named Rasputin!"

Well, I've been warned, Kirk thought wryly. There was only one other navigation trainee, an orange Sacker who hung back from the other two. "And you?" he asked.

The orange Sacker's head drooped forward. She did not answer.

"The Chekov has not yet seen fit to give that one a name," Ivan explained.

Kirk noticed the other Sackers turned their heads away, as if embarrassed. He made no comment but turned his attention back to the seated Sacker. "Well, Ivan, you're the one in the navigator's seat. What are you doing?"

"Sir, I am instructed to keep this seat warm until the Chekov returns."

"I see. Carry on." Kirk decided it would seem logical to continue questioning the Sacker apprentices. "You three—communications. Report."

"Sir," the one that must have been named Rose said, "we are learning the—"

"Report *here*," Kirk interrupted, pointing to the side of his command chair. "Babe, here's a chance to check up on your crew. Question them, find out how much they know."

The three Sackers made their way to the command chair, leaving Uhura alone at the communications station. Babe stood on the other side of Kirk and started her questioning. She showed a knowledge of communications that surprised him, and Kirk warned himself not to take her lightly simply because she was a youngster. It didn't take Babe long to find out that Iris was lagging far behind the other two, and she gave him a dressing-down that made even Kirk's ears curl. *She sounds just like me,* he thought wonderingly.

Kirk peered between Jon and Rose and saw Uhura nod at him. The interior visuals shield was down! He waited until Babe finished chewing out Iris, and then ordered the three trainees to return to their stations.

Spock was watching; Spock was listening.

Kirk sat quietly for a few minutes, getting his thoughts in order.

Everyone on the bridge of the *Enterprise* except Mr. Spock was making a face. About half of them were saying "Ugh!"—or some slight variation thereof. A couple of the more sensitive souls among them had lowered their eyes; the sight of Sackers even on a screen wasn't easy to take.

The main viewscreen showed Captain James T. Kirk firmly ensconced in the Sacker command chair. To his left stood a flaming red Sacker, while a duller brown one was on his right. The captain was wearing a shaded helmet of some sort and rather strange-looking clothing, while the two Sackers were garbed in cloaks that failed to conceal their bodies completely. Their heads were bare, and repulsive; both Sackers were wearing something over the bottom halves of their faces.

"Wide view, Mr. Wittering," Spock said.

The three figures on the screen shrank as the picture widened to show more of the bridge. "There's Uhura!" someone cried. As they watched, the black Sacker seated in the navigator's chair got up to let Ensign Chekov take his place.

"That's three of them," said Dr. McCoy.

Kirk-on-the-screen stood up.

"In close," Spock ordered.

Captain Kirk's head and shoulders filled the screen. "Commander Babe—I think we're going to have to get Chief Engineer Scott up here on the bridge."

"And that's four!" McCoy cried happily.

There was a brief outbreak of cheering. Sulu said, "What did he call the commander? It sounded like 'Babe'."

"Babe, Sweetie Pie, Sugar Plum—what's the difference!" McCoy laughed. "They're alive!"

"The captain definitely said 'Babe'," Spock remarked. "A feminine nickname, I believe."

"Doesn't that beat all!" McCoy said. "We should have known he'd end up sitting in the command chair! *Their* command chair!"

"Doctor, please be quiet," Spock said quickly.

Captain Kirk was speaking. "Babe, we'll need to try some more complicated maneuvers *later.* You're almost ready for them, but *not yet.* We mustn't attempt anything *too soon.* If we rush it, you'll end up looking like *a bunch of kids.* You're all *learning* very quickly, but *wait for my signal* before you try too much. Everything in its time. The tricky stuff will come *later.*" He took a deep breath—and lifted off his helmet just long enough to rub his first two fingers against his cheek, the other two held together but apart from the first. The only time in history the Vulcan peace sign had been used to scratch an itch.

"Return to wide view, Mr. Wittering," Spock ordered.

Helmet back in place, Kirk said, "So for that reason we're going to put off battle maneuvers until we learn how to prepare for battle first. Babe, I saw this ship go from cruise mode to battle mode once, when you moved to put the planet Holox between yourselves and the *Enterprise.* The transition was impressive to watch, but it seemed to take forever. I think you can do better than that."

The red Sacker on the screen spoke. "Much of the transition is automated, Captain."

"Understood. Let's work on the parts that aren't. Take the conn, Babe. Blue—look sharp!"

The *Enterprise* bridge crew watched as the red Sacker sat in the command chair and started giving orders. Captain Kirk stood next to her, ready to make suggestions when needed.

"How can he stand being so close to them?" Sulu shuddered. "And that red one—that's 'Babe'?"

"Evidently," Spock said. "They do accept names given to them by outsiders."

The communications officer said, "Do I call Lieutenant Berengaria, Mr. Spock?"

"There is no need for security, Mr. Wittering."

The young man looked puzzled. "But . . . but didn't you say if we knew where on the ship Captain Kirk was, we could probe for a weak spot in their shielding and—"

"Relax, Lieutenant," McCoy smiled. "Even *I* got that message. Captain Kirk just told us to wait."

"He did?"

"Play the tape back," Spock ordered. They all listened to Kirk's speech again, with its emphasis on *later* and *not yet*. "He has told us something else as well," Spock remarked. "The Sacker ship is being operated by young people who do not know their jobs. Something has happened to the Sackers, something disastrous."

"Good," Sulu muttered.

"This means Captain Kirk's command of their ship is only temporary, until the Sacker commander is ready to take over—Commander Babe, that is. When the captain signals, we must be ready to move immediately."

"Spock, how about sending a new message to the Sackers?" McCoy suggested. "One that would let Jim know we got *his* message. You could address this Babe by name—that would let him know he got through."

"Unfortunately, it would also inform the Sackers that their visuals shield is down," Spock answered. "Obviously the captain—or more likely Lieutenant Uhura—has lowered the shield without the Sackers' knowing. The minute they find out, we will lose visual contact."

"Mm, that's right," McCoy conceded. "Dammit! There must be *some* way we can let him know."

"There just might be a way," Spock replied thoughtfully. "In the early days of aviation, there was a maneuver known as the Immelmann turn. It involved, as I recall, making a half-roll in the middle of a loop. Such a maneuver is of no use to a starship, naturally, but—"

"But if the *Enterprise* did one, Jim would understand we were receiving him!" McCoy interrupted elatedly. "What a great idea, Spock!" Then doubt appeared on his face. "He *would* understand, wouldn't he?"

"I have every faith in the captain's ability to interpret the significance of the *Enterprise*'s performing such an unquestionably useless maneuver. Have you been listening, Mr. Sulu?"

"With both ears, Mr. Spock," Sulu grinned. "I've always wanted to try an Immelmann."

"Then here is your chance. As Captain Kirk would say, let 'er rip."

Mr. Sulu let 'er rip.

* * *

They were enemy engines, but Scotty had to respect good engineering wherever he met it. It wasn't a Sacker design anyway; a group of now-dead Zirgosian geniuses had built these engines, and Scotty gave them a silent salute as he prepared to leave for the bridge.

Yesterday Captain Kirk had said he wanted Scotty to be able to control the power feed to the thrusters from the bridge. That way the helm would respond quickly when the captain wanted it to, and sluggishly all other times. Scotty could see the advantage; they were involved in a game of cat and mouse with the Sackers, and the response time of the helm was one of the captain's best weapons. So Scotty had spent eleven hours sabotaging his own sabotage, redirecting control of the feed to an auxiliary board on the bridge.

One more quick tour to make sure everything was in order. Scotty was confident that Mr. Green could handle the day-to-day operation of the engines without too much trouble, but any serious emergency would be beyond him; he was green in more than just his sac fluid. When Captain Kirk had told him these Sackers were just kids, Scotty had been shocked. *Bairns canna fly starships!* he'd protested.

But they were flying *this* starship, and they were doing a fairly good job of it, considering. Scotty began to feel a new respect for Mr. Green. *He's a boy,* he kept reminding himself, *only a boy.* A boy doing a man's job. And a boy who looked to Chief Engineer Montgomery Scott of the U.S.S. *Enterprise* for guidance in his rite of passage. Scotty stopped and looked at the "plasmicophic ferangulator", still clicking and whirring away. He felt a stab of guilt.

He shook off the feeling and headed down the companionway to the lower deck of the engine room. Mr. Green was waiting for him. "Ah, laddie, it's all yours now," Scotty said. "Today is graduation day. It's a great responsibility ye'll be takin' on."

"No one is more aware of that than I, sir. My greatest hope is that I will not disappoint you."

Scotty paused a moment and then said: "Y'won't disappoint me. An' y'won't disappoint yourself, either. Y'are a good lad, Mr. Green. Bright an' industrious an' eager to learn. I have complete confidence in your ability to do the job."

The Sacker's body shook a couple of times and his head drooped forward. "Oh, thank you, sir—thank you! I was so worried you were not pleased! I cannot tell you how grateful I am for those gracious words."

"Here, now, none o' that," Scotty said gruffly. "Y'are in charge here now. Hold yourself proud!"

Mr. Green's body stopped shaking and he raised his head; Scotty thought he did indeed look proud. "I have something I want the Scott to hear before you go," the Sacker said. "Please attend."

"Go ahead."

The Sacker switched off his translator and said something in his own language.

Scotty shrugged. "I canna understand."

"Can ye understand me now, laddie?"

Scotty's eyes bulged. "Was that you? *You,* an' not the translator?"

"Aye! I am learnin' by listenin' you. I dinna have no another teacher."

"Why, Mr. Green!" Scotty threw back his head and let out a roar of laughter. "'Tis wonderful, that's what 'tis! English! Y'are speakin' English!"

"Are ye pleased?"

"Oh, laddie, I'm more than pleased! I am delighted! Y'couldna have given me a nicer goin'-away present. I do thank ye."

"No, sir, 'tis me who owes the thankin'. Ye'll always be me teacher."

They parted on better terms than ever before enjoyed in the troubled history of Sacker-human relationships.

Captain Kirk had a reason for wanting Scotty on the bridge other than to fiddle with the power feed to the helm. Kirk had not much liked the idea of his chief engineer being alone in the engine room with the Sackers. True, Scotty did seem comfortable enough with his Mr. Green; but Kirk felt better having all his people where he could keep an eye on them. Now Scotty was seated at a console off to one side of him, Uhura was to the other, and Chekov in front of him. Besides, he didn't want Scotty anywhere near the engine room if he could bring off what he was planning.

"Run it again," he ordered.

For the past two days he'd been forcing the bridge crew to watch the tape of the Immelmann turn the *Enterprise* had surprisingly executed. Kirk had had to swallow a laugh when he saw the starship indulging in a loop designed for the early monoplane. But he got the message. *Thanks for letting me know, Mr. Spock.*

"This Immelmann," Toots said, "is it a frequently used maneuver?"

"Oh yes," Kirk said. "It's the best way of evading enemy fire and returning to your original position quickly. Unfortunately, it's rather tricky to execute. But see how smoothly the *Enterprise* makes that half-roll? That takes experience. I don't know another helmsman in the fleet who can do the Immelmann as well as Mr. Sulu."

Blue twitched.

"But . . . but no one was firing on them," Babe said, clearly puzzled. "Why did they do it at all?"

"Practice maneuver," Kirk said shortly. "We need to do a few of those ourselves. Battle mode, please." He lifted the forefinger of his left hand, his signal to Scotty that the helm was to receive full power.

The ship made the transition from its rectangular cruising shape to the multibranched ovoid shape that was its battle mode, and it made the change swiftly and smoothly. The helmsman's primary job during the transition was to hold the ship steady—and steady it was, like a rock.

"Good, Blue, good!" Kirk said with fake enthusiasm. "You may develop a touch for the helm yet."

The Sacker jiggled with pleasure. "Thank you, sir!"

"Babe, come here. You too, Brownie." When they were both in close, Kirk said, "This ship has the capability of assuming more than these two shapes, rectangular and ovoid. The schematics show its best battle mode would be a starburst, with the various sections radiating out from a central point—the ship would be hardest to fire upon in that mode. It would be like trying to hit one spine on a cactus. Have you ever taken the ship into starburst mode?"

"No, Captain, no one ever has," Babe said. "Starburst puts the biggest drain on the engines of all the ship's modes, so it was decided not to use it unless absolutely necessary."

"So the prior commander didn't execute shakedown maneuvers?"

"No, sir. Even before the accident that killed our command personnel, there'd been no need."

Kirk raised his voice. "Misterma'am!"

"Sir?" answered the science officer.

"Status of the *Enterprise*."

"Still tracking, and within firing range of us."

Kirk looked at the Sacker commander. "Do you think there is no need now?"

"I take your point, Captain. You wish shakedown maneuvers for starburst mode?"

"With your permission."

"Granted."

Kirk called for the ship's schematics to be projected on the main screen, trying to still the flutter of excitement in his stomach. He would be the first man in history to execute this maneuver. "Electromagnetic shields down," he ordered, giving Scotty the signal for full power.

Step by step he took his kid Sackers through the complicated procedure of converting to starburst mode. Kirk half wished he could have been on the *Enterprise* to see it; it must have been an impressive sight. Well, he could watch the tape later. If there was a later.

He answered all of Babe's questions, and Brownie even asked one or two. When the procedure was complete, Kirk made a point of congratulating everyone who had participated—except Blue. He didn't criticize the helmsman's performance; he simply didn't mention him. Blue twitched.

"Captain, incoming message," Uhura said. "Visual only."

"On the screen."

A message in the Sacker language appeared on the viewscreen, and the minute the Sackers had had time to read it, a buzz of excitement ran through the bridge. A few of the Sackers were jiggling with pleasure.

"What is it?" Kirk asked. "What does it say?"

No one answered him. Babe and Brownie were consulting, their heads waggling in agreement. Among the jiggling Sackers were Ivan and Rasputin, one of whom carelessly waved a hand . . . and hit Chekov on the shoulder.

Chekov's scream put an end to the Sackers' excitement. He fell to the deck, his shoulder smoking. Kirk, Uhura, and Scotty rushed to him, only to find he'd passed out from the pain.

"Medteam to the bridge," Rose said at the communications station. "Human burn—emergency."

Scotty said, "Canna we do something 'til they get here? Are there nae first aid supplies on this bridge?"

"Not for humans," Babe said. "The medteam will be here shortly."

The medteam when it arrived consisted of two Sackers wearing heavy mitts and pulling an antigrav gurney. One of them sprayed something on Chekov's shoulder.

"What's that?" Kirk demanded.

He was told it was a temporary pain reliever. The two Sackers carefully placed Chekov on the gurney and took him to the nearest turbolift. They themselves stepped into another, even though Chekov was unconscious and would not have been aware of their presence in such close proximity.

Kirk whirled on the two black Sackers. "All right—which one of you did it?"

Rasputin hung his head. "I regret exceedingly that I have damaged the Chekov. It was not done intentionally."

"Of all the stupid, careless things to do!" Kirk fumed. "You know what happens when you touch a human! You have to be on guard *all the time*!"

"It was an accident," the Sacker said in a pleading tone.

"It's the kind of accident we can't afford to have!" Kirk snapped. "Now who's going to plot our course back to the Beta Castelli system? You?"

A dead silence hung over the bridge. Kirk turned to Babe. "What does that message say?"

"It does not concern you, Captain."

"Dammit, Babe, how can I—"

"I repeat, it does not concern you."

He turned his back to her. "Uhura—what does it say?"

Uhura didn't bat an eyelash. "One of their ships that has been having engine trouble is now repaired and in orbit around Starbase Four," she said evenly. "All other Sacker ships are in position and ready to proceed to step three of the Plan."

Rose made a sound. "How long have you understood our language?"

Uhura didn't answer.

Kirk said, "What's this plan? What are you up to?"

"The Plan will be revealed to you at the proper time, Captain," Babe said. "There is another matter to be attended to first."

"And what's that?"

"That too will be revealed in its proper time."

Kirk realized he wasn't going to get any more out of her. Whatever they were up to, they simply weren't going to tell him about it until they were good and ready. Here was one area where bullying wouldn't do the trick. Abruptly he headed for the turbolift.

"Where are you going?" Babe called. "I did not give you permission to leave the bridge."

"I'm going to see about Chekov, so you'd better call

down and have one of your armed muscleheads meet me at whatever level sickbay's on, because *I'm going.*"

"Level ten," Brownie said helpfully.

"We are still in starburst mode," Babe protested. "It is causing a drain on the engines."

"Let it," Kirk said coldly as the turbolift doors closed.

Chapter Nine

CAPTAIN KIRK FOUND CHEKOV lying on an air mattress in sickbay, between two of the vats of gelatinous substance the Sackers used for beds. The young navigator's helmet was off and he was conscious.

Kirk removed his own helmet and breathed in air only slightly tainted with the Sacker smell. "Chekov? How are you feeling?"

"Not too bad, Kepten. A little shaky, but the pain has been neutralized. Permission to kill Rasputin?"

"Granted," Kirk smiled. "What are they doing for you?"

"Vell, the doctor vants to make sure there is no infection before spraying on the false skin. She vill know soon, she says."

"A kid doctor," Kirk muttered.

"But a good vun, I think. She says she has been studying burn treatment for humans ever since ve beamed aboard, because she vas afraid something like this vould happen."

"Thank heaven for that. I'll bet you've named her."

Chekov smiled innocently. "I call her Bonesovna."

"Don't tell me. Daughter of Bones?"

"*Da*. Do you think Dr. McCoy vill be pleased?"

"I'd . . . just as soon not be around when you tell

161

him. Speaking of names, why did you name your two black Sackers but not the orange one?"

"Sewing dissension in the ranks, Kepten. Ivan and Rasputin now look down on the orange vun and treat her like an inferior, and she grows more resentful of them by the hour." Chekov sighed. "But it is not fair. The orange vun vorks harder than the other two and is the vun I vould pick to do any real navigating. I vill give her a name vhen I get back."

"Are you feeling sorry for her? Chekov, we can't feel sorry for them. It wouldn't make any sense to feel sorry for them!" Kirk gnawed his lower lip. "So why do I feel like a rat every time I give Babe or Blue a hard time?"

"Is wery difficult," Chekov agreed.

The captain accepted his navigator's assurances that he would be able to return to his post before long. In the corridor, he told his escort he'd like a look at the baryon reverter; the Sacker flatly refused. Kirk had tried getting in to see it before, always with the same result. He was worried that the reverter might be too large to beam over to the *Enterprise*.

On the bridge, the first thing Kirk noticed was that the yellow Sacker—Jon?—was seated at the communications station. Then he saw Babe, Brownie, Rose, Iris, and Misterma'am forming a half-circle around the hatchway leading to the head. "What's going on?" he called out.

The Sackers divided enough to let him see Scotty standing before the hatchway, his arms flung out in a protective posture. "Ah, Captain!" the engineer sighed in relief. "Will ye tell these . . . people to back off!"

"Babe, please get your people away from him,"

Kirk said. "Do you want to send another of us to sickbay?"

Babe gave an order; the others fell away. "It's the Uhura, Captain," the Sacker commander said angrily. "Misterma'am found out she'd lowered the visuals shield!"

"Well, of course she lowered the shield," Kirk said reasonably. "Our friends have been worrying about us. That was the only way we had of letting them know we were still alive."

"The *Enterprise* has been watching everything we've done! They'll know we are trainees now!"

"They'd figure that out anyway, Babe. Just from watching the maneuvers. It's nothing to get excited about."

"I want the Uhura placed under restraints! Order her to come out immediately."

"Whoa, wait a minute! Lieutenant Uhura was just following my orders. If anybody's going to be placed under restraints, it'll have to be me."

"An' I knew about it as well," Scotty said stoutly. "So y'might as well restrain me too."

"Well?" asked Kirk. "What's it going to be? Are you going to lock us *all* up? It's your decision, Babe. You're the commander."

Babe thought it over, without consulting with Brownie. "No," she decided. "You are still needed. But if there is any other irregularity—"

"It's the brig for all of us. Understood."

"And starting right now, you will train us in the use of the weapons systems."

"But there are still several other—"

"*Right now*, Captain."

He didn't press; her voice had danger signals in it.

Scotty stuck his head through the hatchway. "It's all right, lass. Y'can come out now."

Uhura emerged, looking shaken. She and Scotty both wanted to know how Chekov was doing. Kirk told them he'd be all right.

When he returned to the command chair, he found Chekov's orange Sacker waiting for him. The Sacker asked, "Sir, did I understand you to say the Chekov will recover?"

"Correct. He's going to be all right."

The Sacker made a noise that might have been a sigh. "This one is much relieved."

Kirk examined her closely; she really did look woebegone. "Ah . . . why don't you go down to see him? I think he has something to tell you."

The Sacker made a murmur of surprise, but checked with Babe and then left. Ivan was seated in the navigator's chair, but Rasputin was nowhere in sight. When he asked, Kirk was told the latter had been temporarily banished from the bridge for his carelessness in burning Chekov. Kirk nodded; that seemed right. He took his seat and announced, "Target practice."

In addition to the usual phasers and photon torpedoes, the still-unnamed Sacker ship had short-burst laser flares for close fighting. Kirk decided to ignore the latter for the time being. He ordered targets released, and the weapons training was under way.

This time the forefinger of Kirk's left hand stayed down. Scotty did his bit, and the helm was agonizingly slow to respond. The two young Sackers manning the weapons-system station showed a good sense of timing. They got so they could hit the moving target from a stationary position; but every time they had to fire on the run, they missed by a mile. And the reason was that the ship was always too slow in getting to where it was supposed to be; weapons and helm were out of synch. Everyone on the bridge was staring at Blue.

"Blue, I don't know what to say to you," Kirk said with simulated sadness. "I tell you and I tell you, you must *anticipate* these moves. You have to develop a touch for the helm. Mr. Sulu would have made twelve turns in the time it took you to complete one."

Blue was steaming. "The helm is sluggish in its response! I would like to see the captain do any better!"

Aha! A challenge. "Well, I'm no Sulu," Kirk said, getting up from the command chair, "but I think I can make a simple turn faster than that."

Blue slid out of his seat. "Please."

Kirk sat at the helm. "Babe, you give the order."

She waited a few moments and then said, "Hard to starboard."

The ship whipped around nicely. "You see?" Kirk said innocently. "The helm *does* respond."

"But . . . but you did nothing more than what I do!" Blue protested.

"I anticipated. You don't anticipate." Kirk moved back to the command chair. "Let's try it again."

They tried it again. And again. And again. Kirk didn't even have to yell at Blue, because Babe was doing that for him. And then Brownie joined in. Then Misterma'am. Before long every Sacker on the bridge was yelling at Blue. Kirk let it all go on for a few minutes before standing up and raising his hands to silence them.

"Blue," he said, "if Mr. Sulu were in command of this vessel and saw what you were doing at the helm, he'd be using *you* for target practice. I've been trying to figure out what your problem is—and as far as I can see, you're just not concentrating."

"I am concentrating!" Blue yelled.

"We should have taken the Sulu with the others," Brownie said to Babe.

"But you're obviously not concentrating enough," Kirk went on. "You're allowing yourself to be distracted. You've got to learn to shut out all other sights and sounds—only the helm matters. When Sulu is on duty, he never——"

"Sulu! Sulu!" Blue screamed. "I am choking with nausea at the name of Sulu!" He jumped out of his seat and whirled to face Kirk.

"You're away from your post, mister!" Kirk snapped.

"Sir?" said Misterma'am.

"Not you. *Him.* Return to your post, Blue. You'll never be a Sulu if you act like this."

"That name again!" Blue shrieked. "I am tired of hearing about your wonderful Sulu! And I am tired of having to wear these ridiculous things because of you!" He ripped off his cloak and his translator and stood there defiantly.

Kirk's stomach heaved at the sight of the white wormlike objects oozing around in Blue's intestines, but he forced himself not to look away. "And I am tired of having to wear this thing over my head because of *you.*"

"He cannot understand you, Captain." Babe switched over to her own language and said something to her rebellious helmsman. He started to answer her without the translator—and all three humans on the bridge instinctively tried to slap their hands over their ears, but ended up just smacking their helmets. Babe stopped Blue with a sharp word, and he charged toward a turbolift and was gone.

A tension-filled silence reigned for a moment or two, and then Babe said to Rose, "Consult the duty roster and summon the next helmsman trainee."

Kirk sighed. "We're going to lose a lot of time, you know."

"I know," Babe said. "But it is clear to all of us that Blue cannot do the job."

"She's on her way," Rose reported.

"I think you'd better get Blue back up here," Kirk advised. He hadn't thought Blue would break so soon. Kirk swore to himself; he must have lost sight of the fact that in spite of his seven-foot-plus, Blue was still just a kid. His bolting like that—well, it was something to worry about. If the replacement was no better than Blue had been, Babe might start suspecting there was indeed something wrong with the helm.

They waited, until the turbolift doors opened and a Sacker shorter than the others walked on to the bridge. "Here I be!" she announced.

Kirk, Uhura, and Scotty all did a double take. *"Pinky?"*

Babe turned to Rose. "I thought [*untranslatable*] was next up."

"She is," Rose said, "but she has been in sickbay the last two days. Pinky is next."

Pinky plopped down at the helm. "So what do I do?"

Kirk looked up at Babe and cocked an eyebrow.

"I had not anticipated this," the Sacker commander said agitatedly. "The one who backs up Blue has had some training. Pinky has had none."

"You have a problem, Babe," Kirk said expressionlessly. "Part and parcel of being a starship captain."

That was the moment one of the other turbolift doors opened and Chekov's orange Sacker came bouncing in. She was excited and impervious to the air of gloom on the bridge. "I am named!" she announced gleefully. "Do you all hear? I have been given a name of my own! Henceforth you will address me as Orangejuiceandwodka!"

Kirk groaned and covered his eyes. "I could use one," he said.

Dr. Leonard McCoy sat glumly at his desk in the chief surgeon's office, staring at his terminal that he'd keyed in to the main viewscreen on the bridge. The screen showed the Sacker ship changing shape, releasing a practice target, firing, missing. Over and over. Endlessly. What did Jim have in mind? Was he just trying to wear them down?

A shadow fell across his desk. McCoy glanced up and said tiredly, "Ah, sit down, Mr. Spock. Sit down and tell me what's going to happen next."

"I shall sit down," the Vulcan said, doing so, "but I fear I know no more of the future than you do. Once we lost interior visuals, we also lost knowledge of what is occurring on the Sacker bridge."

"More of the same, I'd guess. Jim's waging some kind of psychological warfare over there."

"That is what I came to see you about, Doctor. Our record banks contain no information about the Sacker young. We cannot assume they will react to pressure the same way human young do."

"The human young don't always react the same," McCoy said.

"Exactly. Human and Vulcan youngsters would either withstand the pressure or else break and run. Or—they could rebel, although for Vulcans that would be unthinkable in most circumstances. But we don't know what the Sacker young might do. They could turn on Jim. I am concerned that his tactics may be placing him and the others in danger."

"I've been wondering about that too. But we don't know the situation over there, not really. Jim knows what he's doing, Spock. He always does." McCoy thought a moment. "Well, almost always."

Spock shook his head. "Three men and one woman against perhaps a thousand Sackers? The odds are too great."

"So what do you want of me?"

"An explanation. I want you to tell me how the sonic hypnosis-inducer works."

McCoy smiled tiredly. "You're gonna hypnotize the Sackers? Good luck."

"Doctor. As long as the Sackers' defensive shields remain operational, the only access we have to that ship is through their communications system. Sound is our only possible weapon at the moment. If there is any chance that we can put the Sackers into a trance—"

"That's crazy, Spock! The sonic hypnosis-inducer is configured to the *human* brain and auditory system. Any fool can tell just by looking at them that the Sackers aren't built the same way we are!"

"I am well aware of that, Doctor. But the hypnosis-inducer's configuration can be changed, I assume."

"Yes, but to what? We don't have anything to go on!"

Spock pressed his lips together. "We may have one thing. The record banks say the Sacker voice is piercing, penetrating. That would suggest a higher pitch than a normal human range."

McCoy looked interested for the first time. "Raising

the frequency level of the sound waves the hypnosis-inducer sends out is easy. I can even adjust it up to ultrasonic if we need to go that high, but it will take a little work. There's no therapeutic value in the ultrasonic for humans, so the designers didn't build it in."

"We can use only the frequency levels higher than those liable to produce a trance state in Jim and the others," Spock pointed out. "They have to remain conscious in order to lower the shields, or else the whole exercise will prove futile."

McCoy scowled. "Is that a problem? They're wearing helmets."

"Helmets that evidently do not block sound. They are able to converse."

"Mm, that's right." McCoy thought about it a while and then slowly nodded, realizing the plan just might work. "It might make our people drowsy, but we can keep it high enough not to send them into a trance."

They both fell silent, staring at the Sacker ship on the viewscreen. It had resumed its rectangular shape. As they watched, one section unfolded from the bottom to a perpendicular position, and another unfolded from that, parallel to the ship. The ship looked for all the world as if it were kneeling on one leg.

The doctor stirred. "You understand, Spock, I don't have the foggiest notion of what it takes to hypnotize a Sacker."

"Understood. I would suggest an escalating scale of various frequencies, each to be transmitted for the same time duration."

"It will be hit-and-miss, you know—trying to find the exact level that induces a hypnotic trance in monsters."

"If, indeed, they can be hypnotized," Spock remarked with something close to a sigh. "I shall be happy to assist you if my services are needed."

"Oh, I can use your help, all right," McCoy said, getting up and heading toward the lab. "Come along, Svengali—let's get started."

Blue was back.

Nothing had been said on the bridge, no explanations were offered. But Babe had got him back, one way or another. Now Blue sat stonily silent at the helm, defiantly not wearing his cloak. Iris—the rebellious one—had also cast his cloak aside; Uhura was on her rest period or he might not have found the courage to try it. But when the two Sackers seated at the weapons systems station saw Iris, they'd quietly slipped out of their cloaks as well—giving Scotty a few bad moments, as he was seated at the station next to theirs.

Babe was growing suspicious of Scotty. Kirk had said he wanted the engineer on the bridge to help Blue, to try to feed in more power at those times Blue claimed the helm was sluggish. But since Blue's performance remained abysmal for the most part, Babe was wandering over in Scotty's direction more and more frequently. Kirk decided it was time for Blue to shine a little.

He gave Scotty the signal. "Full reverse."

The ship boomed backwards as if fired out of a cannon. The Sackers were surprised, and none more so than Blue.

"Very good," Kirk said calmly. "Now full stop."

Without even a hint of vibration the ship halted its backward flight.

"Why, Blue, I do believe you're getting the hang of it. Hard to port."

The ship shot off to the left. A couple of the Sackers started jiggling in pleasure. Kirk let Babe take over, and the amazing performance continued. Scotty slowed down the power feed a couple of times to keep it all from looking too easy, but by the time Babe called a halt, the other Sackers were actually congratulating Blue.

Babe ordered a series of six targets released, to be fired upon while the ship was in motion. They hit five out of six.

Blue was jiggling in his seat.

Kirk said, "That was good work, Blue. And you, too, Engineer." He smiled.

"Thank ye, sir," Scotty smiled back.

The captain decided the time was ripe, now while the Sackers were in a self-congratulatory mood and their guard was down a little. Now he could—

But he didn't get a chance to put his plan into operation. Babe unexpectedly announced, "I think we are ready. Rose, you may send the message."

Silence immediately fell on the bridge, and Kirk felt an ominous prickling at the back of his neck. "What message?" he demanded. "What are you talking about, Babe?"

"Put it on audio," she told Rose.

The message was in English.

ATTENTION: STARFLEET COMMAND. THE RACE OF BEINGS YOU ARE PLEASED TO CALL SACKERS HAVE IN THEIR CONTROL THE MEANS TO STOP THE EXPANSION OF THE NEW UNIVERSE WITHIN YOUR OWN. YOU WILL SURRENDER ALL YOUR STARBASES TO US WITHIN TWENTY STANDARD HOURS OR THE EXPANSION WILL BE ALLOWED TO CONTINUE. THERE WILL BE NO

NEGOTIATION. YOU HAVE ONLY ONE CHOICE:
SURRENDER TO US OR WE ALL DIE.

"That's suicide!" Kirk cried. "Have you no more respect for your own lives than you do for others? How can you throw your lives away like that?"

"Lass, this is foolishness!" Scotty implored of Babe. "What do ye want to be doin' a thing like that for?"

"It is the Plan," Babe said simply.

"Plan!" Kirk exclaimed. "I keep hearing about a plan! *What plan?*"

"It is our Plan, and you now have a part to play in it. Captain Kirk, I am giving you an order. You are to shoot down the *Enterprise,* and you are to do it now."

Kirk was so stunned he couldn't answer.

"Oh, lassie!" Scotty moaned softly.

Kirk recovered. "You're out of your mind. I won't do it."

"If you do not shoot down the *Enterprise,* Captain, I will. We have a better chance with you in command, but—"

"You have no chance at all!" Kirk said heatedly. "Look, Babe, we need to talk privately. Let's go into the readyroom."

"There is no need for talk. Will you open fire upon the *Enterprise*?"

"No, and neither will you. There are things I haven't told you. Ten minutes, Babe. You can give me ten minutes."

Before Babe could answer, Rose spoke up. "Message from the *Enterprise.* Audio only."

"Pipe it in," Babe ordered.

The bridge was suddenly filled with the soft sound of a shimmering, specially augmented tone, oscillating gently between a major keynote and its minor. Then as they listened the tone modulated to a higher pitch.

"Music!" Brownie exclaimed. "Why is the *Enterprise* sending us music?"

After a few minutes the pitch changed again. "I like it," Orangejuiceandwodka volunteered.

Jon, the yellow Sacker, began rocking from side to side without moving his feet. After a minute Rose joined him, the two swaying in unison as the *Enterprise*'s "music" continued its climb up the scale.

"This makes no sense," Babe said, puzzled, "unless it is a code of some sort that the humans can decipher and we cannot. Is that what it is, Captain Kirk? Captain?" When he didn't answer, she whirled around quickly, for a Sacker. "Captain!"

Kirk had collapsed into the big command chair, his arms cradling his head on the control panel in the armrest. He was sleeping peacefully, a faint smile on his face.

"He's asleep?" Brownie couldn't believe it.

"The music!" Misterma'am cried, suddenly understanding. "It was the music that put him to sleep— they are trying to put *us* to sleep! Turn it off—quickly! Quickly!"

Rose shut down the transmission from the *Enterprise.*

The young Sackers exchanged uneasy glances, momentarily rendered speechless by their close call. "These humans are full of tricks," Babe finally said. "We must all be on our guard." She bent over the sleeping captain. "Captain Kirk! Wake up! *Captain Kirk!*"

"Give him a good shake," Blue growled.

"Captain!"

Kirk drowsily opened his eyes; the sight of Babe peering at him from six inches away completed the waking-up process. "What happened?"

"Your friends aboard the *Enterprise* tried to put us asleep," Babe answered, straightening up. "As you see, we are not as susceptible to seductive music as you humans."

Seductive music? Kirk tried to think. Spock must have done something with that thingamajig from sickbay, the instrument Bones sometimes used to hypnotize trauma patients. A good notion, with bad results. Kirk sighed heavily—and was startled to hear the sound of rusty machinery starting up.

It wasn't rusty machinery; it was Scotty. The engineer lay sprawled in his seat, head thrown back, snoring up a storm. Kirk walked unsteadily over to him and shook his shoulder. "Scotty—wake up. Wake up, Scotty." He slapped the engineer's cheek lightly four or five times with his fingertips. "Mr. Scott— *wake up.*"

Scotty woke up, reluctantly. And realized he'd been asleep. He was appalled. "Oh, sir! Sleepin' on duty!"

"Not your fault, Scotty. Mr. Spock played us a lullaby—it got me too."

"Captain Kirk!" Babe called impatiently. "Before you took your little nap, you were about to direct an attack against the *Enterprise*. Return to the command chair."

Kirk fought against a feeling of letdown as he walked back and planted himself in front of the red Sacker. "Before I took my little nap, Babe, I was asking you for ten minutes' private conversation. Is your Great Plan so inflexible it won't allow me ten minutes? What happens to your mission depends on what you do next. You can't make a command decision without knowing as much about the circumstances as you can learn."

Brownie hovered behind the Sacker commander, ready to offer advice. Babe didn't ask for it. "Very well, Captain. Ten minutes only. Brownie, you have the conn."

The brown Sacker twitched. "I?"

"You're in training for a command position, aren't you?" Babe asked sharply. "So command! Take the conn." Unaware of how much like James T. Kirk she'd sounded, she led the captain into the readyroom as Brownie gingerly lowered himself into the command chair.

Most of the readyroom was taken up by a strategy table, currently not activated; the small space was even hotter than the bridge proper. The first thing Babe did was toss aside her cloak. The message was clear; the Sackers were through catering to human peculiarities. Babe's sac fluid was thinner than human blood, but "bloody" was the word that popped into Kirk's mind. Yet his stomach did not heave, much to his surprise. Was he actually getting used to these repulsive-looking beings?

He got straight to the point. "If you fire upon the *Enterprise*, that will be the biggest mistake of your life."

"I do not see why. We have the superior weaponry."

"Ah, but the *Enterprise* has something you *don't* have, and that is a pointy-eared Vulcan named Mr. Spock. Babe, you're nowhere near ready to challenge Mr. Spock. I'm not sure *I* could take him, and I hope never to have to put it to the test. And there's still the problem of Blue. He had a good run just now, but he's still a neophyte. And remember he'll be going up against the best helmsman in the fleet."

"I cannot allow the *Enterprise* to interfere with the Plan."

"The *Enterprise* is not going to interfere! Say Starfleet does surrender its bases to you—the *Enterprise* is going to want to make sure you get back to the Beta Castelli system safely so you can stop that destructive influx of heat. But say you attack my ship. Mr. Spock will retaliate, you can count on that, even though you have the four of us on board. Your shielding system is good—the best I've ever seen, frankly. But no shield is perfect. What if the *Enterprise* hits the place where you're storing the baryon reverter? What happens to your wonderful Plan then?"

The Sacker commander twitched; she obviously hadn't considered that. But when she did consider it, she began to sag.

"What happens?" Kirk persisted.

"The Plan fails," she admitted.

"You didn't think of that, did you?" Kirk pressed. "Babe, when you're in command you have to think of everything. It's part of the anticipating I keep telling you about. You can't just react, you have to act first. Like the time Blue stormed off the bridge. You should have been ready for that. And you should never have let him go. But when he did go, you should have called Security and ordered him placed under restraints. You don't ever let a crewman walk out on you—not *ever*. And I could name a hundred other things. Babe, believe me—you're not ready to take on Mr. Spock. You don't want to risk the reverter. You're in over your head."

She sagged even further. "I have failed," she said heavily. "I have tried to learn, I have tried to follow your example. I have given my very best effort—but it is not good enough. I am not fit to command this vessel."

Kirk's throat tightened; this was it. This was what he'd been building toward, the moment he could move in and crush her utterly, when her self-esteem was at its lowest ebb and her defenses shattered. It was the moment he could shatter her ego beyond any hope of recovery. *Do it. Do it now, before she has time to bounce back.*

Do it.

He couldn't do it.

He let the silence between them build as he tried to get his own jumbled feelings in order. Finally he began to speak, in the softest tones he'd ever yet used with her. "Babe, you have the makings of a fine starship captain. I've been telling you all the things you've done wrong because that was my job. But I didn't tell you all the things you've done right—even though that should have been part of my job too, I suppose. But you do a lot of things right. You learn fast. You make sensible decisions. You have the respect of your crew. And you've had the courage to take on a responsibility that no youngster should ever be burdened with."

She lifted her head. "What did you call me? A youngster?"

Kirk smiled. "I know you're not grown up yet, Babe. I know you're *all* youngsters, every one of you on this ship. That accident that put you in charge—it killed off every adult on board."

"How . . . how did you find out?"

"It doesn't matter. But we've all known for some time now. And the *Enterprise* knows as well. I sent a sort of message while the visuals shield was down." He laughed awkwardly. "That's one reason I want to avoid a battle. My crew on the *Enterprise* would feel guilty as hell shooting down a bunch of kids."

"You still consider yourself a part of the *Enterprise*?"

"Of course. I always will. You'll soon feel that way about your own ship, if you don't already. Babe, tell me about the Plan. It's out in the open now. It's not *your* plan, is it?"

Babe made one of her indecipherable Sacker sounds and said, "We were not included in the planning sessions, we 'youngsters'. The Plan was formulated before I was taken out of the incubation vat. Our Elders devised the Plan, and every one of us on the ship was trained with only one goal in mind—to make sure the Plan was correctly and efficiently executed when the time came."

"Where are you from originally? Someplace outside the Federation's sphere, I know."

"We originally occupied four planets circling a sun that has no name on your star charts. This was long before I began my life, you understand. But our sun had almost depleted itself of fuel when the Elders of the Four Worlds decided we must find other worlds to live on. And so the search began."

Kirk knew what was coming. "And you found yourselves unwelcome wherever you went."

"Yes. At first no one knew why. The computer has records of the studies made of local laws and customs, and of our attempts to honor them. But gradually the truth came out. The sight and smell of us make other races ill. Our voices can cause deafness. If we touch you, you burn. No one wanted us to stay."

"So you decided to take by force what you couldn't get peaceably."

"Not exactly, and not immediately. Captain, can

you understand what it is like to spend your entire life being rejected because of physical attributes you were born with? Everywhere we went, for over fifty years, every race we contacted turned their backs to us. My race did not know there was anything unusual about us until we left our homeworlds. And when we did leave, it was to find ourselves being treated as worse than lepers."

Kirk remained silent, understanding her pain.

"Our computer is full of recorded instances when some well-meaning human made suggestions as to what we could do to get rid of our odor, or change our appearance, or the like. It was always assumed that we would not only be willing to alter ourselves to accommodate your prejudices, but also that we should be glad of the opportunity to do so. No human ever suggested altering himself to accommodate us."

Kirk grimaced. "Yes, that's the human race for you, I'm afraid."

Babe went on, "Eventually the Elders became convinced there was no place at all for us in your Federation. So the years of ignominy eventually came to a head, and the Plan was devised to *force* you to learn to live with us. If we were the rulers and you the underlings, then you would have no choice but to adapt. So when the Zirgosians perfected their technique for tapping into a neighboring universe, the Plan was put into action."

Kirk had suspected it must be something like that, but hearing Babe put it into words made it more real. This takeover plan was not hers, but she was doing her damnedest to make sure it worked. But all the Sackers were in on it, not just this ship. And because of the accident that robbed this ship of all its adults, the entire Sacker race was forced to rely upon a youngster to get the job done. Why didn't they just wait until some adult Sackers could be beamed aboard from another ship?

Because that would have upset the Plan, Kirk told himself. He remembered the signal they'd received from the other Sackers saying that a recently repaired ship was now in orbit around Starbase Four. Probably every Starbase had a Sacker ship circling it now, ready to accept the base's surrender. Or perhaps several ships—nobody knew how many Sackers there were all together. To pull one of those vessels away long enough to meet Babe's ship might have upset some distribution of power they'd arranged. And there was something else. Scotty had said each ship carried one "clan"; perhaps beaming adults aboard from another ship would have violated some clan taboo. But whatever the Sackers' reasons, it was now up to Babe and her crew of kids to make the Plan work.

Kirk finally spoke. "So none of this was your idea. But there's one thing that *was* your idea." He paused. "Holox."

"It was necessary," Babe said quietly. "We could not allow the colonists to endanger the incubation vats."

"There were ways to stop them other than by killing them, Babe. And you killed two of my people as well, a woman named Ching and a man named Hrolfson. That makes you a murderer, Babe. Doesn't that mean anything to you at all?"

"A hundred alien lives are of less value than one of our own."

"That's something else that sounds memorized. Besides, all lives are of value."

"That is a comforting thing to say, Captain, but do you truly believe it? The stranger who attacks your friend—is his life of equal value to that of your friend?"

Kirk grunted. "Well, there's one thing I'll have to take back. Maybe you're more grown up than I gave you credit for. But the killing was wrong, Babe. No argument in the universe can justify what you did to those people on Holox."

The readyroom didn't have space enough for any serious pacing, but Babe managed it anyway. Three steps in one direction, three steps back. "Captain Kirk, from the day I was old enough to understand language, I was taught that I must harden myself against other races. Every one of us on this ship has been taught to kill when killing is the solution to a problem that might interfere with the Plan. It is a doctrine I accept. I not only accept it, I embrace it. As much as I have come to respect you, Captain, I will kill you rather than let you interfere. Make no mistake about that."

Kirk's heart pounded. He took off his helmet to wipe an arm across his sweaty forehead. "And you're willing to kill yourself and the rest of your race rather than . . ."

"Rather than continue as lepers. Yes."

"Oh, Babe, Babe!" Kirk groaned. "You've lived your whole life on a ship—you don't understand what it is you're destroying! You have the rest of your life ahead of you, and you don't have to live it inside these bulkheads. It doesn't have to end this way. . . . let's talk. We can work something out."

"We tried that. No one listened."

"Then let's try again. I don't think anyone understood what it was like for you."

She stopped pacing. "It is no longer in my hands. The Plan is under way."

"Contact the other ships. Tell them—"

"Captain," she interrupted him abruptly. "Your helmet. You did not put your helmet back on."

He'd forgotten. The minute she mentioned it, though, Kirk's stomach started to churn. He forced down the feeling of nausea and said, "You see? We can adapt. You just didn't give us enough of a chance."

Babe stared at him, unbelieving.

He said, "Do you really want to kill me, Babe?"

She took her time answering. "I do not wish to kill anyone. But I will, if I must. It is my duty."

"Your duty, but not your conviction."

"My duty and my conviction."

"I don't believe you."

If it was possible for a Sacker to look shaken, Babe did. She sat down at the strategy table opposite Kirk. "You have said much to disturb me, Captain. I need to think."

"Take your time. And while you're thinking, call off your attack on the *Enterprise*—it wouldn't succeed anyway."

She was silent a few moments, and then burst out, "No! I cannot listen to you! You are more experienced than I, and you use your experience to twist me and make me uncertain. I refuse to listen to you, Captain James T. Kirk! We *will* attack the *Enterprise*!"

Kirk's heart sank. He'd almost had her! "Babe—"

"No! Say no more! We will attack."

"Then postpone the attack a while. There's one basic battle maneuver you must know if you're to have any kind of chance at all, and we haven't even started on it. Babe, I'm not quite so eager to die as you are. At least wait until I've had time to teach the others this one maneuver. You can't protect the baryon reverter without it."

"Are you telling me the truth?"

"Damn right I am. You *have* to know how to perform the invitational."

"Invitational? That is the name of the maneuver?"

"Yes." Kirk had just made it up. "It's a way of luring your opponent into an unfavorable position."

She thought about it. "Very well. You have slightly less than twenty hours."

"That's not enough time!"

"It will have to be. If we do not leave for the Beta Castelli system in twenty hours, we will not be able to get in close enough to use the baryon reverter. The reverter's range is not infinite."

"I see." Kirk mulled that over. "Where did you get that figure of twenty hours? How do you know how long we have left?"

"I asked Orangejuiceandwodka to plot a course to the Beta Castelli system and estimate a time of arrival."

Kirk nodded. "Well, Chekov says he'd trust her navigating."

"We are wasting time. Come. Let us learn the invitational maneuver."

Kirk rather apologetically put his helmet back on. "Sorry, Babe, but I don't think I'm ready for more than one of you at a time yet."

"It does not matter. We will return to the bridge now."

"Yes, now."

And now he knew what he was going to have to do.

Chapter Ten

STARFLEET COMMAND had decided to fight back.

More specifically, Starfleet had decided the *Enterprise* would fight back. Help was promised, but not in time to do any good; the nearest starship was six days distant and the Sacker deadline now only seventeen hours away. The *Enterprise* would have to go it alone.

Mr. Spock received his orders from Admiral Quinlan, whose visage filled the main viewscreen on the bridge. Spock surmised that Starfleet probably had terms of surrender drawn up and ready to offer the Sackers should the *Enterprise* fail. But there'd be no overt talk of surrender as long as there was any chance at all of wresting the baryon reverter away from the race of strange beings who had stolen it from those who'd designed it for peaceful purposes. The admiral knew he was ordering a suicide mission, but—as Spock would have been the first to acknowledge—it was the only course of action immediately perceptible to him and the other decision-makers at Starfleet Command. It was up to Spock to convince Admiral Quinlan that there just might be a viable alternative.

"Admiral, you are aware that the Sacker ship has three times the firepower of the *Enterprise*, as well as superior shielding," Spock said levelly. "And even if

185

we were to discover a weak spot in their defenses, we still have no way of ascertaining the location of the baryon reverter. We could very well end up destroying the one thing that could save us."

"Not if you beam an armed force aboard the Sacker ship," Quinlan said. "I know their shields are up, but it seems to me your best bet is to probe for a weak spot, Mr. Spock."

Spock waited, but the admiral had no more to offer. "Even if we could beam over our entire security force at once," the Vulcan said, "our chances for success remain minimal. Our people would still be greatly outnumbered. And may I remind the admiral that the Sackers' best weapon is their own bodies? All the Sackers have to do to put us out of commission is to touch us."

The admiral sighed tiredly. "I'm aware of all that, Mr. Spock. It still seems the only feasible solution."

"There is one other possible course of action, sir. Captain Kirk and three of his officers are still aboard the Sacker ship—"

"I understand how you feel," Admiral Quinlan cut in. "But four lives against the total destruction the Sackers threaten? You know there's no real choice, Mr. Spock."

"My point, sir, is that Captain Kirk is in a unique position. We had interior visuals for a time, and we were able to witness the activity on the Sacker bridge. It was abundantly clear that the captain was waging a campaign to demoralize the Sacker crew, and what we observed indicated he was achieving notable success. During this period Captain Kirk managed to signal us not to attack just yet. He will give the word when the time is right."

"Do you still have visuals?"

"No, sir."

"Then Kirk could be dead by now as far as you know."

Spock came as close to sweating as it was possible for a Vulcan to come. "I do not think so, Admiral. Remember these are very young Sackers we are dealing with. They are in dire need of Captain Kirk's expertise—and equally in need, I suspect, of the presence of a strong authority figure among them. They will not kill him as long as he is of use to them."

"So you're saying we should wait to see what plan Kirk is hatching?"

"Yes, sir, that would seem to be the best procedure."

"How can he signal you if you don't have visuals?"

Spock paused. "The captain will find a way, sir." There was no doubt in his mind about that whatsoever.

Admiral Quinlan was frowning in concentration. "I'll get back to you," he said abruptly, and his image faded from the viewscreen.

The tension on the bridge was thick enough to slice. The young man seated at the communications station asked nervously, "What do we do now, Mr. Spock?"

"Now we wait, Mr. Wittering. And I shall do my waiting in my quarters. Mr. Sulu, you have the conn."

The bridge crew was disappointed. The fact that Spock would take Admiral Quinlan's reply in his quarters meant it would be a private communication. They wanted to hear.

Spock hurried down to his quarters, wondering at the extraordinary feeling of alarm growing in him. It was becoming more and more difficult for him to make the coolly detached assessment of the developing situation that he should be making. He had to work at it; he had to force an objectivity that should be coming naturally, automatically. Spock did not understand what was happening to him. This new uneasiness—would it cloud his judgment, color his responses? Had it already done so? The Vulcan was not at all certain he had been adequately persuasive in his communication with Admiral Quinlan.

What happened next depended solely on the reputation Captain James T. Kirk had built up in Starfleet. Time and again the captain had turned certain disaster into triumph, or at least into an acceptable compromise. The man had a talent for survival. His resiliency and inventiveness had made the *Enterprise* the most talked-about ship in the fleet. Surely Starfleet Command would base its decision on those considerations. Surely? Spock wasn't at all certain the admirals would make the logical—and obvious—choice.

Alone in his quarters, Spock seated himself and started calling up those Vulcan techniques of deep concentration that had stood him in such good stead all his life. He shut out everything—the onrushing new universe, the Sackers, the *Enterprise,* his quarters—as he methodically turned his focus inward. Gradually he slowed down his heartbeat, and then his rate of respiration. After a time he had his feelings of alarm under control. If ever he needed the computerlike mind Dr. McCoy was always accusing him of having, now was the time.

Speak of. The door signal sounded, and the familiar voice said, "McCoy."

"Come."

The doctor stood in the doorway. "I won't intrude if you don't want me to, Spock. I can guess what you must be going through."

"Please come in, Doctor. I would be glad of your company."

McCoy took a chair near Spock's, and for a moment the two sat in silence, wrapped in their own thoughts. Then McCoy said, "He'll come through, Spock. He always does."

Spock nodded. "It is not Jim I have no faith in, but in the Sackers' willingness to go on with their training after having issued their ultimatum. They must have reached some level of confidence in their own abilities before taking a step as irrevocable as that one. Jim's time with them may be near the end."

McCoy bit his lower lip. "You didn't mention that to the admiral."

"No."

They fell silent again. Spock reached out and turned on the viewscreen. They watched the Sacker ship still practicing maneuvers, the same ones over and over again. The ship released three practice targets and hit all three of them.

"They're getting better," McCoy remarked. "Did Jim have to be such a good teacher? I wish we could do something instead of just sitting here. It's too bad the sonic hypnosis-inducer didn't work. That was a good idea, Spock."

Suddenly Spock rose from his chair. "How very odd."

"What?"

"This maneuver they are attempting now. It is not familiar to me."

They watched the ship sending out one of its legs from the end of the rectangle. The leg moved upward about forty-five degrees, and then the entire ship tilted forward—nose down, so to speak, up and down relative to the frame provided by Spock's viewscreen. Then the ship just hung there for a while, and eventually refolded itself.

McCoy looked puzzled. "What's that supposed to accomplish?"

Sulu's voice came over the intercom. "Mr. Spock— the Sackers are trying something new."

"I am watching it, Mr. Sulu. Do you recognize the maneuver?"

"No, sir. It's not in any of our manuals."

"Nor in any of theirs, I should imagine."

McCoy's eyebrows shot up. "*That* is Jim's signal?"

"Unlikely, Doctor. It may be simply an imperfect execution of a familiar maneuver. Let us see if it repeats."

It did. Unfold, tilt, refold, straighten up.

"That *is* the signal!" McCoy said excitedly, jumping out of his chair. "Jim wants you to attack!"

Spock did not agree. "We must not jump to conclusions, Doctor. He must have something more in mind than a direct attack."

"No, no—that's it! That's the go-ahead! Let's get cracking, Spock! Jim's yelling for help!"

"May I remind you that Jim himself ruled out an attack on the Sacker ship—even before he was kidnapped? The ship has not lost any of its weaponry since then, nor any of its shielding. It is the same well-protected space fortress it has always been."

McCoy ground his teeth. "Blast it, Spock, must you always be so *cautious*?"

"When caution is called for—always. Think, McCoy. Would you have us sabotage Jim's plan by moving too soon? He would not have gone to such extremes to warn us off unless timing were all-important. If we rush in precipitately, we will undoubtedly spoil whatever he has planned."

McCoy sank back down into his chair, suddenly deflated. "I *hate* it when you're right."

"Indeed, I have noticed that tendency in you before."

"Jim really does have a plan, doesn't he, Spock? Tell me he has a plan."

"He has a plan, Doctor. I would wager my life on it."

"You are wagering your life on it," McCoy muttered. "Yours and everybody else's as well."

The intercom came on; Wittering said, "Admiral Quinlan for Mr. Spock."

"Pipe it through, Lieutenant."

The Sacker ship faded from the screen to be replaced by the admiral's worried face. "Spock, we've decided to give you seven hours," he said without preamble. "If at the end of that time you haven't heard from Captain Kirk, you're to attack the Sacker ship. That will leave a little less than ten hours until the Sacker deadline. That's all the time you'll have to carry out the operation, and that's cutting it close. But do not wait one minute longer than seven hours. Understood?"

"Understood, sir. Unfortunately, Captain Kirk has no way of knowing he is now under a seven-hour time limitation."

"That can't be helped. Seven hours, Spock." The screen went blank.

"Oh boy," McCoy moaned. "If there were just some way to let Jim know!"

"We can but try, Doctor." Without further ado Spock opened the door and walked out.

Surprised, McCoy hurried after him. "You've thought of something!"

"I have thought of the obvious. Since Jim does not know about the new seven-hour deadline, we shall simply have to tell him. We will send a message to the Sacker ship."

"Just like that, huh? What kind of message?"

Spock stepped into the turbolift. "Why, we will offer the Sackers an opportunity to surrender, of course."

Pinky had just brought them a meal in their quarters and left.

Kirk pushed his plate of assorted mystery meats aside and said, "This may be the last time the four of us will be alone together, so let's make sure we've got everything straight. But first—Chekov, did you get a chance to check Orangejuice's course and time estimate back to the Zirgosian system?"

"Yes, Kepten. It is dead accurate." He grinned. "Vhat did you expect? She has a good teacher, you know."

"Mm, but not a particularly humble one. All right, let's count on making our move during this next session on the bridge. Chekov, watch me for the signal. I'm sorry to put this off on you, since you haven't been out of sickbay very long—but that's why you're the logical one to get sick. Make it convincing."

"Do not vorry, Kepten. They vill think I am dying. But I am almost completely recovered. The only reason I vear this thing . . ."—he indicated the sling holding his right arm—". . . is thet Dr. Bonesovna vanted to try vun out." He removed his arm from the sling. "I haf complete use of the arm."

"Well, don't let the Sackers know that. Look as helpless as you can."

Scotty interrupted. "Better eat somethin', Captain. We have a long row to hoe."

Kirk nodded. "I suppose you're right." They all ate in silence for a while, but Kirk kept going over the plan in his mind. He swallowed a mouthful of meat and said, "Uhura, you'll have the farthest to go—from your station over to beyond the weapons station. And you'll have to make it before one of them gets it into his head to stop you."

"It shouldn't be a problem, Captain," she said. "It would seem only natural for me to rush to the aid of my collapsing colleague here."

Chekov grinned.

"And you've got to keep them distracted long enough for Scotty to take care of the E-and-E shields," Kirk went on. "A little distraction won't be enough. Make a scene, Uhura. Lay it on thick. Put them on the defensive."

"Understood, sir."

Everything depended on Scotty's getting the shields down without being noticed. E-and-E was Kirk's shorthand for engines and environment. The environmental control section was on the deck immediately above the engine room, and the two together made up one of the legs the Sacker ship could unfold on command. The Zirgosian designers of the ship had had in mind a means of isolating those two sections in case of a shipboard disaster, but Kirk had seen a way to use it against the Sackers.

With heavy reluctance, he turned to his chief engineer. "I'm sorry, Scotty. I wish there were some other way."

"I understand, sir. What hasta be done, hasta be done."

"Destroying the engines is a last resort, you know. I did try to talk Babe around." Kirk held thumb and forefinger a centimeter apart. "I was *that* close to persuading her. But she's a tough kid—she bounced back and wouldn't give in. So we'll have to do it this way."

"Yessir, I can see that," Scotty said unhappily.

Kirk looked at him closely. "It's not just the engines, is it, Scotty? It's your Mr. Green you're worried about."

"He's a good lad, Captain. I don't like the idea o' puttin' him in danger."

"Neither do I, believe it or not." Kirk played with his food a moment and then gave up on it. Something was troubling them, all of them, and he might as well bring it out into the open. He looked at Scotty, gloomily chewing on a piece of meat he probably didn't even taste. Kirk asked him, "You've actually grown fond of that Sacker, haven't you?"

Scotty sighed deeply. "Aye, I s'pose I have."

"What about you two?" Kirk asked the others. "Any qualms about blowing this bloody-minded species to bits?"

Neither answered at first. Then Uhura said softly, "I wouldn't like to see Rose get hurt."

Chekov nodded. "And I think I vould cry if anything happened to Orangejuiceandwodka," he admitted.

Kirk grunted. "Well, I'm no different. I'd hate it if that red monstrosity I have to deal with got killed. I've developed a healthy respect for Babe."

Chekov asked, deadpan, "Vhat about Blue?"

Kirk laughed. "Poor Blue. I'm going to feel guilty

about him for the rest of my life." Then he sobered. "That's the difficulty, isn't it? As long as they remained a race of monsters and villains we knew what attitude to take toward them, how to react to them. But now that we've come to see them as individuals, it's not that simple anymore."

"Aye," Scotty nodded, "that's the truth."

Kirk continued, "These kids have been brainwashed from the day they left the cradle, or whatever the Sackers use for cradles. Every one of them on this ship has been indoctrinated to one way of thinking, to do one thing and one thing only—and that is to carry out their grand and glorious Plan no matter what the cost. They've been taught that all other life forms are simply obstacles to be swept away as neatly and as emotionlessly as possible. Killing is a tool to be used when needed, that's all. Babe for one isn't any too happy about that, but she doesn't really question it. I doubt if any of them do."

"There's something else," Uhura offered. "Those other Sacker ships. If this were the only ship, maybe the kids would come around eventually. But they know their entire race is depending on them, and that has to be why they're so . . . adamant—about going ahead with it, I mean."

The other three murmured agreement, and they all fell into a kind of reverie. Only a few weeks earlier they would have scoffed at the idea that they'd all four be worrying about the fate of the Sackers. But now . . . now too many things had happened to make that earlier simplistic view of the Sacker race possible any longer. Now, it was hard to hate them.

After a few moments Kirk shook himself and said, "Remember, Scotty—none of the Sackers must see you when you lower the E-and-E shields."

"They won't see me, Captain."

"Good. You manage that, and the rest will be up to Mr. Spock."

Chekov shook his head. "Vhat if Mr. Spock does not ketch on?"

"Watch your mouth!" Uhura slapped at him, only half playfully. "Mr. Spock always catches on!"

That's what Kirk was counting on. Of all the people he had ever met in his event-filled life, Mr. Spock was the only one he could unquestioningly rely on to understand a situation and know what to do about it. If Spock couldn't figure out what Kirk's signal meant . . . well, then they were lost, no two ways about that. There was no contingency plan.

The door suddenly opened. "Finished?" Pinky asked brightly.

Kirk noticed that only Chekov bothered to don his helmet for the few seconds it took Pinky to take hold of the antigrav unit bearing their food trays and depart with it. *They do say you can get used to anything,* he thought, finding a strange comfort in the old truism.

The intercom spoke Captain Kirk's name. It was Rose, summoning them to the bridge. Their rest period was not over yet; something must have happened.

When they got there, they saw that all the Sackers on the bridge had abandoned their cloaks. It was not a pretty sight. Even Captain Kirk hesitated a fraction of a second before stepping off the turbolift. Matters were not helped any by the bridge temperature, which seemed higher than ever.

Babe said to Rose, "Play back the message."

Mr. Spock's image filled the screen. "Attention— Sacker ship. This is First Officer Spock of the starship

Enterprise. I call upon you to surrender your ship and your prisoners within the next *seven hours*. If you surrender within *seven hours,* Starfleet Command will show leniency. If you do not surrender within that time, we will be forced to attack. I repeat—you have only *seven hours*." Rose froze his image on the screen.

"Will it be enough, Captain?" Scotty asked under his breath.

"It should be." But still he wondered why the seven-hour time limit.

So did Babe. She said, "Why seven hours, Captain Kirk? Does the number seven carry some special meaning among your kind?"

"No, it's just the length of a full work shift," Kirk improvised. "On our ship, at least. We tend to think in terms of work shifts."

Orangejuiceandwodka edged closer to Chekov, her eyes not leaving the viewscreen. "Is that a Vulcan or a Romulan?" she whispered.

"A Wulcan," he whispered back.

"What are you going to do, Babe?" Kirk asked.

In response she told Rose to contact the *Enterprise.* "This is Commander Babe speaking." She didn't identify her ship because she couldn't; their human captain hadn't named it yet. "We thank you for your offer to accept our surrender, and we make the same offer to you in return. Surrender to us or leave this sector, and we will not destroy the *Enterprise.* What is your answer?"

The frozen image of Spock disappeared from the screen to be replaced by a live one. "Greetings to Commander Babe," Spock said with no indication that he found her name even a little bit strange. "We decline your offer and repeat ours. Please take the entire *seven hours* to reconsider your decision."

197

All right, Spock, I got it, I got it! Kirk said aloud, "That's a good suggestion, Babe. Take the time to think it over."

"Captain?" Spock said. "Is that you?"

"End transmission," Babe told Rose quickly. "Captain Kirk, I will not have you speaking with your first officer."

Kirk made a show of protesting. "I wasn't even in the picture."

"Nevertheless, he recognized your voice. It will not matter in the long run, however. Now that we have mastered the invitational maneuver, we will attack."

"I don't think 'mastered' is the right word," Kirk said slowly. "Babe, are you certain you want to do this?"

"I will tolerate no more argument, Captain Kirk. I command you to fire upon the *Enterprise.*"

"It's a mistake, Babe." But he took the command chair with a reluctance that wasn't all show, thinking nothing could ever have made him believe that one day he'd be directing an attack against his own ship. Attack the *Enterprise*? Unthinkable. Earth, Starfleet Command, God himself, maybe—but not the *Enterprise.* "Attack mode three," he ordered with a sigh.

They all assumed their posts. Chekov hunched down in the navigator's seat looking helpless, as instructed. Only Ivan and Orangejuiceandwodka stood near him, as Rasputin's term of banishment had not yet ended. Uhura too was down to two trainees; she'd grown tired of Iris's dogging it and told him he'd flunked the course. Brownie had reassigned the would-be commander to Shuttle Maintenance.

The ship unfolded itself. "All right, Blue, look sharp," Kirk said. "You're going to have to be faster than Sulu, remember. Half-turn."

They moved in on the *Enterprise* at an oblique angle. All of them, Sackers and humans alike, were holding their breaths. This was the young Sackers' first taste of combat; every one of them was not only anxious about the outcome, but concerned about how well he or she would perform under fire. The moment was tense; it was their final exam, with ultra-stiff penalties awaiting failure—penalties that included capture, injury, and even death.

"Ready photon torpedoes," Kirk ordered.

"Torpedoes ready," said one of the Sackers at the station next to Scotty's.

"Lock on."

"Locked on, sir."

Kirk paused a moment to let the tension build even more. "Fire." The ship released eight torpedoes.

The *Enterprise* danced gracefully out of the way.

"There! You see that!" Kirk said forcefully. "Blue, did you see how fast Sulu moved the ship? That's what you're going to have to do. About full."

Blue brought the ship about, muttering about the helm's sluggishness. They made another run, with the same results. The *Enterprise* ducked easily.

"You are deliberately mistiming the torpedo fire," Babe accused Kirk.

He slid out of the command chair. "If you think that, you do it."

She did. This time the torpedoes went so far wide that the *Enterprise* didn't have to use evasive maneuvers at all. Chekov stifled a snicker. Babe kept trying, though. Finally she got close enough that her target did have to move—but that was small consolation to a commander bent on blasting her enemy out of the sky.

"You're just not going to hit 'em, Babe," Kirk said tonelessly. "They're too fast for you."

"We'll try phaser fire," she said angrily. "Increase to mark three."

"Now, Babe, you know they're not going to let you get close enough to use your phasers," Kirk lectured her.

"Helm—ahead, now."

"It won't do you any good, Babe. They'll just back away out of range."

"Increase to four."

"Don't you see, they'll just match whatever velocity you—"

"Ready phaser banks one and two."

"You can use *all* your phasers and it still won't make any—"

"Captain Kirk—*shut up.*"

"Yes, ma'am." Kirk meekly quick-stepped over to stand by Scotty.

As the Sackers approached phaser range, the *Enterprise* simply backed away. Babe increased the speed; so did the *Enterprise.* Babe tried swooping down and coming up from below; the *Enterprise* swooped away in the opposite direction. Babe pursued; the *Enterprise* retreated.

"Misterma'am," Kirk called out, "are you checking distances?"

"Yes, sir. They're staying within torpedo range but just outside phaser range."

"So they can shoot us any time they feel like it," Kirk mused out loud, "but we can't hit them with our torpedoes for love or money. Interesting situation."

"Transporter?" Babe asked.

"Also out of range," Misterma'am replied.

Kirk let the futile chase go on for another fifteen minutes. Then he strolled casually back to Babe. "All right, evaluate the situation," he said in the tone of instructor-to-pupil. "We can't hit them with our photon torpedoes, and they won't let us get close enough to use phaser fire. So what do you do?"

"Lure them closer," she answered promptly. "This is the time for the invitational maneuver?"

"This is the time."

"You had better do this." She gave him back the command chair.

Kirk directed the ship to assume a position not found in any combat manual of any space fleet anywhere. "We look helpless to them," he told Toots. "Now we wait to see if they take the bait."

Then he folded his arms over his chest, his signal to Chekov to begin.

"There it is again!" Sulu exclaimed. "That same odd maneuver! What are they up to, Mr. Spock?"

"What is *he* up to, you mean," Dr. McCoy muttered. "That's Jim's doing, you can bet on it."

Spock said nothing, concentrating on the position the Sacker ship had assumed as a result of the maneuver. It had gone back to its rectangular mode, with the exception of one section protruding from the aft end at a forty-five degree angle. The forward part of the ship had tilted downward, leaving the protruding section more exposed than ever. The ship hung there in space, doing nothing.

"That can't be a regular attack mode," Sulu said. "Could they be in trouble?"

"That is what it appears to be, Mr. Sulu. Or, that is what they wish it to appear."

McCoy asked, "How do we tell the difference?"

"We watch to see what they do next."

They waited. "There's nothing wrong with that ship," McCoy grumbled. "It's a trap. They've been chasing us all over the galaxy, for Pete's sake—now all of a sudden they're helpless? Ha! If you believe that, there's a bridge on the planet Iotia I'd like to sell you."

"I agree with Dr. McCoy, sir," Sulu said. "It's a trick."

"It is indeed a trick," Spock replied. "But whose? Captain Kirk's or the Sacker commander's?"

Then as they watched, the protruding section folded back into the Sacker ship. The ship rotated on its axis until it once again occupied the same plane as the *Enterprise*. A solid-looking rectangle, it did nothing for two minutes, and then it once again assumed its peculiar position—tilted forward, one section sticking up at the rear.

Spock shot out of the command chair. "Ready photon torpedoes!"

It hit McCoy just an instant later. "By golly, they're wearing a 'Kick Me' sign!"

"That is exactly what they are doing," Spock said, "if I understand the allusion correctly. We are being invited to fire upon the exposed section. It is an invitation I think we will do well to accept."

"Photon torpedoes ready, sir."

"Lock in on the extreme end of the protruding section. We do not want to hit the main body of the ship."

"Just nip off the end of the tail," McCoy said happily.

Spock said, "Mr. Sulu, status of the Sacker shields?"

"They're still up, sir," Sulu answered regretfully.

"Then we have a little longer yet to wait." Spock sat back down in the command chair. "The minute those shields are down, Mr. Sulu—"

"Understood, sir."

They waited, but this time with a feeling of anticipation made fervent by the real hope that this long nightmare might at last be near its end. For the first time, they understood what Captain Kirk wanted them to do.

Chekov clutched his chest with his good hand and rose shakily from his seat. "Orangejuice . . . you had better take over."

"Mr. Chekov—what's the matter?" Kirk asked with just the right note of concern.

"I . . . I do not feel so vell, Kepten. I vould like to go to the head."

"Do you need help?"

"No, sir, I can make it." He started to weave his way unsteadily to the upper level of the bridge. He made it just past the weapons station, where he collapsed—taking care to fall on the shoulder that had not been burned.

"Chekov!" Uhura shrieked, and flew past the command chair in a blur. Kirk followed; Scotty had left his station to peer between the two Sackers from the weapons station who were bending over the prone navigator, afraid to touch him. "Look what you've done!" Uhura screamed at the two helpless Sackers. "First you burn him and then you make him report for duty before he's recovered!"

"Chekov—can you hear me?" Kirk asked.

"I . . . we did nothing," one of the Sackers protested faintly.

"A medteam is on the way," Rose announced.

Babe had joined the group around Chekov. "Will he be all right?"

"You!" Uhura exclaimed in her most scathing tone. "What do you care whether he's all right or not? What do any of you care? Look at him! Does he *look* all right?"

"He looks as if he has fainted," Babe replied calmly. "Surely this is not serious."

"Oh, now you're a doctor, are you?" Uhura snapped.

Kirk glanced at Scotty and saw him making a circle of his thumb and forefinger in the okay sign. Kirk felt a surge of adrenaline and said, "All right, everybody—stand back, don't crowd." *Come on, Mr. Spock,* he prayed silently, *we don't have much longer before—*

An explosion jolted the ship. On the bridge, it was felt only as a sudden vibration that threw everyone a little off balance. "What was that?" Ivan cried.

"We've been hit!" Misterma'am exclaimed in a tone of disbelief as he read his instruments. "The *Enterprise* has fired upon us! They actually shot at us!" He sounded ready to break into tears.

"Damage report!" Babe snapped out.

"Ah . . . engine room hit. Environmental hit. Warp engines are out!"

"Do we have any power at all?"

"Impulse only," Blue said, a distinct note of fear in his voice.

Kirk said, "That won't get us away from the *Enterprise.* Babe, you'll have to take evasive maneuvers while Mr. Scott and I see to the warp engines. When you—"

A second explosion rocked the ship.

"Hard to starboard, Blue!" Babe shouted.

"Keep the ship moving!" Kirk yelled as he and Scotty stepped into one of the turbolifts.

"Now, Chekov," Uhura said in a low voice. In three steps she was in front of the escape chute. She grabbed the bar above the opening and lifted herself into the chute feet first. Chekov was right behind her, performing a one-armed lift that protected his injured shoulder and arm.

They left behind them a scene of near-panic. Orangejuiceandwodka was yelling at the Sackers at the weapons station, they in turn were yelling at Misterma'am, Misterma'am was yelling at Blue, Blue was yelling at Babe, and Babe was yelling at everybody. The frightened young Sackers suddenly found themselves in a real battle in real combat with real weapons—and with no humans to help them or to tell them what to do.

Chapter Eleven

THE SACKER ENGINE ROOM was on fire.

Fire . . . neither Kirk nor Scott paused to ponder the irony of the Sackers' natural weapon being turned against them. The two men from the *Enterprise* were more concerned with the fact that the fire-control system had failed to cut in. Something else the Zirgosian designers had not had time to test before the Sackers stole the ship.

Scotty tried activating the sprayers manually; nothing happened. He removed a panel from one of the bulkheads and examined the circuitry. "I think I see what the problem is, Captain," he said, "but it'll take a few minutes to fix. Can ye do somethin' about that blaze in the reactor room?"

"I guess I'd better," Kirk answered. Not for the first time he was thankful for the helmet he was wearing; it protected him from the smoke that was everywhere and which showed no sign of dissipating on its own. He rounded up what Sackers he could find who hadn't been injured in the explosion and organized an old-fashioned bucket brigade. When not slowed down by the smoke, the Sackers turned out to be natural-born firemen; they could walk through flames that Kirk couldn't even go near.

Medical teams arrived, pulling gurneys and applying the Sacker version of first aid. In the midst of all the confusion, a medteam discovered that one of the Sackers in the engine room had been killed. He was a six-foot gray creature who didn't look at all fearsome in death. Kirk stood over him, sick to his stomach. He was just a kid, this dead Sacker, and Kirk's plan had killed him, "I'm sorry," the captain whispered, and moved aside to let one of the medteams load the body on a gurney and take it away. *No one has ever seen a dead Sacker,* the *Enterprise*'s record banks had said. Well, someone had now. Kirk tasted bile in his mouth.

"Captain Kirk!" one of the bucket brigade cried out. "Look!"

The fire had spread out into the corridor and was climbing the bulkheads to the deck above. "Scotty!" Kirk yelled.

"Any minute now," the engineer answered.

Kirk took part of his bucket brigade out into the corridor, but he could see their efforts would be futile. The fire had spread too far; the bulkheads were already starting to melt as the flames licked away at them. Just then the sprayers went on in the engine room. The Sackers still inside gave a brief cry of relief and made their way into the corridor to help fight that fire.

"Scotty!" Kirk called out. "The sprayers aren't working out here either! Where are you?"

Scotty ran through the smoke toward him. "Captain, did ye happen to see Mr. Green?"

Kirk thought back. "I didn't see any green Sackers." Without a word Scotty headed back toward the smoke. "Wait!" Kirk called. "Where are you going?"

Scotty turned his head to look back. "I've got to find him, Jim," he said simply, and waited.

Kirk swore. "Be quick about it, then." Kirk joined

the bucket brigade and did his best to help keep the fire at bay until his chief engineer got back.

Scotty made his way through the smoke, calling Mr. Green's name. The fire in the reactor room was out, and the intermix chamber was safe. He finally found his Sacker, slumped on the deck near the intermix monitoring console, his back against the bulkhead. Mr. Green was holding both hands against his side.

"Mr. Green!" Scotty stared in horror as his protégé's sac liquid leaked out to form a viscous puddle on the deck.

The Sacker looked up at him. "Is it the Scott?" His voice was weak.

"Medteam!" Scotty roared, and heard someone pass on his call. "Aye, laddie, I'm here. Lie still, now. Help is on the way."

"'Twill be no use. I am dyin'. But I'm glad o' seein' ye once more."

"Enough o' that! I won't have ye dyin' on me."

In answer Mr. Green lifted his hands from his side and showed Scotty a great gaping hole in his sac membrane.

Scotty didn't hesitate. He ripped off his helmet and started pulling off the brown tunic he was wearing. He wadded the tunic into a ball. "Now try to hold still, lad. If I touch ye I willna be any use to either o' us." Carefully he poked and prodded the tunic into place; Mr. Green jerked once but didn't cry out. "Sorry I hurt ye," Scotty said. "Now y' are goin' to have to hold it in place yourself. I'm takin' me hands away . . . *now.*"

The Sacker placed his own hands over the tunic. He winced from the pain but still didn't forget his manners. "I thank ye," he said faintly.

"That should slow down the leakage," Scotty said worriedly. "Where is that medteam? *Medteam!*"

This time they came—two of them, pulling a gurney. They examined Scotty's makeshift bandage and decided to leave it in place until they could get Mr. Green to sickbay. They strapped the tunic in place and lifted the wounded Sacker on to the gurney. The last thing Mr. Green did as he was being taken away was turn his head and say, "Ye mustna forget your helmet!"

"Oh. Aye, I've got it. I'll be in to check on ye as soon as I am able!" Scotty called after the departing gurney.

He made his way through the smoke-filled engine room to the corridor on the other side where Kirk and his non-volunteer firemen were fighting a losing battle. Something was seriously wrong with the fire-control design or else the installation had not been complete at the time the ship was stolen; not a single sprayer was working. There was a real danger that the ship could be destroyed by a fire that should have been put out automatically and easily.

"Scotty!" Kirk called when he saw him. "Find the control panel! And hurry!"

"It should be near the hatchway," Scotty muttered. "Ah! Here 'tis!"

Kirk just then noticed that the chief engineer was in his undershirt. "Where's your tunic?"

"Pluggin' up a hole in Mr. Green's side, it is." He got to work.

"Hurry, Scotty. We're right under the environmental control section."

Scotty didn't have to be told. If the fire broke through to the deck above, their entire plan was in jeopardy. Because right above them at that very moment were Uhura and Chekov, who had enough to handle without having to worry about being burned alive.

Chekov's and Uhura's ears were throbbing from the one word they'd heard spoken by the Sacker not wearing a translator. When the Sacker saw his/her voice had brought them both to their knees, he/she backed away hastily. The helmets the two humans were wearing had helped some; gradually the pain in Uhura's ears eased down to a dull buzzing. "Chekov?" she said, touching him lightly on his good shoulder. He gestured helplessly; he couldn't hear.

The Sacker who'd inadvertently spoken out of surprise at seeing them was the only one in the environmental control section. All the others, Uhura presumed, were helping fight the fire on the deck below. She and Chekov had made their way past a few anxious Sackers keeping watch on the crawlways in case the fire should start to ascend that way. Uhura had seen no flames, but the smell of smoke had grown stronger with each step they'd taken on the way to Environmental Control. The moment she'd been dreading was here. The big fire that had been haunting her dreams had caught up with her. A lump grew in her stomach the size of a fist, her throat tightened, and her breathing grew shallow. She'd had great difficulty putting one foot before the other. At one point Chekov had had to grab her by the arm and drag her along the corridor.

Uhura looked around Environmental Control, orienting herself as quickly as possible. Over to the left were the life-support controls, but between them and her stood the Sacker—a big, especially colorful one, with sac fluid that was variegated turquoise and yellow. With a distant part of her mind she noted she was able to stare straight at this new Sacker without wanting to upchuck. That was nice, but getting rid of him/her was the first order of business. She looked a question at Chekov.

He decided to try the nonviolent approach first. He started speaking rapidly to the Sacker and making imploring gestures with his hands, trying to draw the Sacker out into the corridor. The Sacker, of course, understood nothing of what the human was saying, yet Chekov somehow managed to convey a sense of urgency. But to no avail; the Sacker refused to budge from his post.

Uhura sighed. She was the one with two good arms, so she would have to do it. While Chekov kept the Sacker occupied, she started a surreptitious sweep of the place. She'd almost circled the room before she came upon a heavy wrench about a meter long. It took both hands to lift it. Uhura walked quietly up behind the Sacker, took aim, and swung the wrench as hard as she could.

The Sacker was so tall that only the tip of the wrench caught his/her head, but it was enough. He/she fell like a rock.

Chekov and Uhura both checked to make sure the sac membrane hadn't been ruptured. "Now what do we do?" Uhura asked. "We don't want him in here with us."

"True," Chekov agreed. He took off his sling and tossed it aside. "She might regain consciousness before ve are finished. But ve cannot drag her out ourselves."

"Then get some Sackers to drag him out."

Chekov's face lit up. "Yust vhat I vas about to suggest!" He stepped out into the corridor and started calling for help. Uhura took herself and the wrench out of sight.

Three Sackers answered Chekov's call for help, hurrying as fast as Sackers could hurry; one of them, fortunately, was wearing a translator. Chekov told them a story about being on his way to help in the engine room when the door to the environmental control section opened, and he looked in just in time to see that Sacker right there falling down.

The three Sackers tried to rouse their fallen companion. When they failed, they carried him/her out—to sickbay, the Sacker with the translator told Chekov. Chekov started off in the opposite direction, but was back in a few minutes.

"Ve cannot seal the door," he said breathlessly. "The captain and Mr. Scott are not here yet!"

"Then you'll have to stand guard," Uhura replied worriedly. She hurried over to the life-support controls. She looked over the board until she found the temperature regulators and keyed in a command: *Shipwide.* Then she lowered the temperature ten degrees.

They had to wait nearly thirty minutes. They removed their helmets, and the smell of smoke was immediately stronger. Uhura and Chekov both grew more tense as the minutes passed. At the same time they were aware of the dropping temperature—one blessing, at least.

Finally Captain Kirk came running in. "Seal that door!" he ordered.

Chekov sealed it. "Vhere is Mr. Scott?"

"Trying to get this blasted fire-control system to work," Kirk said, taking off his helmet. "That's something I hadn't counted on—no fire control. Scotty got the sprayers going in the engine room, but by then the fire had spread out into the corridor. We've got a regular conflagration down there, and it's working its way up." He saw the expression on Uhura's face. "Uhura," he said, taking hold of her shoulders, "hang on. You've got to hang on."

"Yes, sir," she replied dully.

"Temperature's down, I can feel it. Where's the intercom?"

Uhura pointed.

Kirk slapped the activating button. "Kirk to bridge."

"Babe here," came the familiar voice. "What is happening, Captain? Are the warp engines functioning?"

"Negative," Kirk growled. "It seems your elders didn't give the Zirgosians enough time to test their fire-control design. The fire's spreading, and there's not a hell of a lot we can do to stop it. But that's only one of your problems. Have you noticed a change in temperature on the bridge?"

"The temperature has dropped ten degrees. Has the fire reached Environmental Control?"

"Not yet. But we have."

"Explain."

"We lowered the temperature, Babe. And we're going to keep on lowering it, a few degrees at a time. Remember how your elders died? Do you remember watching their sac fluid freeze solid and there was nothing anyone could do to stop it? That's what's going to happen to you unless you surrender your ship. Do you understand? You're going to freeze to death if you don't surrender. Unless the fire gets to you first."

The answer didn't come immediately. Then: "You would kill us all, Captain Kirk?"

213

"I'm trying to keep you alive, you big red—" Kirk broke off and took several deep breaths. "Now listen, Babe—listen carefully. This is what will happen when you surrender. First, the *Enterprise* will beam over a team with fire-fighting equipment and get that conflagration under control. Then they'll beam over security and medical teams. There are already a few injuries and there are bound to be more. There's been one death that I know of."

A strange sound came over the intercom. "Who?" Babe asked.

"He was gray, worked in the engine room. That's all I can tell you—except that I regret his death more than I can say. Babe, there's no reason for anyone else to die. Surrender your ship. Let me tell the *Enterprise* to start beaming the rescue teams over."

"And the baryon reverter?"

"We take it."

"Never!"

"Think it over, Babe. If you don't surrender, your only options are to freeze to death or to watch your ship burn away from under you out here in space."

"We do not surrender!"

"Then keep an eye on your temperature readings. Kirk out." He slapped the intercom button and nodded to Uhura. She lowered the temperature another few degrees.

Then there was nothing to do but wait. Chekov started to pace.

After a while Uhura said, "Captain, am I imagining it or is this deck getting hot under our feet?"

"You're not imagining it. The fire must be directly under us." He shot a quick look at her out of the corner of his eye. She seemed to be holding up.

They waited some more, and at Kirk's signal Uhura lowered the temperature once again. Chekov paused in his pacing to place an ear against the sealed doors. "Kepten! I think they are out there!"

Kirk had expected that. "Better stand back from the doors."

Chekov's eyes grew round. "Can they get in?"

"I don't think so, but don't take any chances—stand away. According to the ship's schematics, once those doors are sealed, the only way to open them from the outside is to rig a bypass on a circuitry board mounted inside a corridor bulkhead. I'm gambling these kids won't know how to do that."

"Vhat vill they do, then? Try to force the doors?"

"Probably. Those hand weapons they carry won't do the trick. And if they use photon grenades, they'll destroy the entire environmental section."

"I hope they know thet," Chekov remarked nervously.

Whatever the Sackers had tried, it didn't work. Then a heavy *thump* sounded from the doors—they were attempting to force their way in.

Uhura gasped at the sound. "Are they using a battering ram?"

"Sounds like it." *A last resort,* Kirk thought with a surge of excitement. The battering continued at a gradually increasing rate, but the doors held; the Zirgosians had built well.

At last the thumping stopped. Kirk shot a grin at the other two and hit the intercom button. "Kirk to bridge."

"Yes, Captain."

"It didn't work, Babe. The doors are still sealed, we are still here, and the temperature is still going down."

"We are prepared to die, Captain Kirk."

"Mm, very noble. Is that something else you were taught from babyhood? Babe, your dying won't change anything. We can stand lower temperatures than you can—we'll simply wait until you're all frozen and *then* take the baryon reverter. Of course, you can all fight one another for a place close to where the fire is burning and hope to survive that way. But sooner or later the cold will get most of you." He paused, and then resumed quietly. "This is the end, Babe. You can't put it off any longer."

The intercom was silent.

"Babe, listen to me. You've done everything that could be expected of you—in fact, you've done more. You've acquitted yourself honorably. But part of being a good starship captain is knowing when to stop. Did you hear that? It's time to stop, Babe. Let's get the rescue teams over here and save this ship. And then we'll put out that other fire, the one in the sky. We're out of time. You must decide now."

Nothing for a few moments, and then: "I must consult with my officers."

"Of course." Uhura and Chekov were both grinning at him; he could taste victory.

After about two minutes Babe came back on the intercom. "We are agreed. Captain Kirk, I surrender this ship to you."

Uhura and Chekov cheered. The psychological warfare Kirk had waged and the taste of physical warfare the Sackers had had and the fire raging out of control and the threat of freezing to death—it had all just been too much for the Sacker youngsters. "Babe," Kirk said in relief, "that's the best decision you've made yet. Now I want you to instruct your crew to lay down their weapons. Tell them we are to be allowed to move throughout the ship without opposition. And tell them in English, please."

"Yes, of course. One moment please." Getting her thoughts together? Then she started to speak. "Attention, all decks, attention. This is Commander Babe speaking. I regret to inform you that I have just surrendered this ship to the humans from the *Enterprise*. There will be no more hostilities—you are to disarm yourselves immediately. Wherever you are at this moment, put your weapons down on the deck beside you and leave them there. I have given Captain Kirk my word that he and his officers can move freely throughout the ship without fear of reprisal. I repeat, there will be no more hostilities. We will soon be boarded by rescue teams from the *Enterprise*. They will put out the fire and tend to our injured."

She paused a moment, and then went on in a less official tone of voice: "You have nothing to be ashamed of—any of you. You have shown courage, and stamina, and resourcefulness. We knew we might fail when our elders died and it was left to us to carry out the Plan . . . but we did make an effort all of us can be proud of. *I* am proud of *you*. No ship's captain ever had a more conscientious crew. Now let us show these humans that we can face defeat with composure and dignity. Babe out."

The three humans in the environmental control section exchanged wry looks. "That Babe is going to be one hell of a starship captain someday," Kirk murmured. "Okay—grab your helmets and let's go. This deck's getting too hot for me."

Chekov unsealed the doors. Outside in the corridor eight or nine Sackers were standing dejectedly in a half-circle, waiting for them to come out. Their weapons were lying on the deck. They looked so disconsolate that Chekov felt a surge of pity for them. "Sorry, fellas," he apologized and hurried off after Kirk and Uhura.

The fire was eating its way along the unfolded section that held the engine room and Environmental Control, but the main body of the ship was as yet untouched. Their destination was the transporter room, two decks above. While the turbolifts in the main body were probably still operational, they decided not to risk it and instead climbed the ladder through a crawlway. They found only one Sacker on duty in the transporter room; he yielded the control pad to them without being asked.

Kirk studied the figures on the controls and punched in some numbers. Then he spoke the three words he'd been aching to say for so long a time: "Kirk to *Enterprise*."

"Captain! You are uninjured, I trust?"

"Quite uninjured, Mr. Spock, and feeling very well. So well, in fact, that I'd like to invite you over to see my new ship."

"*Your* new ship. Indeed. I take it the Sackers have surrendered?"

"With grace and dignity," Kirk said seriously. He proceeded to give orders as to the teams he wanted beamed over—fire fighting, security, repair, medical. "By the way, that was good shooting, Mr. Spock."

"Why, thank you, Captain. I hope our timing was apt?"

"Couldn't have been apter. Oh . . . tell Mr. Sulu to suit up and beam over with one of the teams. I'll need him to take command of this vessel. I've got the coordinates locked in here—you can start beaming over any time."

"The first security team is suited up and in the transporter room now."

"Good. Beam away."

Almost immediately a team headed by Lieutenant Berengaria materialized in the Sacker transporter room. "Captain! Are you all right?" Berengaria asked.

"Perfectly all right, Lieutenant, and *very* glad to see you. You can probably direct your operation best from the bridge."

"Right. Trucco, you stay here and tell the next team to secure the armory. Then report to the bridge." She glanced at the turbolift. "Does this go straight to the bridge?" At Kirk's nod, she and the others boarded the lift, leaving the one called Trucco behind.

"At least they won't have to smell them," Uhura commented, eyeing Trucco's helmet. "The way we did."

"And they've had a little time to get used to the way they look," Kirk added. "From the bridge visuals— when you lowered the shield. It shouldn't be too rough on them."

The second security team beamed in, got their instructions from Trucco, and left.

"Kepten," Chekov asked with a grin, "are you really going to put Sulu in charge?"

"Absolutely. We owe Blue a chance to meet his hero, don't you think?"

Mr. Spock appeared with the third security team. He quickly stepped down from the transporter platform and three long strides brought him face-to-face with Kirk. "Congratulations, sir. There was a time there when I was quite concerned about your welfare."

Kirk pretended to be hurt. "You doubted me?" He

didn't bother to mention he'd been pretty concerned himself. "The Sackers won't give us any trouble, Spock. They know it's all up. Now it's just a matter of getting the baryon reverter over to the *Enterprise.*"

"When we have the time, I would be most interested in learning how you brought about a surrender without hostile resistance."

"I'll give you all the details later. Right now what we need are some fire fighters."

"They are coming next."

Just as Spock was speaking, the first team of fire fighters beamed in. Kirk gave them directions and sent them on their way. "Spock, you three go on to the baryon reverter—Chekov knows where it is. I'll join you there shortly."

"Where will you be, Captain?"

"On the bridge. I have one last thing to attend to." He stepped into the turbolift. "I don't know how big the reverter is," he said as the door closed.

One last thing to attend to. It could wait, he supposed; but he felt he couldn't leave without reassuring Babe that she had indeed done the right thing.

He stepped from the turbolift into a scene that might have been funny if it weren't so serious. It was a toss-up as to which side was more frightened of the other, the humans or the Sackers. But this time it was the humans who held the weapons, and the *Enterprise* security guards were pointing them. The young Sackers were twitching with anxiety, Misterma'am so much so that he looked as if he were afflicted with some strange nervous disorder. Blue, on the other hand, was stiff as a board, too scared to move. Berengaria was at the communications console, giving orders—and staying as far away from Rose as she possibly could. The command chair was unoccupied.

"Where's Babe?" he asked.

"Here, Captain."

He hadn't noticed her standing by the weapons station. "What are you doing over there?"

"I am no longer in command of this vessel. It did not seem fitting that I occupy the command chair."

"Ah. Well." Kirk cleared his throat and spoke so that everyone on the bridge could hear. "I am beaming an officer over from the *Enterprise* to assume command. I'm sure he would appreciate all the help you can give him, Babe. Are you willing to help?"

"I will do all I can to make the transfer of authority as smooth as possible."

"Good, good. So, until he gets here . . .?" He gestured toward the command chair.

Babe walked with measured steps back to the chair. With a tense regal dignity, she seated herself.

"Lieutenant Berengaria!" Kirk called out. "Do you suppose you could get your people to point their weapons at the deck instead of at me?"

She didn't have to say a word; the weapons were lowered. Reluctantly.

"Ah, that's better." He leaned one elbow casually on the back of the command chair and bent in close to Babe. The other humans on the bridge stared at him in astonishment; he wanted them to see that the Sackers weren't as monstrous and as fearsome as they appeared to be. "If you're thinking that's the last time you'll ever sit there," Kirk said to Babe, "don't count on it. You'll be back."

"How can I be, Captain?" she answered tightly. "If your Federation does not execute us, we will surely spend the rest of our lives in a penal colony somewhere."

He raised his voice again; they should all hear this.

"Well, nobody's going to execute you, and I seriously doubt that you'll end up a hardened convict. You'll probably go to some sort of juvenile rehabilitation institution where you'll be re-educated."

"*Re*-educated?"

"Babe, you and your crew have been taught to hate us and even to kill us when you think it's necessary. That's not natural to you—it's something you had to learn. We've got to undo that conditioning. There's no reason why, in time, you can't all become functioning members of Federation society. We want you with us, not against us."

"You would do that? After what we have done?"

"Well, the adults in those other Sacker ships aren't going to be welcomed with open arms—frankly, I don't know what's going to happen to them. But if they're willing to give up their notion of ruling the Federation, I don't see why we can't sit down and talk. But however that works out, you people on this ship are safe. We've never known a starship to be operated entirely by youngsters before. Starfleet isn't going to let that kind of talent go to waste. Babe, you have a natural gift for command. You belong in a command chair. Sooner or later, you'll be sitting in one again. And speaking of this ship, don't you think it's about time we gave it a name?"

Every Sacker on the bridge turned and looked at him. "You . . . you have a name for our ship?" Babe asked, almost afraid to believe it.

"I do indeed. I've decided that from now on, this ship will be known as the *Babe in Arms*. In your honor."

There was about two seconds of silence, and then all the Sackers started talking at once. Orangejuiceandwodka was jiggling up and down happily in the navigator's seat. Babe was stunned.

"Captain Kirk," she said, "you . . . Captain . . . I, I do not understand why you honor a defeated enemy in this way."

"Not an enemy. A friend. A friend and a future ally."

She couldn't speak for a few minutes. "Captain, when you took over the environmental control section, I thought you must be the most duplicitous creature in the universe. Even when you told me you were trying to keep us alive, I did not believe you. I was wrong. You *are* concerned with our welfare— perhaps even more so than the others of our race. I never thought I would be thanking a conqueror, but that is what I am doing. I thank you, Captain Kirk. For everything. I wish there were some way I could show my gratitude."

"As a matter of fact," Kirk grinned, "there is something you can do. Tell me the name of your race. The only reason we call you Sackers is that we don't know what else to call you. What do you call yourselves?"

"You wish to know our race-name?"

"You bet I do. But only if you want to tell me. This isn't one of the spoils of war, Babe. You don't have to tell me if you don't want to."

"But I wish to. I think we would all wish it."

She stood and looked to the other members of the bridge crew. They were all on their feet, wagging their heads back and forth in their affirmative gesture. The sight of so many Sackers all making the same gesture at the same time was a bit unnerving to some of the *Enterprise*'s security team; Lieutenant Berengaria spoke a word of command, and the weapons that had started to rise went back down again.

"Very well," Babe said. "Captain Kirk, we are the Vinithi. That is our race-name."

"Vinithi," Kirk repeated, thinking it was a lovely name for a people whom, even in his most charitable moments, he could never think of as lovely. "I like that much better than 'Sackers'."

"So do we," Orangejuiceandwodka said earnestly.

Just then the turbolift doors hissed open, and an *Enterprise* spacesuit walked on to the bridge. A familiar face looked out through the helmet's visor.

"Aha—here is your new commander now!" Kirk announced expansively. "Welcome aboard, Mr. Sulu!"

"*Sulu!*" The name was spoken aloud by every one of the Vinithi. An audible wave of fear and curiosity swept through the bridge. After all their failed plans, after all that had gone wrong—now they had to suffer the trauma of finding the much-dreaded Sulu suddenly thrust among them! If Captain Kirk had been hard to please, the Sulu would be impossible! What was going to happen to them? Unconsciously they all edged a few steps away from this new human.

Sulu was a little taken aback at this reaction to his name; even Berengaria's security team looked surprised. But Sulu was quick to regain his composure. "Thank you, Captain."

Kirk waited until the murmuring had died down a little and said, "Mr. Sulu, this is Commander Babe. The commander wants to make the transfer of authority as easy as possible, and I think you'll find she'll be of invaluable assistance to you."

"Commander."

"Mr. Sulu." She couldn't quite bring herself to say *Welcome aboard.*

Kirk was pretending not to notice the stir Sulu's appearance had created. "I hereby turn command of this vessel, *Babe in Arms,* over to you. It's all yours, Mr. Sulu."

The murmuring resumed, and Sulu began to get an inkling of what was going on. He was the Bad Guy. For a time they'd all watched from the *Enterprise* as Captain Kirk had ground down the Sacker bridge crew, instilling in them a fear of Sulu that was, in the helmsman's private opinion, totally unjustified. But what an opportunity to play villain! Sulu marched to the very edge of the upper platform of the bridge next to Kirk, slammed his feet down about three apart, and planted his fists on his hips. "I accept command," he said sternly. At the sound of his "command" voice, silence fell. Sulu looked his new crew over and then asked Kirk out of the side of his mouth, "Now what do I do?"

Kirk smiled tiredly. "Wing it, Mr. Sulu," he said as he headed toward the turbolift, "wing it."

Sulu examined the bridge personnel one by one, and then picked out the one who was cowering the most. "You! Helmsman! Come here!"

The last thing Kirk saw as the turbolift doors closed in front of him was the sight of poor Blue, slowly shuffling forward to meet his doom.

Chapter Twelve

DR. MCCOY HAD a decision to make, and whichever way he decided would put his patients in danger.

He'd beamed over from the *Enterprise* with a medical team and headed straight for the Sacker sickbay, sending the rest of the team to the site of the fire. Fortunately, only four of the Sackers had been hurt in the fire so far, none with burns. All four had been struck by some falling or flying object that had ruptured the membranes encasing their bodies; two of them had lost a lot of sac fluid before they'd been found and could very well die, he'd been told.

The Sacker who'd told him was a horrendous-looking female with black and blue sac fluid. To McCoy she looked like a walking bruise. The doctor had to concentrate on not turning his eyes away from her; at least his suit protected him from the odor and from any accidental touch of her body.

He'd thought he was ready to face the Sackers after studying the visuals transmitted from their bridge, but he'd underestimated the power of their physical presence. McCoy had seen some pretty gruesome things in his time in the medical profession, but this decayed-looking creature standing before him was a *healthy* organism, hard as that was to believe.

Healthy, and sentient. This one seemed to know what she was doing; she'd taken each patient in turn and explained succinctly what was wrong and what she'd done to patch the membrane ruptures. As far as McCoy could tell, her procedure had been impeccable.

It took him a while to get used to his strange surroundings. Many of the instruments he found in the sickbay were unfamiliar to him. Some of the medicines were labeled in English, but many were not. Most astonishing were the vats of gelatinous substance the Sackers used for beds—a lubricant, no doubt, for their tough membranous exteriors. The real problem, of course, was that McCoy knew nothing at all about Sacker anatomy and physiology.

He pointed to the nearest patient, a big Sacker whose sac fluid was a sort of dirty yellow. "Tell me, how much sac fluid can a fellow this size lose before his condition turns critical?"

The walking bruise twitched. "The medical computer says a full liter. But I think it must be less. Our fluid cells regenerate very slowly."

"But what does the fluid do? What's its function?"

"It keeps us warm. We are not low-temperature dwellers like humans. The sac fluid prevents ice crystals from forming in our internal organs."

"My God," McCoy said, amazed. "Antifreeze!"

"Pardon?"

"Nothing, nothing. Why don't you just give this fellow a transfusion? You must have a supply of the sac fluid on hand."

"The fluid does not preserve well in its natural state. An artificial substitute must be made up."

"Well, did you make some?"

Her head drooped forward. "I do not know how."

McCoy reminded himself that this "doctor" was little more than a child. "Do you want to explain that?" he asked encouragingly.

The Sacker waggled her head back and forth and said, "The medical computer has the formula and the steps to follow in making it up. I read it and I read it, but still I do not understand! There are too many questions, and no one to ask . . ."

"I understand. What language does the programming use? I don't mean computer language—is it in your language?"

"No, it is in two other languages, Zirgosian and Universal English. The Zirgosians did not know our language."

"Then there shouldn't be any problem. Call up the formula for me, and let's take a look."

He read the formula on the viewscreen and studied the procedure for making it. He told the young Sacker to assemble the ingredients. They sat down at a table in the sickbay laboratory and together they mixed up a batch of artificial sac fluid. McCoy answered all her questions, and laughed when he saw her jiggling with pleasure at finally understanding something that had eluded her for so long. "Let me ask you a question," he said. "The computer said nothing about different formulas for different sac colors. Are you sure this same formula will work for all four of those people in there? We've got four different color patients, you know."

"Oh, that is not a problem. Coloration has nothing to do with the composition of the fluid—nothing essential, I mean to say."

"Then why are you all different colors?"

"Why do all humans not have the same color eyes? Or hair? Or physical attributes of other kinds?"

"Ah. It's simply a matter of individual characteristics."

"Yes, that is so."

He thought that once there must have been many Sacker races, and the varied hues he saw now were the result of some long-ago dissolving of barriers between the races. "You're going to have to do the actual work," he told his colleague. "This suit I have to wear makes me clumsy. Besides, I've never treated one of your race before."

She made a sound McCoy couldn't interpret. "*I* have treated a human!"

"You have? Who? What?"

"The Chekov's shoulder was accidentally burned— not badly. But I treated him."

"Tell me what you did." He listened as she described how she had treated Chekov for pain and sterilized the burn area and then checked carefully for infection before spraying on the new skin. "That sounds all right," he told her. "I'll have a look at his shoulder later, but you did everything the way you're supposed to. By the way, what's your name?"

She raised her head proudly. "I am named Dr. Bonesovna. The Chekov named me."

"Bonesovna!" McCoy looked at the black and blue space monster across the table from him and thought: *My daughter?* But he recognized Chekov's brand of humor at work and merely smiled. "That is an honorable name."

"It is?" She sounded surprised.

"Yes indeed. Did you know it means 'Daughter of Bones'? Bones . . . well, I'll just say he's a famous and distinguished Starfleet surgeon. A remarkable man."

"I did not know that! And I am given his name? Oh, thank you for telling me!"

"You're welcome," Bones said dryly.

McCoy did little more than watch as Dr. Bonesovna hooked up the transfusion apparatus. She worked quickly; he noticed there was very little waste motion in her work. Finally the last Sacker was taken care of, a green male with a gaping hole in his side. The young would-be doctor courteously stepped aside and invited McCoy to check the patients himself. He went through the motions, but he could think of nothing to suggest. He congratulated Bonesovna on her efficiency.

When he was sure the patients were all resting comfortably, McCoy took some time to look over the rest of the sickbay. He wandered into a side room where he found what could only be a coffin. He asked Bonesovna about it.

"He was killed in the engine room. When the *Enterprise* fired upon us."

McCoy hadn't known there'd been a death. "I'm sorry, Bonesovna. We were hoping no one would have to die. We didn't want it this way." He stopped to think. "I'm going to have to beam the body over to the *Enterprise.*"

She twitched. "To perform a post-mortem examination. I thought perhaps you would."

He didn't like distressing her. "If we're to help you," he said gently, "we're going to have to know more about you."

"I understand, Dr. McCoy. I do. I do not believe you mean us ill."

Glory be, he thought, *she trusts me!* He was extravagantly pleased. He felt like a kid who'd been paid a compliment by an approving adult, even though he was the adult here and she the kid.

About that time McCoy became aware of a growing

warmth and adjusted his suit temperature control for the second time since he'd beamed aboard. That led him to his dilemma. As long as that fire was still burning, Bonesovna's four patients would be safer on the *Enterprise*. But all the equipment and medicine they needed were right here, as well as the specialized Sacker medical computer. He could keep them here and risk their getting killed in the fire, or he could transfer them to the *Enterprise* sickbay and risk killing them himself through his own ignorance. Some choice. He could take Bonesovna with him, but he didn't want to have to rely on her limited experience alone; he needed their computer.

He called Spock on the communicator and asked if the fire was under control yet. Spock told him it had been extinguished in the engine room and in the environmental control section, but flames had escaped up a few of the shafts. The unfolded leg of the ship was safe, but now the main body was in danger of catching fire.

McCoy hadn't seen Jim and the others since he'd beamed over, but he accepted Spock's reassurances that they were unharmed except for Chekov's burn, which didn't seem to be causing him any trouble. But it was Uhura that McCoy was worrying about. Finding herself caught on a burning starship—that could only compound her nightmares and make her lose whatever ground she'd gained in conquering her fears. She shouldn't be here.

He decided to keep the Sacker patients where they were for the time being. He could always beam them over later if the fire got closer. But surely they'd have it out before long.

He and Bonesovna went back to check on their patients—and found the green one struggling to sit up. "Whoa, there!" McCoy said. "Take it easy—that's a pretty big rupture you have in your side."

"Aye," the Sacker said, "but I'm feelin' so much better I thought I'd move meself about a wee bit."

McCoy blinked. "What . . . did you say?"

"I said I'm feelin' better. What's the matter? Am I not sayin' it right?"

"Oh, you're saying it right. You wouldn't happen to know a human named Montgomery Scott, would you?"

"Aye!" the Sacker said enthusiastically. "He's me teacher!"

McCoy smiled. "I never would have guessed. Ah . . . you must be an engineer."

"Aye, that I am. I'm hopin' to be chief engineer someday. Just like the Scott."

"Well, you've picked a good man to model yourself after—there aren't many like Mr. Scott. In the meantime, stop that wriggling and lie still. Bonesovna, isn't there something you can do to make him keep still?"

"I could hit him over the head." Both she and the green patient started jiggling.

McCoy rolled his eyes. Sacker humor. Just what they needed.

The Vinithi had stored the baryon reverter in their ship maintenance section, high up on a platform where it would be safely out of the way until needed. The maintenance area was the largest open space aboard the *Babe in Arms,* crisscrossed with catwalks and hanging gear. The reverter itself was a black, primarily rectangular affair with two domes on top and an extruding section holding the controls. It was enclosed in fiberglass netting still attached to the multiple-geared pulley that had been used to raise it up to the platform. Captain Kirk, Mr. Spock, Uhura, and Chekov had discarded their helmets and were now moving around aimlessly on the main deck, craning their necks to look up at the reverter.

They were moving around because the hot deck under their feet made standing still more than a little uncomfortable. The fire had left the shafts and reached the main body of the ship, burning furiously one level below. The engines were safe, and Environmental Control—but with none of the ship's fire-control sprayers cutting in automatically, the fire had gone on burning far longer than it should have. And now it was beneath them; they needed to get the baryon reverter to the transporter room as quickly as possible.

"We will need to lower the reverter to the main deck before we can attach antigrav units, Captain," Spock said. "The standard antigravs cannot be sufficiently strong to lift the weight of the reverter to that height, or else the Sackers would not have troubled rigging the pulley."

"Vinithi," Kirk said. "They're called Vinithi."

"Indeed? I am gratified to learn their name at last. Vinithi."

"It docs look heavy, doesn't it?" Kirk mused. His eyes followed the power line of the automated pulley from the baryon reverter across to a smaller platform where a control panel had been mounted. "There!" he said, pointing. "Uhura, I want you to climb up there and see if you can figure out which one of those switches controls that pulley."

"Yes, sir." She hurried to a nearby ladder and started up to the catwalk.

"I'll go up to the platform and guide the reverter down. Spock, you and Chekov are going to have to—Scotty! What are you doing here?"

The chief engineer took off his helmet and wiped the sweat from his face. "I'm not needed at the fire, Captain. The heat has fused the circuits controllin' the sprayers for this section of the ship. I checked 'em in the adjoinin' sections, an' I *think* they'll be comin' on if they're needed."

"What about the fire fighters? What are they doing?"

Scotty did a little dance as the heat from the deck worked its way through the soles of his boots. "They've laid down a wall of flame-retardant foam all around this section here, so they've confined the fire to this area, at least."

"They've got it under control?"

"Just about, sir. It's only a matter o' time."

"Well, that's something," Kirk said. "There's the baryon reverter, Scotty—up there. See it? We've got to get it down."

"Looks heavy."

Spock explained the plan to him as Kirk started climbing the ladder to the platform where the reverter was stored. The ladder was attached to a bulkhead that was about a meter from the edge of the platform. Kirk stepped across the open space and called, "Uhura?"

"I've found it, sir. When you're ready."

"One second." Kirk waited until the three below were in position and then called out, "Now!"

A long catwalk away Uhura reached for the switch—but didn't make it. An unexpected *cr-a-a-a-ck!* made her jump. The switch was forgotten in the shock of what she witnessed happening. Numb and horrified, she watched in stunned disbelief as the center of the main deck collapsed with a roar. Pieces of repair equipment and machinery started a slow-motion slide into the newly created abyss, and Uhura looked down through the open-grid platform under her feet at the tongues of flame shooting up from below.

This was it. This was the fire she'd been dreaming of.

With a surge of fear she remembered the three men who'd been standing on the deck and jerked her head around to look for them. What she saw made her heart pound. Chekov and Scotty had managed to jump to safety. But Scotty was lying on his stomach at the very edge of the chasm, holding one of Mr. Spock's arms with both hands. Chekov scrambled over Scotty to the other side, where he could reach down and grab the other arm. Together they managed to pull Spock up to what was left of the deck, a perimeter of two or three meters circling what was now a flame pit. The knot in her stomach eased somewhat when she saw the Vulcan stand up unaided, apparently not harmed by his close call. Someone was calling her name.

Someone was calling her name? Yes . . . it was Captain Kirk. He was yelling at her to pull the switch.

Pull the switch.

What switch? Which one was it? She knew only a minute ago. But now . . . Uhura slapped her forehead to wake herself up. There. That one.

She pulled the switch.

The pulley's automation hadn't yet been put out of commission by the fire. The baryon reverter in its fiberglass net lifted smoothly from the platform, and Captain Kirk steered it toward the edge. The pulley line slanted at about a forty-five degree angle between the platform and that spot on the deck perimeter where the other end of the pulley line was anchored. If the anchor had been placed another two or three meters away from the bulkhead toward the center of the work area . . . Uhura's mouth grew dry when she thought of what that meant.

The reverter cleared the platform. It had barely started its journey downward . . . when the automation went out. The instrument they were all counting on to save them hung suspended over the flames, halfway between Kirk on the platform and the other three below.

Something had to be done! "Manual override!" Uhura shouted. "It has a manual override!"

But she couldn't make herself heard over the roar of the flames; the noise had become deafening within just the past sixty seconds. She jumped up and down and waved her arms to attract the attention of Spock and Chekov and Scotty. When she got them looking at her, she pantomimed hauling on the pulley chain. They understood. As soon as all three had taken hold of the chain, she switched to manual. The reverter descended in jerks to the safety of the deck perimeter.

But the surge of satisfaction Uhura felt at seeing the reverter safe was cut short. With a series of sounds like small explosions going off, the ladder she and Captain Kirk had both climbed pulled away from the bulkhead and dropped into the fire pit.

She could see the captain staring in horror at the place where the ladder had been attached, as shocked by this loss of their escape route as she was. The same idea came to her that must have occurred to the captain. If the fire could destroy the ladder supports, how long would the platforms and the catwalks hold up?

This is where I'm going to die. The thought had come unbidden; but try as she might, she couldn't drive it away. *This is where I'm going to die, high up on a flimsy platform in the belly of an alien ship. This is where I'm going to burn to death.*

She looked down; the flames were only inches beneath the scorched soles of her boots, and the waves of heat were making her dizzy. But there was no way to get off the platform. *No—wait,* she thought. The ladder that had fallen into the fire couldn't be the only one in this place. Hastily she looked around, trying to spot another way down; but the heat and smoke were making her eyes water, and she was having trouble seeing.

Then she saw the first tongue of flame spurting up through the open grid she was standing on, not more than a foot away from her left boot. She couldn't move. She couldn't breathe, she couldn't swallow, she couldn't take her eyes off the flame. During a seconds-long break in the roar of the fire, she heard her name again.

It broke the spell. She looked over to where Captain Kirk was gesturing to her frantically with a come-here motion. The three men below had sent the grappling hook back up, the one that had lifted the net holding the baryon reverter. The captain had gripped the hook with one hand and was gesturing to her with the other. They were going to lower him down . . . over that pit of fire.

And he wanted her to descend with him.

But how could she, when she couldn't move? Between Uhura and Captain Kirk stretched a long catwalk that bisected the fire area below. It was wide enough to permit the passage of only one person at a time, and the guard rails must be blistering hot by now. And it was a certainty that the catwalk would collapse at any moment. But her only chance of getting out of there alive was to cross it—directly over the inferno. Uhura shuddered in spite of the heat. It was impossible. Unthinkable. Mad. Was the captain crazy, expecting her to walk out over that hungry, merciless fire? She couldn't do it; didn't he know she'd lost the use of her legs?

No, there was no way she could go out over that fire. She knew she'd never make it. And the longer Captain Kirk stayed on that platform waiting for her, the greater the chance was that he'd never make it either. With a heavy heart she shook her head at him, *No*. She gestured with her whole arm that he should go down alone.

But he didn't go.

She could see his face contorting as he yelled something to her. He kept gesturing to her to come; she kept gesturing back that she couldn't. Yet still he would not go, foolishly risking his own life in the vain hope that somehow she would float over that fire untouched and they both could escape the danger. Why didn't he leave? Why did he keep hanging on, and yelling, and gesturing to her . . .

The memory of a responsibility not fulfilled.

Long ago someone close to her had died because she'd let the flames of a raging fire drive her back. Was it going to happen again?

It was clear the captain wasn't going to budge without her. How could he do this? How could he put the responsibility for his life . . . upon *her*?

She looked down to where Spock and Scotty and Chekov were all waving their arms, pointing up toward Captain Kirk. She could see their mouths moving, but she couldn't hear a word. *Go,* they must be saying.

Uhura was split in two. There was the ineffectual, immobile Uhura, too terrified of the fire to take the steps that would save her life as well as that of the captain. And then there was the "outside" Uhura, the one who looked with annoyance at her paralyzed self and said aloud, "Pick up your right foot and put it down in front of you."

She picked up her right foot and put it down. And then her left. And then her right again.

She was out on the catwalk. Straight ahead she could see but not hear the captain yelling encouragement. Like a zombie she moved out over the fire, keeping her eyes on the captain, looking neither right nor left, and not permitting herself to look down into the incinerator waiting for her. She couldn't go any faster. She couldn't go any slower. She couldn't stop. One step. Another. Another.

Another.

And then Captain Kirk was grabbing her and laughing and sweating and laughing some more. "I knew you could do it, Uhura! I *knew* it!"

"You did?" she said weakly.

"Of course I did! Look, you're going to have to hold on to me. We're not going to have time for two trips." He grabbed the grappling hook with both hands.

Uhura stepped behind him and wrapped her arms around his waist, locking her right hand around her left wrist. "Ready," she said.

"Here goes."

As they left the platform, her grip on his waist slipped a little but she managed to hold on. She wondered vaguely about the strength in his arms—

they had to support the weight of two people, after all. She noticed with a curious detachment how large the flames beneath them had grown. She was calm.

And then they were down. They had made it. They were safe. She had not burned to death. It was all right.

Scotty greeted her with a cheer and a sweaty hug.

Spock said, "I commend you on your courage, Lieutenant."

Chekov just stared at her wordlessly for a moment and then blurted out, "I vas afraid you vould not make it!"

"So was I," she answered in a tone meant to reassure, "but we did."

Scotty and Spock were fitting antigrav units to the baryon reverter. Kirk stepped out into the corridor for a look around. When the reverter was fitted and towed out of what remained of the maintenance section, the captain said, "That way is cut off—the flames are starting to eat through the deck. We'll have to go this way." He headed off in a direction away from the quickest route to the transporter room, the other four following with the reverter in tow.

The turbolifts were out, so they were looking for a crawlway. The Vinithi must have been evacuated from that section of the ship because there was no one in sight. No fire fighters, either. They were in some sort of storage area; the corridor was lined with fitted bins on both sides.

"There, Kepten!" Chekov ran toward a crawlway at the end of the corridor. He leaned in to see if the crawlway was clear of flames—and jerked back as a geyser of white foam spurted up at him and overflowed into the corridor. "Vhat is *thet*?"

"That's the flame-retardent they're usin'," Scotty

said. "The fire fighters must be fillin' all the shafts they can find."

"So how do ve get out?"

"That's a good question, lad."

Kirk held his hand out. "Spock—your communicator." Spock gave it to him. "Kirk to fire fighters, come in. Kirk to fire fighters!"

The communicator crackled with static and then a voice said, "Captain Kirk! Are you all right?"

"For the time being. Where's the fire now?"

"We've got it localized, Captain. We've blocked off the exits and filled the crawlways and air shafts with foam. It's just a matter now of foaming down the main blaze. That fire'll be out in half an hour, forty-five minutes at most."

"But where *is* it?"

"We've got it confined to just two corridors—let's see, now. According to the schematics, they're labeled H-2 and G-2."

"Uh-oh," said Chekov, and pointed. Painted on the bulkhead under an unreadable Zirgosian symbol was a big black G-2.

"We're in G-2," Kirk told the communicator tiredly. "Five of us, and a piece of equipment that's more important than any of us."

"Captain, find cover—quickly, don't waste any time. Look for a compartment you can make airtight. Anything—but hurry."

"Right. Kirk out." He looked at the others. "You heard the man. We've got to find us a hiding place."

They all looked around helplessly. There were no living quarters in this corridor that could be sealed, no rooms of any kind that they could see. What to do? Kirk couldn't think. He was tired; he'd already lived a hundred years that day.

"Captain," Spock said, "perhaps inside these storage bins? One of the larger ones should be ample to hold the baryon reverter."

"Oh, good, Spock," Kirk sighed with relief. "Of course—the storage bins. We'll have to empty the largest ones . . . come on."

The two largest bins were directly opposite each other at the far end of the corridor. The first one contained crates of nonperishable food supplies which slid out easily on belts that fell into place when the side-loading door was raised. They stacked the crates out of the way and guided the baryon reverter into its new hiding place. Spock latched the door and remarked that the fittings looked airtight.

"This one unloads from the top," Uhura said of the other large bin directly across from the one now holding the baryon reverter. She opened the lid to reveal a supply of the cloaks the Vinithi wore when dealing with other races.

Whoosh. The other end of the corridor burst into flames.

"Get that stuff out of there!" Kirk yelled. Uhura was already pulling out the cloaks as fast as she could move; the others pitched in, getting in one another's way more often than not. Scotty tripped over Chekov and went sprawling.

"We are not well organized," Spock commented in the understatement of the century.

But the bin got emptied nevertheless. "All right, everybody in," Kirk ordered.

"Captain!" Scotty exclaimed in dismay. "We canna all fit in that one bin!"

"We're going to have to—we don't have time to empty another one. Come on—move!"

They scrambled in, in a tangle of arms and legs.
"Wait," said Uhura, "I can't get my—"

Ker-thunk. The lid fell closed while they were all
still maneuvering for position. There was much grunting, some swearing, and a great deal of muttering
under the breath.

"It's pitch black in here," Kirk grumbled. "Didn't
anybody bring a light?"

"Mr. Chekov, if you could move your knee five
centimeters to the—"

"Thet's *not* my *knee,* Mr. Spock!"

"Oof! Who's sitting on my stomach?"

"Lassie, at any other time I'd be happy to have ye
breathin' in me ear, but—"

"I can't move my head! Somebody has a foot right
in back of—Captain, is that you? Could you move
your foot?"

"Love to, but somebody seems to be using my leg as
a stepladder."

"Captain, I am merely attempting to achieve a little
leverage to facilitate a shift in position that should
prove beneficial to all of us. I am not intentionally
using any part of your anatomy as a stepladder."

"Ow! Thet is my bad shoulder!"

"Sorry."

"Please! Whoever it is in here who's got roving
hands, you're trespassing on private property!"

"I do beg your pardon, Lieutenant."

Cough. "Somebody's got an elbow up against my
windpipe!"

"Sorry, Captain, I was tryin' to get me right arm
free an'—"

"Uhura, I hate to ask you, but could you possibly
scratch my nose?"

"I hef a cremp in my leg."

"If two of us could possibly manage to elevate ourselves sufficiently to allow the other three to draw their bodies into a more compact configuration—"

"Somebody's mashin' me favorite right hand an' I don't want to be mentionin' any names but if she doesna move soon—"

"Everybody shut up!" Kirk roared, effectively deafening all of them. "We have only so much air. Suffer in silence."

They suffered, and in near-silence. They were all panting, taking short, shallow breaths in the close, confined area. Packed together like sardines, none of them could even get a hand free long enough to wipe off a sweaty brow. The heat was unbearable. Someone's stomach growled. Time dragged.

They waited.

Then: "Kepten, do you think thirty minutes hef passed yet?"

"No."

They waited some more.

Then: "Mr. Spock, is your internal clock a-runnin'? Have we not been in this oven long enough, do y'not think?"

"Not quite half an hour yet, Mr. Scott."

They waited still longer.

Then: "I wish we could hear something," Kirk complained. "It ought to be safe enough by now to take a look, at least. What do you think, Spock?"

"I would surmise that an adequate amount of time has elapsed to enable the fire fighters to bring the blaze under control. At any rate, I question our ability to survive under these conditions for much longer."

"Uh-huh, I want out too. Somebody open the lid—my arms are pinned down."

There were the sounds of two people grunting, and then Uhura said, "It's stuck!"

"Not 'stuck', Lieutenant," Spock said, "but evidently held in place by some sort of safety catch operable only from the outside."

"Oh, that's dandy, that is!" Scott exclaimed. "What do we do now?"

"We yell for help," Kirk answered, and proceeded to do just that. Then they were all yelling and banging on the top and the side of the bin and thoroughly driving one another crazy.

But their cries for help were heard. The lid opened suddenly, and they all squinted against the sudden glare of light. As their vision adjusted, they looked up to see the face of Dr. Leonard McCoy peering in at them, his left eyebrow arched up almost to his hairline.

He said, "Do you want me to go away and come back later when you're finished?"

Kirk erupted from the bin, followed closely by Uhura and Scotty, with Chekov scrambling out right behind them. Spock was the last to emerge, struggling hard to maintain his dignity in such unseemly circumstances. They were all hot, grumbling, sweaty, rumpled, and irritable . . . and desperately glad to be alive.

Chapter Thirteen

THE FIRST THING Chief Engineer Montgomery Scott had done back aboard the *Enterprise* was head straight to the part of the ship he called home and plant a big, sloppy kiss on the engineering systems monitoring board. Mr. Spock found the gesture melodramatic and said so.

"Ah, Mr. Spock," Scotty replied, "if ye'd been the one to bide a wee among the beasties instead o' me, ye'd not be so quick to criticize. It's good to be home."

"And I am extremely gratified to see you returned safely to your post, Mr. Scott," Spock commented, "but we do not have the time for emotional displays at the moment, regardless of how well merited they might be. The installation of the baryon reverter has first claim on our attention."

"Aye," Scotty said, settling down to business, "and to figurin' out how the little beauty works."

The first problem was that the Zirgosians had built the reverter for their own use, when and if it was ever needed. Not expecting any other race to have to read the control panels, the Zirgosian inventors had quite naturally labeled all the switches and dials in their own language alone. So the first thing Spock did was ask the language banks in the ship's computer for translations. Once he had them, the problem of puzzling out the baryon reverter began in earnest.

After a while Spock said, "As well as I can interpret these controls, the baryon reverter does not revert baryons into something else. It seems the Zirgosians found a way to revert leptons into baryons."

"*What?!*" Scotty cried, flabbergasted. "That's impossible! Y'canna change leptons into baryons!"

"Normally I would have agreed with you, Engineer, but evidently the leptons first transform into mesons and then into the heavier baryons. The reverter uses antiparticles instead of particles."

"Let me see." Scotty studied the control panels and shook his head. "The minute the baryons pass through that barrier separatin' our universe from the one next to us, they'll all decay, Mr. Spock, ever' blessed one o' them."

"And that, presumably, is why the Zirgosians used antiparticles. When the antiparticles pass through the barrier, they will undergo the same sort of reversal, only in their case it will result in antidecay."

"And the baryons are reconstituted on the other side, in the other universe?" Scotty mused. "Aye, that might do it—like puttin' a heavy particle patch on the inside o' the rupture. But ye'd need a power source larger than this ship to do it!"

Spock folded his arms and stared at the baryon reverter. "But this is what we have, Mr. Scott—this one instrument. The only possible way this reverter could work would be by means of some miniaturized internal power generator we do not have in our technology."

Scotty's face glowed. "When this is all over—if it works, o' course—y'think we might be openin' it up to take a peek inside? A miniaturized power generator!"

"The same thought had crossed my mind," Spock admitted. "I too would be most interested in examining such a magnificent leap in technology. But we are getting ahead of ourselves. The reverter will need some sort of external start-up power."

"That's nae problem. There's a port here on the side."

"And we'll need a way of directing the antiparticle stream. If we cannot control the stream's bearings, our chances of hitting the exact location where the rupture between the two universes took place are minuscule."

Scotty was walking around the reverter, inspecting for the tenth or eleventh time every visible part of the instrument. "I've been thinkin' about that. There ought to be a way o' directin' the stream through our phaser banks."

"The phaser banks," Spock repeated slowly. "That is an excellent suggestion, Mr. Scott. To be controlled from the bridge?"

"Oh, that's the easy part." Scotty hunkered down and removed a small panel near the base of the reverter. "Aha. In-line diverter switches. It'll take some trial and error, it will, but this may be our answer, Mr. Spock."

Without further ado they got to work.

Ensign Chekov had laid in a course for that burning section of the galaxy that had once contained the Beta Castelli star system; the *Enterprise* was headed right back to the place where it had all started. "Estimated time of encounter vith heat front—three hours, twenty-one minutes," the navigator announced.

He sounds tired, Captain Kirk thought. *We're all tired.* Kirk was sitting in his own command chair once again, and openly exulting in it. They'd taken the time to shower and change into uniforms and eat, but what they all needed most was a long stretch of worry-free sleep. He could have ordered Chekov and Uhura to get some rest; but he knew they'd want to be here for the moment the baryon reverter was put to the test. After all, it might be the last moment they'd share together. He glanced over at his communications officer; Uhura's back was erect and her head held high. Why didn't *she* look as tired as the rest of them?

Kirk slapped a hand on the armrest control panel. "Kirk to Spock."

"Spock here."

"Report, Mr. Spock. Have you and Scotty figured out a way to make the reverter work?"

"We believe so, Captain. We have computer-tested it, and it checks out. Mr. Scott is currently devising an interior shielding to protect the phaser banks from the antiparticle stream that will be passing through them."

Kirk paused. "We're going to plug up the hole by shooting antiparticles at it?"

"That is what the baryon reverter is designed to do," Spock said. "A wide-beam steady stream of a minute's duration should accomplish the task admirably."

Kirk blew air out through his lips. "I hope the Zirgosians knew what they were doing."

"That is my sincere wish also, Captain."

"Kirk out."

Chekov had turned in his seat and was staring at the captain. "Antiparticles?"

"Antiparticles."

The navigator shook his head. "Thet is dangerous stuff."

"Very dangerous."

"Ve should be vorried."

"Yes, we should."

"But I am too numb to vorry."

Kirk smiled. "I know the feeling, Mr. Chekov. Too much has happened, and we're all tired. If you wish to be relieved—"

"No, sir!" Chekov interrupted emphatically. "I vish to be right vhere I am, Kepten! I do not vant to be relieved!"

"I didn't think so," Kirk murmured. "What about you, Uhura?"

"I'd also prefer to stay, Captain."

Kirk nodded. "Yes, we should all be here for this."

They lapsed into silence. The bridge was unusually still. What speaking was necessary was done quietly, in lowered voices. Even physical movements were soft and noiseless—*like a funeral,* Kirk thought. Showing respect for the dead. Hushed tones, somber faces, quiet movements. It made Kirk edgy. *We're not dead yet!*

The intercom broke the silence; it was Dr. McCoy. "Jim, I've finished the post-morten."

"I'll be right there." Kirk headed toward the turbolift. "Uhura, you have the conn. Let me know when we get within half an hour of the heat front."

On his way down to G Deck, Kirk tried not to think what would happen if the baryon reverter didn't work. Then he caught himself: that was exactly what he *should* be thinking about. Lord knows he'd told Babe often enough that a starship captain has to think ahead. He must be more tired than he thought.

In sickbay, Dr. McCoy was putting the results of his post-mortem into the medical computer. He broke off when he saw the captain and said, "Have a seat, Jim—you're in for a surprise."

Kirk sat down. "Did you find out what that sac fluid does?"

"It keeps them from freezing to death. Dr. Bonesovna—I find it hard to keep a straight face when I say that—anyway, Bonesovna had already told me about the fluid. But I checked it and she was right. It regulates the Vinithi body temperature. It not only keeps the internal organs warm, but it's also their early warning system when temperatures fall to dangerously low levels. Didn't you tell me the older Vinithi died when their sac fluid froze?"

"Yes, that's what we were told."

"They never felt it. They had to have died long before the fluid solidified—it would have been the last thing in their bodies to freeze. The kids that survived can take lower temperatures, but even they would be uncomfortable if they had to spend any length of time in a temperature like, say, the one we maintain on the *Enterprise*."

"I can believe it. They kept their own ship like an oven—and told us they'd lowered the temperature to accommodate us. But what's this surprise you have for me?"

"Well, it seems the Vinithi are a long-lived race. *Very* long-lived. As close as I can pin it down, their period of childhood and adolescence lasts well over a hundred of our years. Since your Commander Babe is the oldest, I'd put her age at about a hundred ten, maybe twenty."

"What?" Kirk was astounded. "Over a hundred? That means . . ."

"It means that those kids you made dog food of are about eighty years older than you are."

Kirk stared at him. "I'm glad I didn't know that."

251

McCoy laughed. "It might have changed your approach?"

"No question. Whew."

"But they're still children and adolescents, Jim, no matter what our way of measuring time tells us. They're still going to need adults for a while."

Kirk was silent for a few moments. "Bones, you've just told me that Babe has lived for more than a century without ever putting foot on a planet."

"Oh, surely not! They—"

"The adults never took their offspring with them when they visited different worlds. Remember that incubation dome the kids put up on Holox? That was the first time they'd ever been planetside. The ones that didn't go down, like Babe, have spent their whole lives on board ship. Not on *that* ship, but on the one the adult Vinithi abandoned when they stole the unfinished *Babe in Arms* from the Zirgosians."

"A hundred years . . . cooped up inside a ship." McCoy shook his head. "It's a wonder they stayed sane."

Kirk nodded; the same thought had occurred to him. "We are the first 'aliens' they've ever had any sustained contact with. Remember, only the adults ever went planetside—the young ones were always kept on board. After the accident killed all the adults, a few of the kids did talk to the Zirgosian delegation that wanted them to leave Holox. And they had the three Gelchenites on board for a while, long enough to persuade them to do that dirty poisoning job. But we're the only ones they've seen up close for any period of time."

"So we're just as strange to them as they are to us. Well, maybe not so strange now. But we still have a hell of a lot to learn about these people."

"It makes me wonder about the other Vinithi youngsters," Kirk remarked, "on those other ships. They've undoubtedly been brainwashed just as thoroughly as *our* Vinithi kids were. What's going to happen to them?"

"You can't save everybody, Jim."

"We were damned lucky, Bones, you know that? What if that ship had been filled with adult Vinithi?"

They were interrupted by the intercom. "Captain Kirk, Admiral Quinlan is on subspace."

"Pipe it through to sickbay, Uhura."

The admiral's face appeared on McCoy's screen. "Captain Kirk—again, congratulations on a job well done. I'm happy to see you back on the *Enterprise*."

"Thank you, sir. You don't know how glad I am to be here. But the job isn't done yet."

"No. Any problems with the baryon reverter?"

"None that we can see at this point. We won't know whether it works or not until we try it."

"Of course. Nevertheless, I've ordered the *Bellefonte* to rendezvous with the Vinithi ship— they're carrying extra crew who'll take over for your people on the *Babe in Arms*." Admiral Quinlan snorted. "*Babe in Arms*! What an absurd name for a starship."

"You think so?" Kirk asked innocently.

"Anyway, we're taking your recommendation that the young Vinithi be re-educated under consideration. Off the record, Kirk—just how feasible would such an undertaking be? They are killers, you know. In your honest opinion, *can* they be re-educated?"

"In my honest opinion—absolutely," Kirk replied with emphasis. "And they are not killers by nature. They're kids, Admiral, a tremendously gifted group of youngsters who've been mercilessly conditioned into thinking they have the right to take by violence what their elders failed to win through peaceful means. The Vinithi did try to establish amicable relations with the Federation, you know. They tried for years."

"I know. We obviously fell short there. Well, if you think these youngsters are salvageable—"

"I do, Admiral, without any question. And they're a likable bunch, once you get used to their appearance. And their smell."

"And you had time to acclimate yourselves?"

"We were just beginning to." Kirk cleared his throat. "In fact, we were on a first-name basis with a lot of them."

"Indeed? That bodes well for future Federation–Vinithi relations. Too bad the other Vinithi are not so amenable."

"Ah, yes . . . what about those other Vinithi ships?"

"They've disappeared. Simply vanished. Once they learned we had the baryon reverter, they left their starbase orbits and took off for parts unknown. That's a problem we'll have to deal with in the future. If there is a future."

Kirk knew that was his cue to say *There will be, sir*, but he couldn't quite bring himself to say it. He settled for stating the obvious: "We'll know in a couple of hours."

"Yes, we will." Silence. "Well, good luck, Kirk. Good luck to all of us." Admiral Quinlan's image disappeared.

"We'll need it," Kirk murmured to the empty screen.

Dr. McCoy, who'd moved out of the picture when the admiral came on, pulled up a chair near to Kirk. "Jim, doesn't it strike you as ironic? After all we've been through in all these years, our very survival now rests not on ourselves but on a piece of untested equipment that we didn't even develop! Doesn't seem right, going out that way."

"What a pessimist you are, Bones. We've got a good chance of not 'going out' at all."

"How good? Can you quote me odds?"

"I'm not Mr. Spock. But yes, come to think of it, I can quote you odds. Fifty-fifty. It'll either work or it won't."

McCoy grunted. "Believe it or not, I'd already figured that out for myself. But none of us has any idea whether that thing will work or not. Spock doesn't know, Scotty doesn't know . . . you don't know. The Zirgosians themselves didn't *know* it would work."

"The Zirgosians were sure it would."

"That's not good enough, dammit! It won't work, I know it!"

"It will work."

"How do you know?"

"Because," Kirk answered simply, "it has to."

The heat front was only twenty minutes away.

Kirk glanced over to where Scotty was seated at the weapons station, nervously checking his connections for the umpteenth time. Chief Engineer Montgomery Scott had faced death before, and the death of his shipmates as well. But never before had any of them had to grapple with the idea that the near-simultaneous death of *everybody* was imminent, every living soul in the universe; and all they had to prevent it was an instrument no one had used before. No wonder Scotty was making sure he hadn't made a mistake.

Scotty wasn't the only one who was nervous.

McCoy was pacing back and forth behind the command chair, muttering to himself. Even the normally stalwart Mr. Spock seemed jumpy—and that made everyone more nervous than they already were. They'd all fallen into the habit of expecting their Vulcan first officer to remain rock-steady no matter how serious the crisis. Seeing him so ill-at-ease like that . . . everyone was strung-out, wired.

No, not quite everyone, Kirk thought. Uhura was an oasis of calm in the midst of a bridge crew ready to jump out of their skins if anyone so much as said boo to them.

Right then Uhura was serenely looking at the main viewscreen, which showed a starfield that was gradually growing lighter the nearer they came to the heat front. She became aware that Captain Kirk was watching her, and looked a question at him.

"All right?" he asked.

She smiled. "All right."

Kirk smiled back; she was indeed all right. Uhura understood as well as any of them that these might be their last moments. But she was prepared to die in the celestial furnace they were heading toward if that was to be her fate. The thought of fire no longer terrified her; it was a fact of existence, a source of warmth as well as a danger to be faced. And she would face it. Uhura had conquered her demon.

The temperature was growing uncomfortably high. Kirk got up and moved silently over to stand behind Spock at the sciences station. "Spock, I—"

The Vulcan spun around. *"Yes?"* he barked.

Kirk let his surprise show.

Spock sighed. "I am sorry, Jim. I find myself possessed by a strange uneasiness. It will not happen again."

The uneasiness wasn't the only thing that was strange; Spock had always been careful never to call him Jim on the bridge. A small distraction seemed to be called for. Kirk said, "I wanted to ask you about the Zirgosian woman, Dorelian. Where is she?"

"She beamed down to Holox immediately after you had been kidnapped by the Vinithi. I did not tell her what had happened."

"Just as well. I'm sorry I didn't get to say goodbye."

"She said the same thing, Captain. In fact, she gave me a message to deliver to you."

"Which is?"

"She said I was to tell you that she holds you to your promise."

Kirk nodded. "To stop the Vinithi—only we were still calling them Sackers then. Well, we've stopped them. But we still have to stop what they started."

"It won't work," McCoy muttered, not even pausing in his pacing.

"Doctor," Spock said in an unusually cold tone, "do you think you could possibly find a place to *sit down*?"

"I don't want to sit down!"

Chekov turned to face them. "There is an empty seat at the veapons station," he said pointedly.

"I tell you I don't want—"

"McCoy—siddown," Kirk ordered. "You're getting on everyone's nerves."

The doctor grumbled, but he went over and plopped down next to Scotty. The engineer didn't even notice; he was busy running another check.

"It can't work," McCoy told him just the same.

"It can and it will," Kirk said with an optimism he was far from feeling. He went back to the command chair; only when he was seated did he notice that every face on the bridge was turned toward him, and those faces were wearing expressions that could only be described as dubious. Even Uhura's.

Kirk punched a button. "Attention, all decks. Now hear this. It *will* work! Kirk out."

"That should reassure everybody," McCoy remarked dryly.

A tension-filled silence reigned for a few minutes. The heat was oppressive. Then Spock said, in an almost dreamy tone of voice, "And still we cannot measure it."

"What's that, Spock?"

"I said we do not have the technology to measure the amount of energy leaking into our universe, Captain. If the baryon reverter does not stop the flow from the neighboring universe, what will happen? If the outpouring is large, the inhabitants of other planets will suffer the same heat death as the Zirgosians. The Zirgosians had no knowledge of what was going to happen. Without warning, their sky lit up with the brightness of many suns, and their planet was wrapped in a searing flash of radiation. Farther away from the source, death would come more slowly."

"That's a cheerful thought," McCoy remarked.

"But even if the flow is small enough that it will be attenuated by the time it reaches a distant populated planet, there will still be disaster. The gaseous matter and the cosmic dust of the two universes will oscillate violently and start emitting large quantities of radio waves. What if only a small flow reaches Earth, for instance? The friction between Earth's surface and the particles of dust and gas could leech away Earth's mechanical energy and force it into a smaller orbit. Say Earth lost half its store of mechanical energy that way—its orbit would shrink to half its present size, putting it about forty-six and a half million miles from the sun. Earth would receive four times as much light and heat as it does now, creating thermal conditions that would be quite unsuitable for life."

"Spock," McCoy asked, "is this supposed to make us feel better?"

"That close," Spock went on, unheeding, "the sun's tidal action would act as a giant brake on Earth's rotation, slowing it to a standstill. Earth would then present the same side to the sun at all times, so that one half the planet would be in perpetual darkness. On the side facing the sun, all the vegetation would burn off the surface. All the lakes, rivers, and oceans would start to boil, and would eventually evaporate. Only an unlivable desert would remain. The dark side of Earth, on the other hand, would be covered with layers of ice several thousands of feet thick. Also, if the—"

"Mr. Spock," Kirk said quietly. "Enough."

Silence returned to the bridge. Kirk ran his eyes over the people around him at this most critical moment of his life. Scotty had stopped checking his instruments and sat without moving, waiting tensely for the moment he'd be called upon to activate the baryon reverter. McCoy huddled next to him at the weapons system, arms folded and legs crossed tightly . . . making himself small. The two men at the engineering station and the two security guards were familiar faces, but at the helm sat a woman named Raina whom Kirk didn't know very well. Maybe it had been a mistake to leave Sulu on the *Babe-in-Arms* —no, she had to be qualified or she wouldn't be here. But Raina looked every bit as tense as everyone else.

"Four minutes to heat front," Chekov announced.

The bridge temperature was by then in a range that was barely tolerable. Kirk moved over to the environmental systems monitor; the temperature was up all over the ship. "Spock, how much more of this can we take?"

"Approaching critical now, Captain."

Spock and Scotty had agreed that Captain Kirk should take the *Enterprise* in as close to the heat front as possible. Although they knew the range of the baryon reverter, there was no way to measure the exact distance to the rupture between the two universes. Thus, the closer the better.

"One minute," said Chekov.

"Helm, full stop," Kirk ordered.

"Full stop," Raina said.

"Reverse engines. Match rate of retreat to that of the heat front's advance."

"Aye, sir." The *Enterprise* began moving back.

"Spock?"

"Temperature is still increasing, Captain."

"Then this is it," Kirk said. "Reverter ready."

"Ready, sir," Scotty replied.

"Activate."

There was nothing to see, no dramatic spectacle, no way of watching or listening to the billions of antiparticles that went streaming out of the *Enterprise*'s phaser banks toward the rupture between the two universes. On and on they poured, until the reverter's preset automatic cutoff stopped the flow. "That's it, sir," Scotty announced. "Our baryon patch is in place."

Everyone on the bridge was thinking the same thing: *But will it hold?*

"Temperature?"

"Holding steady."

It would take a while for any decrease to show. The temperature would continue to rise as long as it was fueled by new energy pouring in from the other universe; the front would begin to lose heat only if the source were completely sealed off. The residual heat could still do damage, but there was nothing anyone could do about that; eventually it would dissipate. All they could hope to do was prevent its growing larger.

They lived through an eon of anxiety before Spock spoke the magic words: "Temperature down half a degree!"

"Wait," Kirk said sharply, cutting off any premature surge of hope.

They waited a little longer. When Spock was sure, he announced, "Now it's down a full degree . . . a degree and a half . . . two . . . Captain, the heat level is definitely on the decline!"

"Ah *ha*! Got 'im!" Kirk laughed out loud in relief and slapped a button on the armrest. But while he was announcing their success to the rest of the crew, an uproar of whooping and cheering erupted on the bridge that forced him to yell to make himself heard.

When he'd finished, he gazed at his normally well-disciplined crew in astonishment. Scotty and McCoy were hugging each other like brothers who'd been separated for twenty years. The two men at the engineering station were shaking hands and pounding each other on the back and screaming congratulations. The two security guards were punching each other like a couple of small boys whose team had just won the Big Game. Uhura was doing a little dance in front of her station, providing her own music and snapping her fingers to the beat. And Chekov and Raina—oblivious to everything around them, Chekov and Raina were locked in a passionate embrace.

Kirk wondered if the rest of the ship had gone as mad as the bridge. He opened his mouth to tell them to knock it off—but then shut it again. *Oh, why the hell not.*

And then they were all over him—pulling him out of the command chair, slapping his back, shaking his hand, shouting congratulations at him. Uhura gave him a hug which he didn't have time to enjoy because Scotty grabbed his hand and was doing his damnedest to shake his arm off. They all kept touching him, giving him little pats of approval. Kirk was not one to pass up a development like that, so he went with the flow and gloried in the moment—until he caught sight of Spock standing stiffly apart from the others, distancing himself from the celebration.

Eventually the furor died down and the crew cheerfully drifted back to their posts and Kirk sank down into the command chair. Only then did Spock approach him. But instead of offering his congratulations, he said, "Captain, permission to leave the bridge."

Kirk was surprised. "Is something wrong?"

"I need . . . to return to my quarters. Permission to leave?"

"Granted."

Kirk stared after his first officer as Spock disappeared into the turbolift. Dr. McCoy too had noticed something was amiss. He leaned in close to Kirk and said, low, "Something is troubling our Vulcan friend, Jim. Perhaps I should—"

"No, I'd better go. If he needs help, I'll call you." He vacated the command chair. "Uhura, notify Starfleet Command that the baryon reverter did its job."

"You betcha, sir!" she sang.

"Scotty!"

"Sir?"

"Take over." Kirk headed toward the turbolift.

"Aye, sir!" Scotty boomed heartily. "Mr. Chekov! Do y'think it'd be possible for ye to find us a nice safe route out o' these burnin' heavens?"

"Oh, I think thet vould be possible, Mr. Scott!" Chekov allowed happily.

Kirk wasted no time in getting to his first officer's quarters. "It's Jim," he said to the door speaker. The doors hissed open.

Inside, he found the Vulcan in a physical posture he'd never seen once in all the years he'd known him. Spock was seated, his elbows resting on his knees and his face buried in his hands.

Despair? Kirk thought, shocked. *Spock?* Spock lifted his head and Kirk tried to read his expression—but the Vulcan mask was back in place.

"I have just realized I was remiss in the matter of offering my congratulations," Spock said formally. "You have brought about a successful conclusion to a catastrophic situation and you deserve the highest commendation. I should have said so on the bridge."

Kirk deliberately adopted a casual manner as he dropped into a chair and said, "Well, you didn't have much chance. Discipline on the bridge kind of broke down there for a minute or two. It was a special situation."

Spock did not respond to the friendliness in Kirk's voice; he said nothing, offering no clue.

Seize the bull by the horns. "Spock," Kirk said earnestly, "I want you to tell me what's wrong. I'm not ordering you to say anything. But I'm asking you, as a friend."

Spock was silent for so long that Kirk thought he wasn't going to answer. But at last the Vulcan said, "I am overcome with awe, Jim. I have understood for the first time something humans have had to deal with their entire lives. Can you imagine what it is like to feel a brand-new emotion for the first time? Something that you have known about for years, that you have a name for . . . but which you have never experienced firsthand? Jim, for the first time in my life, I have felt fear."

Oh-h-h-h, Kirk groaned silently, *so that was it.* If he were to answer Spock's question, he would have to say no, he could not imagine what it was like for a mature man to experience fear for the first time. That was beyond him; no one could imagine that. He just knew that it must be a terrible thing indeed. Especially for a man as disciplined and self-controlled as Mr. Spock.

He chose his words carefully before he started to speak. "You know, Spock, fear is not altogether a bad thing. Believe me, I've had lots of experience with it. But fear is . . . full of opposites. It can paralyze you, or it can galvanize you into actions you never thought yourself capable of. It can make you rash, or it can make you overly cautious. It can fill your veins with ice—or it can pump you so full of adrenaline you can't wait to get going, to do something, anything."

Spock's head sank forward to his chest. "A highly contradictory and destructive emotion."

"Not necessarily. It's a question of directing your fear into channels that help you, making it work for you instead of against you. It's a question of control." Kirk paused. "And I don't know of anyone in all of Starfleet who's better equipped to find that control than you, Spock."

Spock repeated the key word: "Control."

"Yes! Don't deny your fear. Use it. You'll see, it will add a whole new dimension to your life—you'll start seeing things in a way you've never seen them before. Anyone with human genes in him who's never known fear—well, he's not . . . whole. Oh, Spock, don't you see? You've found a part of yourself that was missing. Don't despair, Spock! Rejoice! *Rejoice.*"

For a long moment there was no response. Then the Vulcan slowly lifted his head, looked his friend straight in the eye . . . and rejoiced.

The *Enterprise* went home, leaving the universe next door to develop in its own time and, as it always should have been, in its own space.

THE EXPLOSIVE NEW

STAR TREK®

HARDCOVER

PROBE

by
Margaret Wander Bonanno

Pocket Books is proud to present PROBE, an epic length novel that continues the story of the movie STAR TREK IV.

PROBE reveals the secrets behind the mysterious probe that almost destroyed Earth—and whose reappearance now sends Captain Kirk, Mr. Spock, and their shipmates hurtling into unparalleled danger...and unsurpassed discovery.

The Romulan Praetor is dead, and with his passing, the Empire he ruled is in chaos. Now on a small planet in the heart of the Neutral Zone, representatives of the United Federation of Planets and the Empire have gathered to discuss initiating an era of true peace. But the talks are disrupted by a sudden defection—and as accusations of betrayal and treachery swirl around the conference table, news of the probe's reappearance in Romulan space arrives. And the *Enterprise* crew find themselves headed for a final confrontation with not only the probe—but the Romulan Empire.

Copyright © 1990 Paramount Pictures. All Rights Reserved.
STAR TREK is a Registered Trademark of Paramount Pictures.

Available In Hardcover
from Pocket Books

POCKET
B O O K S